CALL OF THE WILD

Sam Benally's sigh came through the earpiece. The humming static of the long-distance telephone connection rushed in. At length Sam said, "I hate to say this to a veterinarian, but I sure as hell hope it was a dog. Dogs can go wild, can't they? Return to nature and all that? You see, my sister's husband has decided it was a wolf. Hell of a big one, from the mess it made. But the worst of it is, my grandmother is convinced it's a werewolf."

"MOORE'S FIRST DETECTIVE NOVEL, *THE DOBERMAN WORE BLACK,* WAS A STUNNING DEBUT . . . HAPPILY, *THE WOLF WHISPERED DEATH* IS EVEN BETTER."
—*The Denver Post*

"ENOUGH TWISTS AND SURPRISES TO KEEP READERS GUESSING THROUGHOUT."
—Bill Pronzini and Marcia Muller,
San Francisco Chronicle

Other Novels by Barbara Moore

Hard on the Road
The Fever Called Living
Something on the Wind
The Doberman Wore Black

THE WOLF WHISPERED DEATH

Barbara Moore

A DELL BOOK

Published by
Dell Publishing
a division of
The Bantam Doubleday Dell Publishing Group, Inc.
666 Fifth Avenue
New York, New York 10103

ISBN: 0-440-20117-9

Reprinted by arrangement with St. Martin's Press

Printed in the United States of America

Published simultaneously in Canada

August 1988

10 9 8 7 6 5 4 3 2 1

OPM

To Joel Goldman, D.V.M.,
who solves the medical mysteries

THE WOLF
WHISPERED
DEATH

CHAPTER 1

The day started unluckily for the abandoned dog. There had been thunder in the night, which terrified him, but no rain fell. Neither the arroyo east of his home nor the dry bed of the Rio Puerco to the south had water, so the dog had to make a three-mile round trip to drink at a windmill pond. His route took him beside Interstate 40, and he always counted on breakfasting along the way, but a coyote had passed by earlier and cleaned the night-drivers' aftermath of small animal corpses from the highway. The dog went home with only water in his stomach.

The dog's home was a roadside park near the Arizona-New Mexico state line. From a hiding place under a clump of greasewood, the dog watched cars that stopped at the rest area, but that day they left more pop cans and disposable diapers than food scraps. It did rain in the afternoon, a brief downfall so fierce that the dog took refuge in a stripped Ford junked in the arroyo. When the rain was over he tried again for a meal, going to the river banks to dig at the burrows of pocket mice. But even the digging was futile.

When evening neared, the dog's hunger drove him four miles along a gravel road to a ranch. It had a big house and a little house and a barn and crumbling log hogans and a small circlet of grass surrounding an empty swimming pool. Better, there was an unused pool house with a broken door in which the dog could lie and wait, because, best of all, there were rabbits.

Luck seemed to improve. It was nearly dusk when the rabbits came, but even so they were early. They came for the succulent grass that was watered each morning by the owner of the ranch.

These were large rabbits. Some were marked rather like the dog: light tan throat, white chest, white underbelly, although the rabbits' backs were mostly desert gray, while the dog's back was a brown-and-black brindle. Big white rabbits, which the owner had turned out of a rabbit coop one year after tiring of them, had mixed with wild rabbits to produce an oversized strain. The dog's mix was less certain. Some German Shepherd, maybe. Some large hound, obviously, from the shape of his skull and his size. He was a young dog and had still been growing when he was dumped in the desert. By now his flanks were hollow and his ribs showed so clearly they could be counted, even on a good day when he had dined on rabbits.

When a rabbit suddenly materialized outside the pool house in which he waited, the dog rose slowly from the dusty floor. To the west, a wild radiance of reds, oranges, and pinks faded with the setting sun, but the dog moved much slower than the fading of the colors. He lifted one foot to take a cautious step. He waited. There were three rabbits this evening. They moved through the grass, nibbling. They moved closer to the open door of the pool house.

Before the dog could charge, another door beyond the grass closed with a muffled click. Both dog and rabbits stiffened and sniffed the air. The rabbits hopped a retreat toward one side of the pool house, and the dog slid silently to hide behind lumber stacked against the other side. The man was coming. Then the dog picked up another scent. Oiled metal. His hackles rose, and his lips drew back. He growled low in his throat. The man was bringing his gun.

Hugh Fawkes carried a .30-.30 rifle that evening when he came out of the guesthouse at dusk. He didn't come for the rabbits. They had eaten his vegetable garden to the ground in the years he had tried a garden, but they did little damage to the pleasing bit of lawn that he kept alive in back of the big house. Fawkes knew a dog had been coming to the place for almost three months, and he hoped to shoot the dog.

Almost got him, back in early May when the dog first came.

Came straight to the guesthouse, as if he could tell by smell that the big house was unoccupied. Came to the screen door of the little kitchen that Fawkes's second wife and the architect had included in the guesthouse. Stared in, looking frightened, as lost dogs look. Looking hungry. Fawkes got off one shot before the dog zigzagged out of sight. Drew blood. But he must have only grazed the dog, because the next time he saw it, it wasn't even limping.

As Fawkes regarded things, he had nothing against dogs, but even though he now ran barely two hundred head of cattle, he still considered himself a rancher, and he wanted no predators hanging around his stock. Fawkes was always after his Navajo ranch hand to keep the coyote population down with M-44 cyanide devices, leghold traps, and Compound 1080. How Fawkes's coyote controls had missed the dog was more than he could fathom. He was eager to rid his lands of the intruder.

Fawkes had no patience with human intruders, either, and he frowned as he heard the sound of a heavy motor on the road that fronted his property. The road belonged to Fawkes. It stopped directly in front of the big house. Or changed, actually, since Fawkes permitted his Indian neighbors to use the road. It became a two-rut track snaking west onto the Navajo Reservation, twisting here to miss a rock outcropping, detouring there through junipers to avoid a badly cut section where one of the Navajo pickups had gotten stuck last rainy season.

Fawkes was getting on in years. When he had turned seventy he had become hard of hearing in his left ear. He couldn't place the direction the vehicle was traveling, but he assumed it was coming north from the highway. The motor noise stopped. Fawkes shouldered the rifle and started for the front of the big house. He had recently forbidden his daughter to come to the ranch. He'd be sure that it wasn't she, driving up with some new demand. If it was just a pickup filled with a Navajo family, he'd see what they wanted. To Fawkes's way of looking at things, he got along well with the Navajos.

No vehicle met Fawkes's eyes as he rounded the house. He saw no headlights. Nothing was there but gathering darkness. Since

vans and RVs had become so common, though, the occasional
tourist had been known to pull in, looking for a place to spend
the night but too dumb to drive on up the interstate to find the
roadside park. They would cook their steaks outside on their
grills. Take their showers in their tiny bathrooms. Empty their
waste tanks the next morning on the clean earth and drive away
raving about the purity and grandeur of the high desert country.

Fawkes walked to the road and stood listening for a long time.
Again, nothing. He looked back toward the big house, admiring
its graceful adobe contours. He had to say that much for his
second wife: even though Fawkes found the big house too much
trouble to live in, it was beautiful to look at. It was then, while he
spared a disinterested thought to one of his several ex-wives, that
Fawkes belatedly heard the steps in the gravel behind him,
bounding, crunching. He turned and looked.

He screamed.

At the first scent of the man's gun, fear overcame the abandoned dog. The fugue state lasted an unknowable span of time.
Then, as suddenly as fear came, it diminished, and the dog was
himself again. He rose, tail between his legs, filled with confusion.
There had been sounds. A human's brief, terrified cry. An animal's deep coughing. A tearing, rending sound of jaws on flesh.
There had been an all-permeating reek of fresh blood. There had
been a Something. The Something was huge and white, and it
smelled of blood. It came toward him. There was a final sound.
The Something had stopped. It turned. It had moved beyond the
abandoned dog's ken.

Now there was nothing except a scent that said death and
spilled blood slowly drying in the road. The dog's empty stomach
rumbled. But fear still tugged at him. He couldn't stay here to
wait again for the rabbits. When he finally moved, he detoured
wide of the house and cut across the country. The desert night
had come, stunningly starred. By starlight, the dog trotted back
toward the roadside park and the trash barrels that maybe, if the
day's bad luck had fulfilled itself, would now have scraps enough
to stay his chronic hunger.

CHAPTER 2

Gordon Christy had a patient waiting, but his fishing buddy's question sounded oddly urgent. Christy stopped and thought a moment before he said into the phone, "Yeah, Sam, it's been known to happen. There was a case a couple of years ago in Florida. A neighbor's two Pit Bull Terriers attacked and killed an elderly lady while she was just walking down her driveway. But do you really think it was a dog that killed this man down in New Mexico?"

Sam Benally's sigh came through the earpiece. The humming static of the long-distance telephone connection from Denver rushed in. At length Sam said, "I hate to say this to a veterinarian, but I sure as hell hope it was a dog. Dogs can go wild, can't they? Return to nature and all that? You see, my sister's husband has decided it was a wolf. Hell of a big one, from the mess it made. But the worst of it is, my grandmother is convinced it's a werewolf. It's a lot of nonsense, of course, but I guess the old lady won't sleep too well until she gets the idea out of her head. She's old style. A lot of my family are."

"Heck, Sam, I'm no expert on wolves," Christy said. "Feral dogs, either. But Dr. Anderson got back early from his vacation, and he's due at the clinic tomorrow. Why don't I come along with you to your family's place? Maybe I can help out in some way. Reassure your grandmother."

"Well . . . how soon do you have to get back to Vail?" Sam asked. "A week?"

"Two weeks if I want it," Christy said. "My girlfriend's out of town, and Dr. Potter has everything under control there. I could take off tomorrow and meet you at your grandmother's place. What's the address?"

"She doesn't have a street address," Sam said. There was a trace of the irony that had made sitting with him over innumerable cups of coffee on the Colorado State University campus such a pleasure back in Christy's student days. "They barely even have a road. I guess we could stick to the original plan, and I could rendezvous with you there in Durango. I'll leave Denver within the hour and drive on down. Well, maybe two hours. Make me a reservation at the Strater Hotel, will you? Tell them I'll be in late. Damn, I hate to drive Wolf Creek Pass at night, but it might even take me three hours to clean up here at the office. Can you leave your Bronco at Dr. Anderson's? We can go on together in my car."

"No, let's take the Bronco," Christy said.

"We'll flip for it. Give me a wake-up call in the morning at the hotel, and we'll meet for breakfast. Then we can get my little family problem out of the way and still go catch a few brookies up at Granite Peaks. Bring the tent and stuff. My ancestral home doesn't run to guest rooms, but what the heck, we were going to camp out anyway. There's a pretty spot by the spring. Sound okay?"

It was fine with Christy. The only Navajo he had ever met was Sam Benally, Ph.D., geology, and the only glimpse he'd ever gotten of New Mexico was on a short trip to Santa Fe. The thought of a few days on the Navajo Reservation sounded fascinating. But Christy paused for another second after putting down the phone. He and Sam were fishermen, not hunters. Christy didn't even own a gun, and if a wolf was terrorizing the countryside, a hunter sounded in order. He chuckled a little to himself. Or, for a werewolf, a hunter with silver bullets. He straightened his face as he hurried toward the examination room. Gregory's owner was beyond humor.

Like all the animals brought to Christy at the efficient little clinic in Durango, Colorado, the dog named Gregory was only temporarily Christy's patient. Veterinarians in one-man practices had a hard time taking vacations, and Dr. Noah Potter, Christy's senior colleague at their practice in the ski resort of Vail, had loaned out Christy's services to a friend. This was Gregory's second siege of acute gastrointestinal distress, and Christy had duly followed the absent vet's earlier prescription of a pink kaolin-bismuth solution, with a little neomycin and atropine, sixty cc's to be given by mouth every four hours.

But Gregory was a pathetic sight. His furry black chin had turned pink. Both front paws were pink, as well. There were traces of pink on his floppy ears, and his runny, mucus-clogged nostrils were outlined in pink.

Gregory obviously felt despondent, too. Instead of throwing himself on Christy and licking his chin, Gregory only whimpered a greeting, tail wagging madly. Christy stepped around the examination table to scratch the dog's ears.

"How's he feeling this afternoon, Miss Merriman?" Christy asked the dog's mistress.

"I think he's better," the young woman said. "Dr. Christy, do I have to keep giving him the medicine?"

"Yes, well, I can see there's a problem," Christy said. He noticed that Miss Merriman also had patches of pink drying in her hair.

"You don't know what he's like," Miss Merriman said in a desperate voice. "Gregory threw up his breakfast this morning, just to prove that I choked him to death by putting a pill down his throat. And that pink gook. There's no way in the world I can get it down him." She reached into her bag for the pink bottle Christy had given her the previous day.

Christy plucked part of the rest of the regimen from Gregory's whiskers. Two disdained pink pills, like the liquid, to coat the bowels and help soothe Gregory's tummy, as Miss Merriman put it. Christy smiled confidently. "Let me show you how," he said. "Did you give him the full dose for his ten o'clock medication?"

"I probably got down only five cc's," the young woman said. "He won't swallow. He holds his breath and blows the medicine out through his nose. Or he holds it in his mouth until I let him go, then he drools it out all over the kitchen. He made teeth at me

when I started to give him the last dose. Dr. Christy, be careful
with him. He says he'll bite."

The dog nudged Christy, telling Christy to keep scratching his
ears, and continued to slobber cheerfully. Dogs didn't know how
to hold their breath. They couldn't refrain from swallowing if the
head was held at a forty-five-degree angle and the medication, in
a dosing syringe or even a small bottle, was inserted into the
pouch between the back molars and cheek. Gregory's nose was
indeed runny, but it was unlikely that a dog could blow medicinal
bubbles through its nose. And while an amiable beast like Gregory might try a bluff on an indulgent mistress—yes, even show
his teeth—he would never bite.

Miss Merriman produced the big thirty-five cc Monoject syringe Christy had provided her, minus needle, of course. Gregory
seated himself comfortably and swept the floor with his tail as
Christy loaded it. "Now what you do," said Christy, reaching for
Gregory's muzzle, "is hold—"

Gregory bit him—not the hand that held his muzzle, but, easily shaking Christy off, the dog swung his muzzle around and bit
the arm that was bringing the syringe toward his face.

At first Christy felt no pain. Then it came, hard. Christy
cursed himself for a fool who was dumb enough to get bitten by a
dog. He didn't try to pull his arm away. Gregory's teeth held too
firmly. Christy had time to feel fury toward Gregory, then the
dog released his arm, sat back a foot, and stared Christy in the
eye, asking if Christy wanted to try again.

"Oh, my God!" said Miss Merriman. "Dr. Christy, are you all
right? Gregory, you're a bad, bad boy."

Christy also felt angry at her. Monstrous Miss Merriman, har-
boring a fiend like Gregory. But this was no time to be silly, and
it was no time to quit. Christy's arm was bleeding freely. He
halted long enough to grab a sterile pad and apply pressure to the
wound. He wiped off the excess blood, took a fresh pad and taped
it firmly over the wound, and instructed Miss Merriman, "Hold
his muzzle, if you will. I'm going to get him up on the examination table."

By now Christy was far less certain than he sounded, but he

stepped to Gregory's side and said briskly, "Okay, Gregory, up you go," and boosted the dog onto the table. Gregory's feet scrabbled. Few animals liked the slick stainless-steel surface. Christy reached under the dog for the far front and rear paws, pulled, and Gregory went gently over on his side, feet paddling in the air. Intimidated by the height of the table and his vulnerable position, Gregory offered no objections as Christy retrieved the syringe full of medication, raised the dog's head, and slowly but steadily emptied the syringe into Gregory's cheek pouch.

"Look," Miss Merriman said, "he's swallowing it."

"We haven't left him much choice this time," Christy said. "But since he objects so much to oral medication, I'd also like to give him an injection of atropine."

"Then I don't have to give him any more of the pink gook?"

"I think it's best not to," Christy said, in what he felt was one of the bigger understatements of his life. "It's one thing for him to nip his vet but quite another to try to nip you. Bad for discipline."

"Your arm's still bleeding. Dr. Christy, I'm so sorry."

"It was my fault," Christy said. He decided to lie by implication. "Getting nipped once in a while reminds us that dogs don't grow teeth just to chew dog biscuits."

Christy refrained from saying he had never been bitten before, not by dog, rabbit, squirrel, gerbil, or even cat, and many cats didn't hesitate to apply teeth and claws in remarking that they had no use for a rabies shot or didn't want to give a blood sample. Christy popped two cc's of the atropine into a shaggy fold of skin at Gregory's neck and lifted the dog from the table. The dog sat and wagged his tail, apparently holding no grudge against Christy for having forced him to bite.

Bite it was, not a nip, and it was deep. A pair of real puncture wounds, top and bottom. Pretty good laceration from the brief grinding of the molars, too. The first thing Christy did after Gregory and Miss Merriman departed was to wash the wound thoroughly with Betadine scrub at the sink in the examination room. The second was to check Gregory's chart and breathe more easily when he found a notation that said Gregory's last

rabies shot was less than three months old. The third was to go
look for Toni Willet, the vacationing vet's chief assistant. All his
anger had gone. Now Christy felt only the pain and the foolish-
ness, which turned his pleasant young face red from his cheeks to
the roots of his sandy hair as he went to confess he had been
stupid enough to become a dog-bite statistic.

Mrs. Willet already knew. She came out of the surgery carrying tape and gauze. "How bad is it?" she asked. "I'm sorry about
Gregory. I should have left a note on his chart. He looks so good-
natured. He *is* good-natured. But he's swung on Dr. Anderson a
few times, too."

"I'll bet Dr. Anderson had sense enough to stay out of fang
range," Christy said.

Mrs. Willet busied herself checking Christy's wound. "Hmm,
nasty," she said. "I've already asked Brenda to tell Dr. Anderson
to come straight in, and I'll call Dr. Melina's office and tell them
you're coming over. Don't let Melina suture that puncture, Dr.
Christy. Tell him I said it needs to drain. He'll listen. Tell him to
get you started right away on antibiotics. There's no sense in
risking blood-poisoning. It looks like mainly soft-tissue damage.
Does it hurt? Maybe I'd better drive you over."

"Thanks, no. I won't have any trouble. It's bad enough to drag
Dr. Anderson away from home on the last afternoon of his vacation."

"I imagine he'll be delighted. Three hours in surgery trying to
patch up one of the poor dogs that are always falling out of the
back of pickup trucks seems far more refreshing to Dr. Anderson
than staying home. It must have something to do with his kids."

True, vacationing with four young children might have had a
bearing on the Andersons' decision to return early from a motor
trip to San Francisco, and, at that, to have driven all night to cut
the trip still shorter. When they'd arrived early that morning,
Mrs. Anderson had looked very happy pulling up in front of her
house to let a flood of lively young Andersons out of the car.

While subbing at the clinic, Christy had stayed at the Andersons' house. Christy's dog, a Doberman named Gala, was polite
with strangers, but he'd brought Gala out to the clinic with him

that morning, stashing her in an outside run. He went to fetch her as he left for the doctor's office. Gala loved car rides and, weather permitting, he took her everywhere with him.

When Christy appeared with her leash in his hand, the black Doberman began to sniff him all over, as she always did when he had been around other animals. The wound caught her attention. She tentatively put her nose a quarter-inch from Christy's bandaged arm and sniffed deeply at a spot of fresh blood welling from the wound. She sniffed, inhaling, and sniffed again, until Christy became uneasy and told her, "Cut it out, Gala. We're going for a ride."

His only major purchase since becoming a full-fledged practicing veterinarian had been a flame-colored Bronco, a four-wheel-drive vehicle that could handle Colorado back country and bad roads with ease. It was Gala's passion. She leaped around his legs, docked tail wagging furiously, making playful stabs as if she was going to nip him. When he finally managed to snap on her leash, she lunged ahead, dragging him to the car.

It was July, but three successive rainy afternoons in this mountainous southwest corner of Colorado had left the area pleasantly cool. Christy found shade under which to park and left plenty of window open, although not enough for the Doberman to leap out if she saw a chipmunk that needed chasing. Christy figured correctly that they would be in for a wait. All bite wounds were contaminated. He spent nearly an hour soaking his arm in an iodine solution before the doctor decided the punctures might be reasonably clean. He got jabbed with a shot of cephalothin and sent away with a prescription for more, plus one for a painkiller in case the pain kept him from sleeping that night.

The afternoon schedule at the animal clinic had looked quiet enough, with only a baby ferret with an eye infection to break the usual routine, but Christy decided to check in promptly and offer to relieve Dr. Anderson. Until tomorrow, Anderson was still officially on vacation.

A mud-covered Jeep pulled in quickly beside Christy as he parked at the animal clinic. Gala grumbled, spotting another dog in the Jeep, and Christy told her, "Quiet, girl." He took in the vehicle with a casual glance. Two men leaped from it and to-gether lifted a big Rottweiler from the rear seat. The Rott's left rear leg dangled uselessly, a jagged edge of the tibia protruding below the stifle joint. The men cradling the Rottweiler staggered into a jog toward the clinic. Christy yelled, "Don't do that!" He jumped out of his car, leaving Gala barking in his wake.

The two men stopped, looking panic-stricken.

"You've got to support that leg," Christy said. He tried to speak very calmly. "Careful now, it looks like he's going into shock. Don't make a big fuss. Just lay him down very, very easily in the shade."

"Are you a vet?" one of the men asked in a small, pathetic voice.

"I'm Dr. Christy. I've been sitting in for Dr. Anderson. That's it. Talk to him soothingly. No, don't try to force him. He'll lie the way it's most comfortable."

The black-and-tan Rottweiler looked like a giant-sized version of Gala the Doberman, with a huge head and heavy muscles. Christy figured him for a hundred and twenty pounds minimum. The dog shivered and breathed weakly. Already in pain, disori-ented, he didn't like being approached by a stranger. At the sight of Christy, he struggled to roll to his chest and even tried to move his fractured leg under him so he could rise. There was real menace in the dark brown eyes that he turned on Christy, and he let out a growl from deep in his throat.

Fear stabbed cold claws into Christy's stomach. He stiffened and had to force himself to kneel by the dog. In a quiet voice he said, "All right, old boy. It's going to be all right."

The dog's master looked anxiously at Christy. It was the sec-ond man who said, "What do we do, Doc?"

Christy glanced up at the man. "Dr. Anderson's in the clinic. Tell him or Mrs. Willet we've got a compound fracture, and we'll have to move the dog on a flat surface. Tell him it's a Rott. Tell him the dog's in shock."

The man ran for the clinic. Mercifully for Christy if not for the dog, the Rottweiler collapsed and rolled to his right side. But his breathing continued. Christy felt for the third rib and the heart.

The pulse seemed steady. A stethoscope was only a few yards away in the clinic, but it might as well have been a few miles. Christy reached for the femoral artery in the dog's groin to double-check. It was all right. No need for heart massage.

The owner swallowed a sob. "Charger's dying, isn't he?"

"Not by a long shot," Christy said. He spoke quickly. "There's a sleeping bag and a blanket on the floor of my car. Get both. Open the door, and I'll call the Dobe. She won't hurt you."

"I'm not afraid of dogs," the owner said.

"Good. Get moving." He looked over his shoulder as Gala started barking again. "Gala, come!" he commanded. "Good girl. Now down, stay."

When the dog's owner returned with Christy's bedroll, Christy placed it under the Rottweiler's hindquarters, raising them slightly. "Put the blanket over him," he said. "We've got to keep him warm." He glanced at Gala. The blanket was hers. But the Doberman, lying obediently in a down position six feet away, made no objections.

The second man returned, Dr. Anderson hard on his heels. The slim, bespectacled veterinarian looked serious and deeply interested. "Instruct me, Dr. Christy," he said. "Will a hammock stretcher do?"

"I think we've got shock and a compound fracture of the tibia, Dr. Anderson," Christy said. He checked the dog again. The Rott was still shivering and his feet and legs were cold, but a little color was returning to the mucus membranes. "Let's see if we can immobilize the limb," he suggested. "Then a hammock stretcher will be fine."

Mrs. Willet waited at the door of the clinic. Anderson called to her for splints and roller gauze, then knelt with Christy beside the dog. The older vet pushed a lock of hair off his forehead and said to the owner, "Exactly what happened here, Mr. Carpenter?"

Carpenter didn't seem to know where to start. The second man answered for him. "Carpenter and Charger were helping us look for that boy that's lost up on Engineer Mountain. Charger was tracking not fifty yards from us. It was rocky. I saw him slip. Just slip, a little. He didn't even howl, but we saw him thrashing around."

"Poor Charger," Carpenter said. He stroked the dog's head.

Dr. Anderson said, "Charger's a strong young dog. It'll take more than a fractured tibia to put him out of business. If you can just move back, Mr. Carpenter, we'll get busy here."

Both vets went quickly to work splinting the fractured leg and moving the dog to a canvas carrier brought by Mrs. Willet. With a glance at Christy's bandaged arm, Anderson beckoned the second man to help carry the Rottweiler into the clinic. Christy was left with Charger's owner and with Gala the Doberman, who, to Christy's mild amazement, had remained quietly in her down position during all the hubbub.

Carpenter seemed to cast about for something other than his injured dog to think about. He nodded at Gala. "Nice little Dobe," he said. "What have you got on her? C.D.X.? U.D.?"

Christy groped a moment for the terms and realized that Carpenter was speaking of obedience trial degrees—Companion Dog Excellent, Utility Dog. He said, "Nothing, actually. Though she was in a pound before I got her. So heaven knows."

"Get somebody that really knows obedience to work her for you," Carpenter said. "They can help you figure out her training. Charger is a U.D. Now I have him in Schutzhund. I'll bet your Dobe'd be darn good at Schutzhund. She looks like she'd have what it takes. Charger and I were just starting on man-work. Boy, does he turn on."

"Man-work?" A newly familiar chill hit Christy's spine. "You mean, like in attack-dog training?"

"Sure. We call it protection training, though."

"You give a command and the dog will attack?"

"You bet your boots. Charger is a natural." The man paused and gulped. "Was, I guess I should say."

Christy preferred the standard chore of soothing clients to talking of attacks by a dog. He said the proper things. Give Dr. Anderson a little time. A fractured tibia could mean nothing but a minor limp, maybe not even that. He would just look in on things, and Mr. Carpenter would be given a report in no time.

Christy put a reluctant Gala back into her run and ducked through the back door to lend assistance to Dr. Anderson. Mrs. Willet intercepted him before he could reach the surgery. "Your arm's hurting badly, isn't it?" she said. "Here. It's Tylenol with a little codeine. I usually keep a few in my purse. I'm prone to periodontal abscesses at extremely awkward times."

Christy's arm was aching actively. He accepted the pill gratefully and said, "Thanks a lot, Mrs. Willet. You're the most organized person I've ever met. How's the Rottweiler doing?"

"Beautifully. No problem in stabilization. Dr. Anderson just can't wait to start repair of the Achilles tendon, but what he's really looking forward to is pinning the fractured tibia. He's in there whistling. His kids had diarrhea all the way through those California deserts, where the nearest service station is a hundred miles away and there's not a single bush to hide behind. Do you want to remove a few sutures from a spayed cat? Or would you rather go into Dr. Anderson's office and lie down on the couch for a while?"

Christy gladly voted for the cat. By three-thirty, the Rottweiler had checked out as a good anesthesia risk, and the two vets set the fractured leg, then moved on to other cases. An hour later they were all caught up, and they had time to sit together and discuss a few non-routine points of cases Christy had handled in Dr. Anderson's absence, including Christy's decision to take Gregory off oral medication. Memory jogged Christy, and he suddenly sat up straighter.

"Darn, I forgot," he said to Anderson. "I was supposed to make a reservation for tonight at the Strater for my buddy, Sam Benally. You don't suppose it's too late, do you?"

"Let me call," Anderson said. "The manager's a friend of mine. Hotels always keep a few rooms open, I guess in case some guest stays over longer than he'd planned. What does your friend want? A single?"

Christy thought of the ache in his arm and the four young Anderson children and the fact that Mrs. Anderson might enjoy having her house all to herself. He fibbed a little. "A two-bed double," he said. "I told Sam I'd spend the night with him at the hotel."

It was soon arranged. Christy didn't know if the hotel accepted dogs, but he was guiltily willing to sneak Gala in. He fibbed some more and declined an invitation to dine with the Andersons, saying Sam might roll in at any time, and at five o'clock he said good-bye to the receptionist and went to look for Mrs. Willet. After a ten-minute bout of packing and a farewell drink at the Andersons' house, he would be off to wait for Sam.

Mrs. Willet was with Charger the Rottweiler. Anderson's clinic was not as fancily equipped as the clinic in Vail, where Christy worked with Dr. Potter. There was no intensive-care area or transport cages in which an animal could sleep off anesthesia. Instead, Mrs. Willet had spread a clean blanket on the floor of an inside run, where Charger had no possibility of rolling off if he thrashed about, as dogs often did when coming out of anesthesia. Just as Christy looked into the kennel, the big dog swung his head suddenly upward and stared at Christy. The eyes were glassy, the dog only partially conscious, but, uncontrollably, Christy jerked back, knowing again the fear that had come when Charger first growled at him.

"Coming up fast, isn't he?" Mrs. Willet said happily. She settled the big dog's head down again. "I'll tell Dr. Anderson."

She left Christy alone with the dog and his fear. Christy asked himself what in the blackest hell had come over him. He couldn't possibly have started being afraid of dogs because of one minor bite. He forced himself to step forward, lean down, and put a hand on Charger's head. Then both hands, arranging the big head in a less strained position. Charger gulped, working his mouth, then subsided again, and Christy slowly straightened and went to the outside runs for Gala. He felt pretty good. The fear, he told himself, had been only momentary.

Gala jumped eagerly into the car. Christy put the key in the ignition and thought for a minute of Charger. A few days learning how real old-fashioned Indians lived, then about ten days pursuing trout near Colorado's Granite Peaks sounded like an even better prescription than Dr. Melina's antibiotic and the

painkiller, which prescription he reminded himself he still had to
fill. That sudden fear he'd felt of a poor dog would be long gone
before he returned to the supercharged atmosphere of Vail.

Christy started the car and turned to give a pat to the Doberman on the seat next to him. She flashed him her smile, putting
her ears back, opening her mouth, and huffing at him. He told
her, "Gala, we're going to a real hotel, and we're going to order
dinner from room service, and your chum Sam Benally is going
to turn up sometime during the night, but he'd better not snore.
Right, girl?"

Gala huffed some more, and Christy smiled, too. For a pleasant change of scenery, there was nothing like having an appointment with a werewolf on the Navajo Reservation.

CHAPTER 3

Christy thought his friend herculean when, despite a very late arrival the night before, he insisted they start as soon as they could get breakfast. Sam approved Christy's four-wheeler with a single nod, arranged with the hotel to garage his own Buick, then climbed into the Bronco beside Christy and promptly went back to sleep, leaving Christy to meditate on how often he failed to understand people's motives. Of course Sam had been willing to leave immediately. He had known good and well he could catch up on his sleep and let Christy do the driving. At least driving was a distraction from the pain in Christy's arm. It was sorer today than yesterday.

New Mexico tended to declare itself the moment one crossed the state border. From any direction, on any highway, a vast, empty vista usually opened up, with at least one remote mesa on the horizon. But the view that greeted Christy when he cleared the town of Farmington, New Mexico, was a huge power plant appearing to the east, smokestacks fouling the sparkling air. Sam roused and grunted, "They're torturing the mountain." Then he went back to sleep again.

Christy wondered until they passed the next town, Shiprock, what his friend had meant, but Sam finally woke up. His dark face lacked animation. He said, "Where'd you put the coffee?"

Christy reached for the thermos on the floorboard. "Who's torturing what mountain?" he asked.

Sam clasped the thermos bottle as though he was warming his hands on it. He grinned. "The likes of me, I guess," he said. "A lot of old-timers don't like the strip-mining in the northern part of the reservation. They think one of the sacred mountains is being tortured, to get out the coal. What can you do? California wants power, and the Navajo people need money."

He yawned. Sam had taught geology for a few years but now worked for the technical assistance center of CERT, the Council of Energy Resource Tribes. If the Coeur d'Alene tribe in Idaho hoped to determine how much uranium it had on its reservation, or the Hopi tribe in Arizona optimistically wanted core drilling to determine depth and quality of possible oil reserves, Sam hopped up to Idaho or down to Arizona to help with the project. The thirty-seven Indian tribes that belonged to the consortium had wearied of poor returns on vast energy treasures lying beneath Indian lands. They wanted to know what they had. They planned to set better terms on what they got for it.

Gala the Doberman spoke up in the back seat. One sharp yap. In her private language, it meant she wanted a stop. Since the dog went along on their fishing trips, Sam knew her signals, and he said, "Let's walk Gala and then drink some coffee. You can pull off anywhere around here. Nobody lives closer than a couple of miles."

Christy obediently looked for a wide piece of shoulder. "Are we already on the reservation?" he asked.

"Sure. You've been on it for the last thirty miles."

They stopped in a wide valley, with a deep arroyo to the east and a tower of red rock far to the west. Dry, purplish mountains rose behind the rock formation. They piled out and addressed themselves to the thermos of coffee while Gala rushed busily to the first clump of brown scrub and began investigating. Sam nodded toward the towering rock. "That's Shiprock," he said. "It doesn't look very imposing from this angle, but at least you can say you've seen a senile volcano."

Christy gawked with interest. "Is that what it is, a senile volcano?"

"The world's leading example," Sam said. "But then, there are a lot of volcanic necks around."

"Where do the Navajos live?" Christy said. "I came to sightsee, and I haven't seen a single Indian so far."

"You nut, they're all over the place. For that matter, you're looking straight at one. But no photographs, please. Not without a fiver changing hands. Us Native Americans will allow tourists to look at us for free, but you'd better do even that politely. No staring."

"I'll try to behave."

"Aw, just be yourself."

"Are you awake yet?" Christy asked. "I've been a little interested in hearing about this werewolf."

Sam glanced at him with hooded eyes. "We won't know too much until we get there," he said. "So far all I know for sure is that an old guy named Hugh Fawkes got his throat ripped out not far from my family's place night before last."

"I'm skeptical," Christy said. "I looked at the moon last night, and it's barely past the half-moon stage."

"What does that have to do with anything?"

"Haven't you seen any old werewolf movies? It's standard to have heavy fog hanging on the ground, and it's got to be a full moon." He recited. " 'Even a man who is pure at heart and says his prayers at night/May become a wolf when the wolfbane blooms and the moon is full and bright.' "

Sam said, "My grandmother wouldn't know your standard Hollywood werewolf if one ate her for dinner. What she's worried about is a Navajo wolf. A human wolf."

"There's a difference?"

"Yeah. Well . . . It's just one of the witchcraft superstitions. But don't kid her about it, Christy. A lot of people still believe in that kind of stuff."

"What's a Navajo werewolf supposedly like?"

Sam looked carefully at his plastic cup of coffee. "It's a person that's gone bad and becomes a witch. They cover themselves with the hide of a coyote or a wolf. At night, of course. Or I guess I've heard of them wearing the skin of a dog or a bear, too. Some people say they go whole hog and actually turn into an animal. In its human state a witch digs up dead men and takes the jewelry they're buried with and sells it, so witches are rich. They practice incest, and they go after victims by blowing corpse poison in their faces or putting a spell on them. Come to think of it, I've never heard of a Navajo wolf tearing out anyone's throat before. You hear of them attacking a sheep or a horse that way, but not a person."

"Do people really believe in this?"

"Some do. But I wouldn't talk to anyone else about it if I were you, Christy. You *bilagáanas* have some crazy superstitions, too. Tell a Navajo it's unlucky to walk under a ladder and he'll have a good chuckle as soon as you're out of earshot. But it's human nature not to like being ridiculed about your beliefs."

"Sam, I'm sorry," Christy said. "I didn't mean to poke fun."

"Of course not. Besides, I don't believe any of that stuff. I don't even know too much about all the taboos and what not. That's what happens when you spend most of your life off the reservation going to school. I guess I might not have heard about Navajo wolves, except . . ."

"Sam, we don't have to talk about any kind of wolves," Christy said. "Tell me about this Hugh Fawkes instead."

"No, you ought to know this. We'll probably find that some people avoid us—me and my family, at least. It's better if you understand. You see, one of my great-uncles was killed about twenty years ago over near Dinnebito Wash. Some poor guy's four children all died, and the guy got it into his head my great-uncle was a Navajo wolf who'd killed them. So he went after my uncle with a hatchet. It was pretty bloody. Then the man committed suicide. A tragedy, all because of superstitious hogwash. But a little bit of a stigma sort of stuck to the family. Mr. Fawkes's death seems to have brought it up again. My sister was crying yesterday afternoon when I talked to her. She'd gone down to Lupton to call me, and a dozen kids hanging around the chapter house ran away the minute they saw her."

"Your poor sister," Christy said.

"Ruthy will be all right. She's a strong woman," Sam said. "Thank goodness it wasn't my younger sister, Irene. She'd still be in tears, but with Ruthy a storm never lasts long. Besides, I set it up for Ruthy and her husband to drive over to Gallup and meet us for lunch at her favorite restaurant. That always gives her a

kick. And I figured we could get all the details about Mr.
Fawkes's death from Harley and not have to talk about it in front
of the rest of the family." He checked his watch. "Call Gala and
let's hit the road."

The two-lane Highway 666 ran straight south, requiring no
driving skills except in passing a slow pickup or car. Tipped off
by Sam, Christy realized that most of the drivers were Indian. He
didn't know what he'd been expecting. Laughing Boy wrapped in
a blanket and riding by on a spotted pony? A Navajo woman
weaving rugs outside a dirt-and-log hogan? Instead, three dark-
haired teenagers riding in the back of a pickup ahead of them all
wore jeans and windbreakers, and two adults in the front of the
pickup seemed to be dressed just as ordinarily. He concluded that
all the mobile homes and small rectangular houses he'd been
passing must be Navajo residences. There, that was a six-sided
hogan, but it was pink stucco with an asphalt-tile roof. Christy
laughed silently at himself. Knowing Sam Benally—expert fly
fisherman, Denver Bronco fan, history buff, resident of a modern
condo in the Denver suburb of Englewood—how could he have
overlooked the possibility that other Navajos might be every bit
as modernized?

They passed a cluster of cricket pumps—three pumping oil,
two sitting idle—and Christy asked, "About this Mr. Fawkes,
was he in oil or something? What was he doing on the reservation?"

"He lived right next to the reservation, not on it," Sam said.
"He was a queer old duck. Bought four or five sections back in
the fifties when land there was going for about five dollars an
acre. Hell, it's still not worth anything."

"What did he do for a living?" Christy asked.

"Fawkes had independent means from some source. Not serious wealth, but enough that he didn't have to bother making
money if he didn't want to. But he was always dabbling with
something. Ran some cattle. Had a bunch of mining engineers in
during the uranium boom, but they didn't find anything. Built a
trading post on the highway, then leased it out after a while. He
even plowed up a wash on his place one year and planted pinto

beans. Darned if I don't believe he got a pretty good crop, but he never kept on with anything."

Christy tried to find a slot to fit the man in. "A hermit living out in the desert," he decided. "I've heard of people like that."

"Hardly a hermit," Sam said. "His main hobby was getting married and divorced. He even married a Navajo woman or two. One of the Anglo wives had a really beautiful house built. Santa Fe style, so it's a little out of place, but it's still an eye-popper. The last I heard about Fawkes, though, he was living by himself for a change, happy as a robin. Grandmother knew him pretty well. He helped her get a horse untangled from some barbed wire once. He didn't mind being helpful, if he was in the mood for it. Of course, I don't believe he spoke more than a half-dozen words of Navajo, so there was the usual communication barrier."

"Did he have any children?"

"Not living with him," Sam said. "I believe he had a few kids by this wife or that, but they're surely grown up by now. He was a pretty old guy."

Sam fell silent, leaving Christy to learn that New Mexico had gorgeous clouds, Bill's Produce accepted food stamps, and Crackerjacks could be bought for $15.95 a case, if anyone chanced to want a few cases of Crackerjacks. The two lanes of the highway became a four-lane approach to Gallup, and Sam directed Christy to a hotel named El Rancho on the eastern edge of the busy, crowded town. The hotel looked old and interesting. Just Sam's sort of place, like the charmingly antique Str ter Hotel back in Durango, or Sam's favorite, the Brown Palace in Denver, where they'd gone a couple of times for festive dinners. When Sam drove over to Vail to haul Christy away from the clinic for some weekend fishing, he always claimed he felt out of his element. Vail was a newish resort with no history, as far as Sam was concerned, and he declared he was intimidated by its many English pubs, its restaurants with Austrian Alps decor specializing in prime rib of buffalo, even its Cal-Mex-style restaurants with jungles of hanging plants reaching tendrils toward the crab enchiladas.

The sprawling white hotel must have been a knockout in its

day, Christy decided. He parked Gala and the Bronco a block
away in good shade, and he and Sam walked back, discussing
what to eat.

"The blueplate special or steak," Sam advised. "And please
don't order fish, Christy. Don't even say 'fish.' My sister would
be shocked to know how many rainbows I've consumed in the
last decade. Proper Navajos still don't eat fish. Don't ask me
why. I've forgotten. But whatever's on the lunch menu will probably be all right. The food's not brilliant, but it's always good."

"Why does your sister like the place so much?"

"I guess because my mother always wanted to eat here. When
she finally got to, she thought it was a real wow. She used to tell
Ruthy and Irene and me about the salad. Probably just a plain
green salad, but she was so impressed when the waiter served it
before the entrée. Then she didn't know when she was supposed
to eat it. Before the meal didn't seem right, so she saved it to eat
with her roast beef or whatever. The waiter must have decided
she didn't want it. He took it away, and she never got to eat the
salad."

"So we'll be darned sure to eat the salad the minute it comes,
right?" Christy said.

"You bet. I don't want to give you a wrong impression about
the hotel. It welcomes Navajos and, for all I know, it always has.
But in my mother's day an Indian didn't feel welcome just anywhere. They used to make her sit in the balcony at the movie, I
remember. Whites downstairs, Indians up— Hey, Ruthy! Harley!
Here we are."

Sam Benally's brother-in-law, Harley Tsosie, was a heavy-bel-
lied man dressed in slacks, sports shirt, and a big Stetson. Sam's
sister was a study in contrasts. She had her long black hair
wrapped in a bun and wore a full pleated skirt, like pictures
Christy had seen of old-fashioned Navajo women, but the skirt
only came down to a point right below the knee, and instead of a
velvet tunic she had on a prim white sweater. Both Harley and
Ruthy wore superb bracelets of heavy silver and turquoise, and
Ruthy's fingers were covered to the knuckles with beautifully

worked rings. She kissed her brother and gave Christy a firm handshake.

"So you're Sam's New York friend," she said.

"I just grew up there," Christy said. "I live in Colorado now."

"Yes, Sam's told us about you. I'm glad he brought you. I keep telling Harley it's a runaway dog that did that thing, and he keeps saying it's one of Bianca Wilson's wolves over at the trading post. You can straighten Harley out."

Sam said, "When did the Wilsons get any wolves?"

"This spring," Ruthy said. "Your own nephew went out to California with Brad Wilson to get them. I guess Irene didn't want to write you about that. Let's go in and get a table in the corner before the restaurant fills up. We can't sit out in the middle of the room and talk about this kind of thing."

There were cases of magnificent Navajo and Zuni jewelry in the lobby and splendid Navajo rugs on the walls. Christy tabled further thought of wolves until they'd ordered and the inevitable salads were placed before them. Then he asked, "What's this about someone bringing in wolves?"

Harley said, "Fawkes's place, the State Line Trading Post. It's got one of those zoos. 'See the giant rattlesnake.' 'See the grizzly bear.'"

"Good Lord, is there really a grizzly?" Christy asked.

"No. It's just that kind of place," Harley said. "But the woman who's running it now has some real wolves in there. I went and looked at them. One he-wolf and two she-wolves. Bianca says there's no way they can get out, but I keep telling Ruthy, one of Bianca's wolves got out and did it, and that's what I'm telling you. I saw the tracks at Fawkes's ranch."

Sam came to attention. "There were animal tracks?"

"Big ones," Harley said. "Four inches long, or close. What kind of dog has a foot that big?"

Sam's eyes swung to Christy, who put down his fork and admitted, "I've never had occasion to measure a dog's foot, but you're talking about a good-sized animal. Maybe about the size of a Great Dane or a Mastiff. Or maybe even a wolf-dog cross. We're beginning to see all too many of that sort."

Ruthy nodded wisely. "Some dumb Hopi south of Second Mesa crossed his German Shepherd with a coyote. Harley, you know that man I mean. He's half-Mexican himself. He told Annie Deschinny's husband he wanted tough puppies. Macho."

"It's not a good idea," Christy said. "I've met a litter of Dingo —Setter crosses and they're not very reliable canine citizens."

"Then maybe it was one of those wild-dog crosses that went for Old Man Fawkes," Ruthy argued. "Or what about a pack of coyotes? Maybe a whole pack of coyotes attacked him."

"Coyote tracks aren't near that big," Harley said stubbornly. "I tell you, it was one of the Wilsons' wolves."

Sam asked, "Did the sheriff's men take casts of the tracks? We could stop by before we leave Gallup, and Christy could look at them."

"Nobody took casts," Harley said. "I told Tully Kee he'd better take casts, but he said it was on the McKinley County side of the line, and he didn't carry around plaster of paris anyhow."

"So who's investigating?" Sam asked. "McKinley County or the Navajo police?"

"They all messed around awhile, and then they all went away," Harley said. "If you ask me, nobody's investigating, and all the hell they have to do is prove it was one of the Wilsons' wolves and people will stop acting so damned funny about your family. That witch talk this spring already had people stirred up. Now they're acting crazy. I don't want anything nasty to happen to Ruthy or the rest of the family. Something's got to be done. Somebody's got to catch that wolf and shoot it before it kills anyone else."

Ruthy gave Harley a warning glance. She couldn't have spoken more plainly if she had simply said aloud, "Not in front of a stranger, dummy."

Sam's round face registered the reference to witches impassively. He changed the subject and explained to Christy, "Sounds like a jurisdictional dispute. It happens once in a while. The Navajo Division of Public Safety has a substation just a hiccup up the road at Lupton, but the nearest McKinley County sheriff's office is here in Gallup."

Ruthy said, "Well, you know how it is. Fawkes's house is twenty or thirty yards on the New Mexico side of the border, but the New Mexico law is saying he was killed on the road, and the road's in Arizona or on the reservation. They'd have to get a surveyor out to settle it, and all the time that runaway dog is loose, and we'd better not go out of the house at night."

Harley said explosively, "Don't tell me about a dog. Don't tell me about coyotes. It was one of the Wilsons' wolves. You weren't there. I went there. I saw the tracks. It was easy because it rained just that afternoon. Tully Kee and I could see a lot of clear tracks."

Christy plucked Sam Benally's pen from his pocket and drew a quick sketch on his paper napkin. A pad that was more kidney-shaped than it should be. Four egg-shaped toes. Four small tear-drops for the claws. "Did they look anything like this?" he asked Harley.

"Just like that. Is that a dog or a wolf?"

"It could be either," Christy admitted. "It depends on the size. Sam, let's pick up a tape measure after lunch. We can do some measuring. Do you suppose the tracks are still there, Harley?"

Harley seemed disquieted. "I don't know," he said. "I didn't go look again. I didn't like it. Maybe for the same reason Tully Kee claimed he didn't have anything to make a cast with. There was something funny about those tracks."

"What?" Ruthy demanded. "Why didn't you tell me?"

Harley sighed. "So you wouldn't get any scareder than you already are. Kee and I picked up the first tracks on the opposite side of Fawkes's road. We could follow them six, eight feet before they were all over, trampling around, right where the . . . the body was found. Then the tracks went up near the house, and they went pretty near the little house by the swimming pool and there was some more trampling, but then they cut back, heading to the road, and then they . . . were gone."

Sam said in a low, angry voice, "What in hell do you mean, Harley? You lost the tracks? It was rocky, right? But you picked the tracks up again, didn't you?"

"No. We couldn't find a thing. They just . . . vanished."

CHAPTER 4

An hour later, Sam Benally gestured out the car window, encompassing with one wave the vastness of the wild and broken country southwest of Gallup. He said, "Come on, Christy. You can't tell me there aren't wolves running around out here. There are places where I'll bet a person doesn't set foot once a decade. If then. How can anyone really know that the wolves have all been killed off?"

Ahead on the highway, Christy could see a sudden upthrust of red cliffs that began to weave a new pattern into the sand-colored canyons and eroded mesas that surrounded them. He had to agree with Sam. Anything could be hidden in this eerie emptiness. He said, "I can only tell you what the authorities say. There are supposedly only about twelve hundred wolves surviving in Minnesota, with maybe a small population in places like the northern Rockies and Mexico. Loners could be roaming around here, I guess."

"Guess, guess," Sam grumbled. "Some animal expert you are."

"Did I ever claim to be a wildlife authority? I'm just a plain vet in small-animal practice."

"Then how can you be so sure a wolf has never attacked a man in the whole United States?" Sam said.

Christy shifted his bandaged arm. "I read a lot of bite statistics," he said. "Besides, the experts all agree. There's never been a documented case of a wolf attack in the U.S. Even in Europe, with all its Big Bad Wolf stories, there's been only one fully documented case of wolves killing people. It was a couple of centuries ago in France. I hate to keep singing the same song, but the attacks stopped after two huge animals were captured and they turned out to be wolf-dog crosses, I assume with the usual highly unpredictable temperament. Face it, Sam. If a wolf attacks anyone, the wolf's probably rabid, and you've got to blame the rabies, not the natural proclivities of the wolf."

Sam sat up straighter. "That's a sweet thought," he said. "I wonder if anyone examined Old Man Fawkes's body for traces of rabies. Do you have to have the head of an animal that bit someone? Or can you tell from the body of the victim?"

"If you cultured tissue from the bite wound, I guess—"

"No more guesses, thanks. Your message is clear. You're just a plain veterinarian, not a rabies expert, either. Turn in at the first tourist trap, will you? That's Ann Lang's very own handmade Indian ruin. Ann knows everything that happens along the highway. You can make your phone call there, and I can have a chat with her."

Smarting a little at Sam's criticism, Christy slowed down. It wasn't Sam's fault, of course. He had a lot on his mind, what with his family under a twenty-year cloud of superstition and potential danger. Christy wondered how good-natured he himself would be if his mother in New York had to face daily accusations of being a witch from her neighbors. Although she'd probably love it.

Civilization of a sort seemed to cluster at the base of the cliffs. In front of a rambling stockade a sign proclaimed, PAINTED CLIFFS RUIN. TRADING POST. JEWELRY. A quarter-mile farther along there was a second sign, STATE LINE TRADING POST. INDIAN TRADER. WHOLESALE-RETAIL JEWELRY. Across the highway from that, a trio of Navajo women had set up a more modest business establishment, a brush shelter with a clothesline full of Navajo rugs. Two cars had stopped to inspect the rugs. The two permanent trading posts appeared to be doing no business at the moment.

As Christy parked in front of the stockade with the PAINTED CLIFFS RUIN sign, he could catch a tantalizing glimpse of what looked like an ancient multi-storied building nestled into a shallow cave in the cliffs. He asked, "Why did your friend go to all the trouble of building a ruin?"

"She didn't," Sam said. "She bought it after an old desert rat spent about forty years pasting it together. It was real once, and I guess the old fellow didn't know enough not to try to restore it. Ann charges the tourists a couple of bucks a head to climb around in it."

To the right as they entered the stockade, a girl in neat navy blue shorts and blue shirt sat on a stool by a gate, ready to sell admission tickets. She smiled at them and said, "Mr. Benally?"

"That's right."

"Mrs. Lang thought she recognized you." She picked up a walkie-talkie and spoke briefly into it, then said, "She's expecting you around at the house. She's busy unpacking some more books."

"What's she researching this time?" Sam asked.

"Another TV mini-series," the girl said. "Twelfth-century Britain. Lucky me, between tourists I get to read up on medieval looms."

"You're in a good area right here for old-fashioned looms and spinning techniques," Sam said.

The girl offered them another smile. "Yeah, Miss Lang figures I can fish up a nice little comparative study for my anthropology seminar next fall."

To the left, another girl in the same navy blue shorts-and-shirt outfit was washing the display windows of a shop. Sam waved Christy toward a flagstone path. "College kids," he explained. "Ann hires a couple every summer to guide tourists through the ruin. Then she puts them on double-duty helping her on research projects."

"What does she research?" Christy asked.

"General movie stuff. She came out here from Hollywood, and she still gets some freelance assignments. She checks on what kind of sandals people wore in Pompeii. What colors people painted their drawing rooms in Colonial America. Things like that."

"Why in the world would a film researcher move to the middle of a New Mexico nowhere?" Christy asked.

"Why do people move anywhere?" Sam said. "Here she comes. Ask her yourself."

The woman who approached them on the path had nothing Hollywood in her appearance. Her short black hair was graying around her face and she obviously didn't bother with either hair dye or makeup. She wore baggy jeans and a baggy gray sweatshirt with the imprint of a man's tragic face on it. She apparently saw Christy's puzzled eyes staring at her sweatshirt, because she said, "Edgar Allan Poe after a suicide attempt. He swallowed an ounce of laudanum, but the dose was too heavy, and it acted as an emetic. Now I ask you, if Poe was the druggie people say he was, wouldn't he have known how much laudanum to take? He was a plain and simple boozer. But a lot of people nowadays prefer thinking of him as a drug-crazed maniac."

There was a steely look in the woman's hazel eyes as she studied Christy. He didn't want to be on the wrong side of even a theoretical argument with her. He said, "I'm afraid I don't know much about Poe, but I have a friend who's such a big Poe fan that he named one of his Dobermans after him. Cletus disdains drugs. He would never have named his favorite dog after a druggie."

Ann Lang appeared interested. "Cletus?" she said. "After Saint Cletus, the third Pope?"

"Probably not," Christy said. "It must be a family name or something. Sam, you remember Cletus Knight. He's the guy who had us over for veal à la Oskar."

"Who would forget anyone that big? Or anyone who cooks like that?" Sam said. "Ann, this is Gordon Christy. I take him along on fishing trips so he can put grasshoppers on my hook for me. Christy, Mrs. Ann Lang."

Mrs. Lang's handshake was firm and quick. She had a hug for Sam.

"You took your time coming home for a visit," she scolded. "I almost didn't recognize you when I saw you in the parking lot.

Ruthy and Harley went by about thirty minutes ago. Do they
know you're coming?"

"Sure. We met them in Gallup for lunch, but we had a couple
of errands to run before we could come out," Sam said.

"If you had time for errands, you've got time for a cup of tea
with me," Mrs. Lang said. "Come on up. I've been experimenting
with mixing my own herb teas. You can try my newest. Orange
peel, blackberry leaves, hibiscus flowers, and just a touch of datura."

"Datura?" Sam said. "Thanks anyway."

"Just a joke, Sam," Mrs. Lang said.

She about-faced and took them around the shop. It appeared to
have living quarters in back of it, but Mrs. Lang marched on
toward a rectangular white house. Behind it was a garage and an
empty stable, and behind that a windmill squeaked in a light
breeze, pumping up a trickle of water that poured into a pond
lined with reeds. The reeds were the only spot of bright green in
the vermilion landscape.

The living room of Mrs. Lang's house was lined with bookshelves. So was the dining room, and so was the upstairs office-
library to which she took them. Three boxes of books were in the
middle of the floor. A young calico cat was digging in the boxes
energetically, scattering styrofoam packing pellets everywhere.

"I didn't know you had a cat," Sam said.

"This is Margery Kempe. Margery isn't quite a year old yet,
but she took on a bull snake last week that looked every bit of
eight feet long. The nasty thing was out by the windmill pond."

"Who won?" Sam asked.

"It was a Mexican standoff," Mrs. Lang said. "But Margery's
been vomiting almost every day since the great snake encounter.
Hysteria, I'll bet. I'll send off for some cat books. Now that I
have a cat, I ought to read up on the subject."

"Have Christy look at her," Sam suggested. "He's a vet."

"Oh, she'll be all right," Mrs. Lang said. "But if you'd like to
do me a favor, Christy, why don't you kill the snake? No one
around here has been willing to get rid of it for me."

"I'm sorry," Christy said. "I'm not a good person for the job.

I'm not crazy about snakes, but bull snakes are harmless. There's no need to kill it."

The glance Mrs. Lang gave Christy had no trace of friendliness. "No need? The snake might swallow Margery Kempe."

Sam had limited interest in cats and snakes. He asked, "Ann, may Christy use your phone for a long-distance call? He needs to check in with his clinic in Vail, and I want to talk to you about the Fawkes killing."

Mrs. Lang pointed wordlessly to a phone on a desk by the front windows and embarked on a quiet conversation with Sam. Wishing he hadn't succeeded in offending the woman, Christy went to the phone and dialed. There was no immediate answer. Apparently Millie Carroll, the receptionist, and Dr. Potter were both busy. Christy gazed out the windows, noting that Mrs. Lang had an excellent view. He could see Gala's ears as she waited patiently in the driver's seat of his car. He could almost see the license plates of passing cars on the highway. If he had binoculars . . . Yep, there on the windowsill was a pair within easy grabbing distance. No wonder Mrs. Lang knew everyone's comings and goings.

When Miss Carroll finally answered the phone, she sounded overjoyed to hear Christy's voice. But, then, Miss Carroll found cause for joy in much of life's miscellany. She said happily, "Dr. Potter is in surgery. It's Mrs. Russell's Dalmation again."

"More urinary calculi?"

"Yes. But what can we expect? Mrs. Russell can't bring herself to keep Temptress on a low-purine diet. Dr. Christy, Karen Hamilton has been trying to get in touch with you since yesterday. She's still in Houston. She left a number at her father's house there. She said it was important."

Christy took the number. "I'll give Karen a ring and see if I can catch her," he said.

"Dr. Potter may want to talk to you later," Miss Carroll said. "Where are you calling from? Are you fishing near somewhere that we can get a message to you if anything urgent comes up?"

"I'm calling from, um, a tourist attraction in New Mexico,"

Christy said. "We had a change of plans and we're going to be
staying with Sam's family for a few days. There's no phone."

Miss Carroll pressed. "You sound just like Dr. Potter when
he's on vacation—elusive. Are you sure there's no way we can
reach you?"

"Well, maybe I can leave this number," Christy said. He covered the phone and reluctantly made the request to Mrs. Lang.
She looked as though she'd rather see him hanged, but Sam
chimed in.

"Sure, that's a good idea. You don't mind, do you, Ann? If it's
okay, I'll leave your number with my office, too. Don't worry
about long-distance charges. I'll stand good for my calls and
Christy's, too."

Mrs. Lang acquiesced. Christy told Miss Carroll the number,
then hung up and dialed Karen's Houston number. He endured
another long wait before her voice came on the phone.

"My darling lamb," Karen said. "I was hoping and hoping
you'd call. I have something important to ask you. Can you cut
your fishing trip a little short?"

Karen was lonesome for him. Christy turned his back on Sam
and Mrs. Lang to conceal the fatuous smile that spread over his
face. He said, "As a matter of fact, I had to postpone the fishing.
Something came up, and I'm down in New Mexico."

"That's marvelous," Karen said. "You're even closer to Houston. Hop a plane, lambchop, and come straight here. Daddy and
I have had a long talk. He wants to meet you."

Christy lost his smile. The only character flaw he had found in
this otherwise delightful young woman was that Karen was tied
so tightly to her father's bootstrings—or was it his purse strings?
Karen spent most of her time in Vail, while her father and his
second wife lived in Houston. But now it sounded as if Daddy
wanted to inspect Karen's steady beau, and Christy wasn't at all
sure he wanted to be inspected.

"I'm sorry, Karen, but I really can't," he said. "I came down
to the Navajo Reservation with Sam Benally to help him with a
problem about an animal attack. A man was killed. A dog or a

wolf or something has been frightening the area inhabitants. We're going to try to help find out what it is."

There was a cold silence and no more pet names. Finally, Karen said, "So. So you're playing detective again, Christy."

It sounded too sarcastic not to be meant that way. "No, I'm just trying to help a friend."

"I thought I was a friend. Quite a close one."

On the desk beside Christy a walkie-talkie suddenly squawked. "Two cars, one Lincoln with an older couple in it, and one van filled with hungry-looking kids and parents. We got any fresh sandwiches made up?"

"Who's that?" Karen said. "Was that a woman's voice?"

Mrs. Lang hurried to the walkie-talkie, picked it up, and said into it, "I'll be right down to man the sandwich bar."

"Who's *that?*" Karen said.

"Just a minute, Karen," Christy said.

"Who are all those women? Exactly where are you, Christy?"

Mrs. Lang left the room. With Sam unoccupied and at liberty to hear his side of the conversation, Christy tried to sound cheerful as he described his whereabouts. He concluded, "With luck we won't be tied up too long. Maybe . . . maybe I'll be able to get down to Houston after this. I'll let you know."

Karen still sounded miffed when she hung up. Sam took the phone to call the tribal police substation. Feeling goaded by Karen's remarks, Christy headed for Ann Lang's shop. He figured he was at least a good enough detective to find a simple sandwich bar and the puzzling person who ran it.

Mrs. Lang welcomed Christy with a sour smile. The van passengers, sandwiches and pop in hand, were being escorted to the ruin by one of her helpers. The other helper stood next to Mrs. Lang, keeping an eye on a well-dressed older couple as they meandered through the shop.

"They say they're 'just looking,' " Mrs. Lang whispered to Christy. "Tell you what. Pretend to be considering a concho belt. It helps business if the joint looks busy. I don't wait on the real customers if I can help it. I can't imagine why, but I seem to scare them off."

"I'm your man," Christy said. "Can we talk while we look?"

"All right. Just keep it low."

From a case lined with black velvet, Mrs. Lang took three massive silver-and-turquoise belts. The assistant arranged one in front of Christy so he could inspect the stones.

"Wow," Christy said, thinking of Karen. "Do you have any in women's sizes?"

"None that's worth a damn," Mrs. Lang said. "What did you want to talk about?"

"That animal attack the other night," Christy said. "If there's a wild animal on the loose, it's probably been around for a while. I was wondering if you'd heard any reports of recent sheep or cattle killings in the area."

Mrs. Lang took the belt from Christy and arranged another in front of him. She said, "Will you settle for cattle rustling? Old Man Fawkes lost a few head a while ago. I indulged myself in a small *Schadenfreude* binge."

The assistant said, "What's *Schadenfreude,* Mrs. Lang? It sounds German."

"It is. It means having a thoroughly good time thinking about misfortunes suffered by somebody you don't like. Trust the Germans to have a word for it."

Christy said, "I take it Mr. Fawkes wasn't one of your favorite people."

"Is that one of your questions?" snapped Mrs. Lang.

Christy backed off. "No, not really. What I mean is, are you sure the cattle were stolen? Couldn't they have been killed and eaten instead?"

"You're talking about coyotes or something killing cattle," Mrs. Lang said. "I'm talking people stealing them. Fawkes said they were rustled. He accused a Navajo kid who'd been working for him, but of course the kid denied it. So Fawkes fired him and that was that."

"Okay, second question. What's the dog population like in the area? Many strays?"

"Pardon me," Mrs. Lang said. She took the three belts away from Christy and put them back in the display case, then took out a solid silver concho belt. "Now here's the real article," she said. "Stone-set belts only date from the 1920s or later. If you like old stuff, this is it."

"No strays?" Christy prompted.

"Where would a dog stray from around here?" Mrs. Lang said. "The Painted Cliffs area isn't exactly a metropolis."

Her young helper said, "You've forgotten that abandoned dog you told us about, Mrs. Lang. The big dog you said was so skinny."

Mrs. Lang's lips tightened. "It's been ages since I saw the poor thing. It's probably long gone."

"Was it quite a large dog?" Christy asked.

"I don't remember," Mrs. Lang said.

"Did you feed it?"

"Certainly not," she said. "Everybody knows that if you feed stray dogs, they just stay around."

Christy decided to change his approach. "So much for dogs. Now tell me about your cat. In addition to vomiting, is she often constipated?"

Mrs. Lang's hazel eyes looked surprised. "How would I know?" she said. "I installed a cat door for her in the kitchen. She goes outside to do her business. God knows, there's plenty of sand around."

"And she comes and goes at will?"

The older couple had zeroed in on a display case with turquoise necklaces in it. The assistant moved over to take out a strand at which the man was looking. Mrs. Lang's eyes lit up, and she answered distractedly, "No, I close the cat door at night. We've got coyotes all over the place. Margery likes to hunt, but so do they."

"Where does she hunt most? Around your windmill pond, where other creatures come to drink?"

"Yes, but what does that have to do with her vomiting?"

"Colonic impaction is a very common cause of digestive disturbance in a cat," Christy said. "Since she hunts, she probably consumes some quantity of bone. Mouse bone. Rabbit bone. When you get that mixed with feces and ingested hair, you can get a problem. Why don't you set up a cat box for her and try keeping her inside for a few days so we can observe her? Brush her really well twice a day so she won't lick up hair when she grooms herself. Do you have any Kat-a-Lax or Petromalt?"

"No. I'll get some the first time I go to Gallup."

"A teaspoon a day of mineral oil would help in the meantime," Christy said. "Better yet, I think you should let me examine her."

Mrs. Lang ignored the offer. She shot an excited glance at the older couple. The woman was trying on the turquoise necklace. Sales were apparently a cause for rejoicing.

Reminded of money, Christy pulled out his checkbook. He dated and signed a check and handed it over with no amount filled in. "If you don't mind, just fill in whatever our long-distance calls come to when your bill comes."

Mrs. Lang regarded the check. "Are you trying to make a better impression on me?" she said.

"I sure am," Christy said. "Am I doing okay?"

"I'll let you know if your score improves," she said.

Christy was still thinking about Mrs. Lang when he and Sam rejoined the Doberman in the car a few minutes later. He was no reformer, but he thought Mrs. Lang's score could use some improving, too. Ailing cats needed more than a vague intention of buying a cat-care book one convenient day, and homeless dogs needed more than mere pity.

Sam said, "So what's next? There's no point in going on to Lupton. Our local cop's away from the substation. He isn't expected back until later this afternoon. Blast it, we need more facts."

"I may have found out something," Christy said. "Mrs. Lang didn't want to talk about it, but she's seen a big stray dog around her place. My guess is she's seen it more than once and that she's seen it recently."

"Say, that could be our feral dog," Sam said. "Has she told Kee about it?"

"I doubt it," Christy said. "And I'm not sure she will. She says she feels sorry for the dog. Things got pretty chilly when I asked her about it. Maybe you can worm it out of her."

"Now?" Sam said.

A reluctance in Sam's voice snagged Christy's attention. He thought he understood. Whenever he went to see his mother, there was a moment just as he crossed Seventh Avenue to turn into Perry Street that was tinged with eagerness and simple happiness at being home again.

"No, let's go on to your place now," Christy said. "We can watch for feral dogs along the way."

CHAPTER 5

At Sam's direction, Christy drove past the State Line Trading Post and took a right on a narrow gravel road. It bounced north through a break in the cliffs, rounding a point at which a soaring layer of red sandstone was topped by a second layer, which in turn was topped by what looked like five or six stories of buff stone, like some massive, three-layer cake. In the bottom layer was a shallow cave that had attracted the kind of people who Christy figured might regard subway graffiti as an art form. Simon & Avis had dropped by with a can of yellow paint. Shelley F. had come to the cave with black spray paint. Why had they bothered to paint their names on a slab of rock? Merely to say, "I exist"? "I am"?

Christy nodded to the cave. "Are there many caves around?" he asked Sam.

"Look up," Sam suggested.

Christy obeyed, but he saw only that gnarled piñon and juniper had found enough toehold to grow among many of the sloping rock walls.

"What am I looking for?" he asked.

"See all those pits in the rock? Wind. It carves away at the sandstone. Yeah, there are plenty of caves, although few of them have any depth to speak of. Why this interest in caves?"

"I was just wondering where Mrs. Lang's stray dog might have set up housekeeping. Like some handy cave."

Sam looked respectful. "Can it be that you occasionally have a brain cell working?"

Christy grinned. "Once in a while. After all, we need some sort of starting place for hunting our werewolf."

"This is a better start than you might think," Sam said. "I've brought you off on the scenic route. It's the long way around to my grandmother's place, but it goes right by the Fawkes ranch."

Christy's interest picked up. As he followed the dusty gravel road, he counted crossroads. Crossruts, actually. He wanted to be able to find his way again. All ruts headed west, away from the cliffs. That must be where the reservation lands lay. Judging from the occasional small house or hogan that he spotted in the distance, other Navajo families lived in this back country. There were no more mobile homes. Maybe the gravel road was too bumpy to allow access for them.

Ahead, two sheer blood-red mesa walls curved toward one another, not quite meeting. Sam said, "There, that's the ranch house, just before the gap."

A big adobe house sprawled at the foot of the eastward mesa. A man had died here. Violently. Christy wondered how many people had driven by to stare at the house with the same feeling of dread that suddenly tickled his own nerve ends. He didn't look long. The road required attention. If he'd thought the gravel road poor, the track that wound on through the gap was worse. "Which way do I go now?" he asked Sam.

Not at all sincerely, Sam asked, "Don't you want to stop at the ranch? The scene of the crime and all? See if the tracks are still there?"

"We can do that later," Christy said. "Which way?"

Sam hunched forward and stared at piñon trees as if they were intimate friends. "Just follow the ruts off that way," he said.

The track led them along the western mesa wall for almost a mile before the wall curved back. Christy brightened as he saw three towering ponderosa pines tucked into a pocket of rock. They reminded him of the somber forests of his own high mountain country. Sam brightened, too, and he said, "Home. We're right on the other side of those pines. Goose this crate up, Christy."

Sam's home looked to be a thriving place. Separated by a wash in which corn was growing were a frame house and a larger house of concrete blocks. Squash flourished in the red earth of a big garden next to the concrete-block house, and near the other house were a log hogan, a shed, and a corral. A new Toyota was parked by the frame house. Harley Tsosie's pickup was in back of it. A tiny old woman in a flowing skirt and purple velvet tunic was lifting a big sack of potatoes from the bed of the pickup. At the sight of Christy's car, two small black-and-white dogs came racing out from behind the frame house. Gala leaned out her window and gave them a good bark.

Then women and girls appeared from everywhere. Christy shushed Gala and hung back to give Sam a chance to greet his family, but Sam wasn't having that. "Out with you," he said. He looked exhilarated. "Come meet my people."

There was one ancient grandmother. There was one stalwart-looking mother in a repeat of the aged woman's long skirt and velvet tunic. There was Ruthy Tsosie. There was a widowed sister, Irene Laughter, dressed in shorts and a sleeveless blouse. There were two girls, looking about ten and twelve, who wore dungarees and T-shirts and who were introduced as Irene's daughters. From the eldest to the youngest, each acknowledged Christy with one polite shake of the hand. The little grandmother apparently had something urgent to say to Sam. She grasped his arm and led him aside, speaking rapidly in Navajo.

Sam's mother spoke English for Christy's sake. She said to the elder girl, "Lois, you go lie down." Then she pointed at Sam with a thrust of her chin and said, "Why did my son bring you in the back way? Irene sent her boy down to the front road to watch for you."

Should Christy mention that they had driven by the dead man's ranch? Should he even say the name of Mr. Fawkes? He stalled for a moment, watching the girl walk listlessly toward the frame house. At its door, she turned and glanced at him before going inside. Bemused, Christy noted that she, too, wore a shirt with a man's face on it, but this man was Willie Nelson.

Christy opted for the simple truth, at least until he could learn what subjects he should avoid. "We went by Mr. Fawkes's ranch," he said. "I wanted to see where it was. Is Harley around? We picked up a ruler in Gallup to see what we could learn about animal tracks."

"That's a good idea," Mrs. Benally said. "But you don't do that now. You come have a cup of coffee. Harley's over at his house. You'll see him in a little while. Your dog's okay? She doesn't chase sheep? Let her out of your car. Our dogs don't mind other dogs."

Christy was reluctant to invite a confrontation between Gala and two dogs on their home territory, but they had to meet sometime. As a precaution, he put the Doberman on leash. Ruthy Tsosie spoke to the smaller dogs. They kept well away from Gala, but they stared at her, not a friendly sign.

Giving Christy much the same kind of stare, a dark-faced youth in his late teens roared up on a motorcycle from the other direction. He was as typical a young man as those Christy had seen anywhere, with his camouflage pants, T-shirt, track shoes, and long hair, except that the hair was bundled back in the same classic string-tied bun that Sam's older female relatives wore.

"There's George now," Sam's mother said. "You rather have a strawberry pop than coffee, Dr. Christy? George keeps them in the spring with that damned beer he likes. It keeps the pop pretty cold."

"No, thanks, nothing for me," Christy said.

When the youth got off his motorcycle, Mrs. Benally introduced him as Sam's nephew, George Laughter. George had no handshake for Christy. For a moment, he maintained his silence and a hostile stare. Then he spoke to Mrs. Benally in sibilant Navajo.

"Speak English," she snapped at the youth. "Be polite to Dr. Christy."

George said in perfectly unaccented English, "Then don't blame me if the guy gets mad. What I'm saying is, you've got to get him out of here."

"That's enough," Mrs. Benally said. "Dr. Christy can stay. He just can't be too close."

"Have I come at a bad time?" Christy said. By his side, the

Doberman straightened her ears, alert for trouble. All dogs could read voice tone, and Christy had decided most dogs were gifted with a garden variety of ESP. Gala hadn't liked the way the teenager spoke to her master.

Nephew George glanced at Gala with a surly look. He stepped a few steps away from Christy and the Doberman.

"Listen," Mrs. Benally said to Christy. "Don't you pay any attention to a rude kid. We welcome you, and we want you here. It's just that we've got illness in the family. Lois is good and sick. It's *tah honeesgai.* We've got to do something about it."

Ruthy muttered, "Lois doesn't have *tah honeesgai.* She doesn't have anything."

"What?" Mrs. Benally demanded.

"Nothing," Ruthy said.

"Well, all right," Mrs. Benally said. To Christy, she concluded, "So with Lois sick, there's a man coming, and then in a day or two there will be people coming. You understand?"

Christy didn't in the least, but he nodded wisely. "I've got a million things I need to do anyway," he said. "Sam mentioned we might pitch the tent by the spring, but I don't really need to stay here at night."

"Sure you'll stay," Mrs. Benally said. "Down by the spring's a good place. Sam? You stop talking now. You take Dr. Christy and show him the spring. I'll say one thing for this outfit, we've got good water and a pretty place to get it."

Sam's expression was harried as he left his grandmother's side. "I guess now is as good a time as any to set up camp," he said.

"This one can give you a hand pitching your tent," Mrs. Benally said. With a thrust of her chin and lips that Christy realized was the Navajo way of pointing, she indicated young George.

"I'm busy," George said. He walked back to his motorcycle.

Sam said to his nephew, "You certainly look it, slouching around on that Honda, doing nothing at all. Straighten up. Keep your shoulders back. Your posture would look good on a piece of fettucini. Luckily for you, we don't need all your magnificent strength. Christy and I have had plenty of practice pitching tents.

Let's drive over, Christy. No point in lugging this stuff any farther than we have to."

George sullenly kick-started the Honda and spun away in a cloud of dust.

Christy excused himself to the Benally family and followed Sam. Gala the Doberman seemed as glad as he was to leave the silent stares of the Benally dogs. They drove the Bronco down a track past another sheep corral. Near the pines, Sam said, "This is about as far as we can get without ripping out your oil pan. Park anywhere. You bring the tent. Is the Scotch in the grub box? I'll bring that."

"Wait a minute, Sam," Christy said. He let the motor idle. "We don't have to set up camp. Gala and I can take a motel room somewhere on the highway for a few days. That way, we—"

"My mother told you? This crap about Lois having ghost sickness? Or is it your girlfriend that's bothering you? I heard you say something about going down to Houston. Is that what you'd really like to do?"

"Uh, no. I don't want to go to Houston, and your mother just said that Lois was sick. Something about 'taw hon-is-gaw.' "

Sam grinned, looking like his old self. "Your gift for languages astonishes me," he said. "*Tah honeesgai,* that's just a way of saying somebody aches and feels bad. But Mother and Grandmother and Irene are also claiming Lois has a bump under her chin where some bloody witch has puffed her with corpse powder. They thought it all up while Ruthy and Harley were meeting us in Gallup. Now they're dead and determined that I've got to go get a stargazer to come confirm their diagnosis. Ghost sickness my foot. Lois has probably just got an enlarged lymph node. Isn't that typical of some minor infection or other?"

"It could be," Christy said. "But I think wanting your family stargazer to make a house call is all the more reason Gala and I should go to a motel."

Sam looked impatient again. "It's all crap," he said. "Walk over to the spring with me. I might as well tell you what's really going on. Gala, you want a walk?"

The Doberman always wanted a walk. She scrambled out the

door the moment it was opened, then whirled around with her phony threat to nip them as they climbed more slowly after her. Sam didn't look like he was in the mood for games. Christy called the dog sharply to heel. They walked over a smooth dome of gray stone. At its foot, the rock sank abruptly into a crumbled hole, from where a shining ribbon of water flowed into a small pool. The pool was so clear that Christy could distinctly see layers of clean sand spread in a delicate pattern on its floor.

"A sinkhole in the limestone," Sam explained prosaically. But the troubled look on his face faded as he listened to the trickle of living water, the thin, triumphant song of the desert.

A cord tied to a bush descended into the crumbled hole. Sam squatted on his heels beside it and fished up a gunny sack in which bottles clinked.

"Let's raid Harley's beer," Sam said.

"Let's don't," Christy said. "I think it's your nephew's, and I don't think your nephew likes me anyway."

"George's problem is that he doesn't like himself," Sam said. He sighed. "The little bum thinks he's unique, but it's the same problem suffered by half the Navajo nation. I guess it's hard not to feel schizophrenic. Look at my mother. She's educated, a high-school education at least. She's sensible. She's one hell of a successful politician. Did I ever tell you she serves on the Navajo Tribal Council? But when her grandkid comes down with a convenient small illness, all my mother and my grandmother can think of is hurry up, quick, quick, arrange a prayer ceremony."

"If it works, why knock it?" Christy said.

Sam sighed again. "Yeah. And there's no question that it will work. All they're really doing is setting up a public relations campaign, Christy. You call in a stargazer, then you call in a singer, then you mess around for four days with an Evil Way ceremony, and then on the last day all the kin and neighbors come, and then, gosh, gee whiz, Lois is pronounced cured of ghost sickness. And in the process, just by happenstance, you proclaim to the whole world that the members of the family have been victimized by a Navajo wolf. That means they're not involved in witchcraft themselves, so the local loonies needn't start sharpening their hatchets and thinking they'd better wipe out a bunch of witches. Get it?"

Christy thought over Sam's private diagnosis of his family's approach to a real or imagined danger. He began to nod. "That's very tidy," he said. "Lois feels better. Your family feels better. The neighbors feel reassured, and everybody settles down. When you get right down to it, it's a terrific idea."

Sam smiled unwillingly. "Except that I'm the party who gets to do all the consulting and arranging. I'm sorry, Christy. I drag you down here to help me, then I get too busy to stick around. I can't even help you set up camp. I've got to drive down to Slick Rock Wash to set up the stargazer to come tonight. I'll borrow Harley's pickup. You know how to pitch a tent on your own, boy. I've seen you do it. So get on with it."

"The camp can wait," Christy said. "I think I'll take a little drive myself. How about it, Gala. Do you want another ride? Gala, ride?"

"Where are you going?" Sam said. "What about the tent?"

"The tent will take ten minutes," Christy said. "I'm going to go look at the ranch and scout along the highway. Just in case your healing ceremony doesn't work, maybe we can defuse your family's problems by catching that feral dog. You can't blame someone for witchcraft if the werewolf is in the dog pound."

CHAPTER 6

Just as Christy pulled away from the Benally homestead and began the bumpy journey toward the Fawkes ranch, Harley Tsosie, on foot and waving his Stetson, intercepted him. Christy stopped for the big-bellied man. "So there you are, Harley," he said. "I was wondering why I hadn't seen you."

Harley smiled wryly. "Ruthy's mother turned real traditional after she got elected to the council," he said. "She remembered that old Navajos think it's not good for a man and his mother-in-law to look at each other. So now I stay a little bit away. Can I ride along with you? I've got some business back on the highway."

"Climb in," Christy said. He ordered the Doberman into the back seat, wondering why Navajo men shouldn't associate with their mothers-in-law and wondering how Harley knew he was heading toward the highway. Christy hadn't known it himself five minutes before. Could Harley have been near the spring, eavesdropping? He said, "I thought I'd stop by the Fawkes ranch, but I'll take you where you want to go first."

Harley gave him a sideways look. "You're going to look at those big tracks I told you about, aren't you? I'll help you. Then later maybe you can drop me at the ruin. I do some work sometimes for Mrs. Lang."

"You wouldn't mind stopping with me at the ranch?"

"Yeah, I mind," Harley said. "I told you, seeing those tracks made me feel kind of funny. But I personally don't believe there are any witches. No, personally, I don't believe that. Neither does

Ruthy. She was real surprised when her mother and Irene came up with the idea some witch is making Lois sick."

"Do you think they believe it?" Christy asked.

"I don't know," Harley said. "I never heard any of Ruthy's family talk about witches before. Today they say Lois has been having bad dreams, with dogs and wolves in them. Today they say she heard something moving around outside the house the night Mr. Fawkes got killed. But the dogs never barked or anything." He gave Christy another sideways glance, a glance that slid over his shoulder and encompassed the Doberman in the back seat. "You're lucky you've got a mean dog. A lot of people will be wanting a mean dog now. They say they help keep witch-wolves away. That's good, since you'll be sleeping outside with just a little bit of tent material between you and anything that's out there."

Like a cloud passing between him and the sun, a shadowy form floated across Christy's mind. The dog of death. The spectral hound. Humankind had long enjoyed a healthy dread of lycanthropy. He blinked and said in Gala's defense, "Dobermans aren't mean. They're very affectionate, obedient dogs."

"Sure," Harley said.

They drove on, jouncing and jostling across the deeply rutted track. At one point, Christy thought he saw people up near the cliffs, two young men well away from the road, talking earnestly. But as the Bronco growled over a rise, the two figures ducked down out of sight. Christy peered at the cliffs as he wrestled the steering wheel, but neither figure reappeared.

A few hundred yards further along the road, Christy spotted a motorcycle pulled off in the brush to the side of the ruts. It was dusty and silent and alone.

"That's George's Honda, isn't it?" Christy asked.

Harley shrugged and looked impassive. He had nothing to say until the ruts intercepted the gravel road and the ranch house loomed up before them, and then he instructed, "Pull over here. We'll go see if the tracks on the roadside are still looking good."

Christy stopped. He reached to the dashboard, where he always kept a leash stashed. "You don't mind if we take my dog with us, do you?" he asked.

"No. She doesn't have feet anywhere near as big as those wolf tracks. We won't get anything mixed up."

Harley didn't wait for Christy to collect his camera and the little bag of gear he and Sam had picked up in Gallup. He slid out of the Bronco and began pacing slowly alongside the road. Directly opposite a long driveway that led to the Fawkes house, Harley stopped and studied the earth. He walked another ten feet, then slowed down but kept walking.

When Christy caught up, he asked, "Anything?"

"Nothing but tire tracks. Some fool didn't stay on the road." Harley eyed the opposite side of the gravel road and crossed, studying the ground carefully as he walked. Christy trailed after him.

Christy tried staring at the road himself. He could see gravel. Beside it he could see sandy soil. He could see an occasional clump of parched grass and a feathery shin-high weed that he didn't recognize. He could see the top of Gala's head as, attracted by his interest, she got in his way, sniffing the ground to try to discern what could be meaningful about it. He could see nothing of any possible use. When Harley hunkered down beside the road for a close inspection, Christy trotted over to stare. Maybe the ground looked scuffed. He couldn't be sure even of that. A dog's pawprint was a clear pattern in Christy's mind. He had seen them often, in new snow, on a freshly mopped floor, or sometimes in soft mud. Always perfect prints on a perfect surface. Apparently he'd never realized that such circumstances were rare.

"Is that a track?" he asked Harley.

Harley made a noncommittal sound. He cast about, walking in a widening arc, then went back to the driveway and began pacing beside it. Christy gave up and inspected Fawkes's big adobe house at the end of the long drive.

Pseudo-Spanish was an architectural style that Christy had seen occasionally in Colorado. He had also cast a tourist's eye at handsome adobes in Santa Fe, where the inhabitants' yen for old adobe houses was so strong that crumbling buildings thirty miles from the town could be seen sporting "Not for Sale" signs, to fend off the seekers of "restorable" adobes. This particular adobe looked like a classic.

The house faced south, overlooking the widening gap between the two mesas that backed it, a view that reached for eternity. A stunning site, and a stunning structure. It was hard to think of it as the scene of sudden, screaming death. Basically a box shape, the house seemed almost to grow out of the ground to a height of two stories in front, one story in back, with a shady ramada running along both front and sides. Although the building was linear, no single surface of golden adobe looked it; all was smooth and rounded, as if patted into place by hand. It wasn't a self-conscious house. It lounged comfortably near the red cliffs like a golden lion. Surely it was knowing about Mr. Fawkes's death that made Christy think of a lion resting after a kill. Resting, yet ready to spring on any unwary prey that wandered too close. But the house was blind. All windows had been boarded up.

Further along the drive, Christy saw a pickup under a cottonwood tree. He started to ask Harley if they should get permission before they went nosing around, but Harley spoke first.

"Not one track left," he said. "Not one that I can find. Right along here was where Tully Kee said the old man was. There were plenty of tracks. Now they're all messed up."

"Sightseers?" Christy suggested.

Harley gave him the sideways look again. "Not from around here, I guess," he said.

"What about where you said the tracks disappeared?"

"That was back by the road," Harley said. "I couldn't find nothing there, either."

He didn't seem to want to linger. He stepped to the other side of the driveway and knocked one cowboy boot against the other, kicking off dust.

Christy asked, "Harley, did you tell anybody about those tracks disappearing? Say anything to anybody about 'vanishing' tracks?"

Harley looked uncomfortable. "Tully didn't say not to. But, no, hell, I didn't need to tell anybody. Raymond and his wife came up before we left. Raymond Wheatfields. He works on the ranch. He saw the tracks, too, so he knew about them. I don't know who he told."

Christy nodded up the drive at the pickup truck. "Looks like he's working today," Christy said. "What do you think? Should I go ask him?"

Harley turned and stared at the pickup. "Raymond doesn't have a pickup," he said. "He's so poor he doesn't even have his own horse. Whose pickup is that?"

Christy didn't remind Harley that he had no way of knowing. "I'll go check," he said, and he walked up the drive with Gala.

Seen more closely, the house had a neglected look. The smooth finish of the adobe was etched with scabby-looking holes, and when Gala pattered onto the front ramada, she left footprints in a thick covering of dust and sand that had blown onto its red Mexican tile. On the far side of the house, a four-foot-tall adobe wall invited Christy to look over it. There was an empty swimming pool surrounded by a chainlink fence and, of all unexpected sights, a lawn that was beginning to need mowing. The door of an unused pool house sagged open on rusted hinges. A long concrete walk, Christy saw, led past the pool and the pool house to a little guesthouse that sat off by itself on the curve of the drive. Then Christy stiffened. Something had moved on one side of the guesthouse. Gala stiffened, too, staring in the same direction. Her cheeks puffed out slightly. She was about to bark. Christy reached down and gently put his hand around her muzzle, a signal that she was to be silent.

Whatever else Navajo werewolves did, it was unlikely that they drove pickup trucks. Christy called out, "Hello! Is somebody here?"

Behind Christy, gravel crunched. Harley Tsosie was walking up the drive. By the time Christy could swing his head back to the guesthouse, a young man had moved into view. Dark hair. Dark skin. High cheekbones and a high-bridged nose that gave his face almost a hawk's beauty. Surely an Indian face, and a handsome one.

The young man took a few steps toward Christy, then stopped.

He looked at the dog beside Christy with steady, secret eyes, then said, "I've got a right to be here."

Christy stepped toward him. "Then you're in better shape than I am," he said. "We just came by to look around. I'm Gordon Christy."

"Eli Tom," the young man said. His eyes went beyond Christy's shoulder to Harley. He didn't greet Harley. He looked at the toe of his work boot, then at Christy's shoe tips, then at the thin desert air.

Harley also refrained from any greeting. He studied the fender of Eli Tom's pickup, then seemed to study its tire tread.

"Uh, this is Harley Tsosie," Christy said, gesturing at Harley.

"Sure," Eli Tom said. After another pause, he said to Harley, "Did George tell you? My cousin found those three sheep that were missing. They'd wandered off with some neighbor's flock."

"That's good," Harley said.

"Sure," Tom said.

Another pause. Christy couldn't figure out what was going on. He said to Harley, "No luck with the tracks?"

Tom wasn't reticent about that subject. He asked sharply, "What tracks?"

"Maybe magic wolf tracks," Harley said. "Big, big tracks that Tully Kee and I saw the day after Fawkes was killed. You know what they say—magic wolves always leave great big tracks."

"How come you're saying that?" Tom said. "You got some reason for saying things like that?"

"Just that I was wondering what you're doing here," Harley said. "Magic wolves might not just kill once and quit. Magic wolves, they keep on killing. I'd be careful about hanging around where a magic wolf's been if I was you."

Harley sounded malicious. Eli Tom had sounded both frightened and suspicious. Christy tried to ease the situation.

"I've been asking Harley things," Christy said. "I'm, um, helping a friend. Trying to find out what kind of animal it was that attacked Mr. Fawkes."

"Yeah, he's a veterinarian," Harley said. "He knows all about animals."

"But not about their tracks," Christy said.

"You would if you'd grown up herding sheep or looking for a hobbled horse," Harley said. "It's too bad about the tracks. There's almost nothing left. People have been driving in and out a lot, it looks like." His glance touched on Tom's pickup. "Over by the pool house is maybe the best place to look now. That's where the big tracks and the littler ones were. You been walking around over there, Eli?"

The young man hunched his shoulders. "Not me," he said. "I've been sitting in my truck."

"Come on," Harley said. The malice was in his voice again. "Help us look."

Eli Tom may have been reluctant to seek a werewolf's tracks, but unlike Christy he was no wash-out as a tracker. As they moved toward the pool house, he stopped abruptly and gestured to Harley. "Here," he said. "And maybe here. And here."

Harley's stomach jiggled as he hustled over to Tom. After a silent inspection, he said, "Those are the little tracks. The big tracks came cutting across the driveway somewhere around here. Wait. Now we've got it. Here's Big Foot coming. Look, he cut right across Little Foot's trail. Little Foot got here first. Big Foot steps here right on Little Foot's tracks, then he starts following them. You can see that, can't you, Dr. Christy? Big Foot was running. Now he's slowing down. Okay, he stops here. Okay, good, here's what Tully Kee and I saw clear. Here's where Big Foot trampled around again."

They were by the pool house. Christy still could see very little. He put Gala on a down and moved over to look closely. To the side of the pool house there was a stack of old lumber. Some ten or twelve feet to the side of that, like divots on a golf course, there were small, irregularly spaced mounds of soil. A running or plunging animal could kick up soil as the foot forcefully lifted to take the next step, Christy thought. He would have to watch Gala to be sure. He hunkered down, looking, then glanced up to see Harley's amused expression.

"Can you find me a clear print, Harley?" Christy asked.

"There's a pretty good one about three feet to your right," Harley said. Beside him, Eli Tom edged closer to look.

"Man, that's big," Tom breathed.

"Too big for a dog," Harley said. "That's what I keep telling people. It's from one of Bianca Wilson's wolves."

The younger man looked less apprehensive. "Are you sure?" he asked Harley.

"You bet. I was just kidding you about magic wolves."

"That's not a good thing to kid about," Tom said.

Harley said slowly, "Well, Old Man Fawkes is sure dead. And whatever killed him could keep on killing. I wasn't kidding about that."

Christy studied the track Harley pointed out. He finally began to see things. It was like a kid's picture puzzle remembered from childhood, where the artist hides a soaring eagle in a cloud or a squirrel in the sworls of a tree's bark: once seen, you were amazed that you hadn't seen it before. The imprint of a toe. Two more. Should be a fourth toeprint. Good, there it was, splayed to the side. All the toes were splayed, for that matter. Gala's feet left a much tighter imprint. And Gala's feet were much smaller. My God, that couldn't be right. He could distinctly see the entire footprint now, but could any canine leave a print that huge?

Christy stared. The sides of the small depressions made by each toe were crumbling slightly as gravity began to reclaim the grains of sandy soil that had been pushed up. How long had it been since the killing? About forty-eight hours. Probably long enough. Christy couldn't read the exact imprint of the nails, but there was no question of the size of the footprint. He dragged his paper sack from his pocket and produced a can of baby powder, the ruler, and the notepad he and Sam had decided upon. Careful not to disturb the soil, he began measuring and noting.

Harley asked, "What're you going to do with the baby powder? Find the wolf and powder its ass?"

Eli Tom chuckled along with Harley, so Christy found a grin for them. "No," he said. "Sam thought if I couldn't get a clear shot of any prints, maybe powdering them lightly would make them stand out more. Like fingerprints."

"Might work," Harley said.

Christy laid the ruler carefully beside the track and stood to focus his camera. It was a Leica M-4, his mother's somewhat extravagant present when he graduated from high school, and he figured if anything could get a clear shot of the pawprint, it could. He banged off three shots from slightly different angles, then applied a drift of baby powder to the track and shot three more.

Harley helped Christy find another set of tracks. Christy photographed them and lingered over the last. Eli Tom had wandered off.

Harley noticed Christy's preoccupation with the last pawprint. "Something different about this one?" he asked.

"No. It's just a little more splayed. Whatever wolf or dog made these tracks was sure down at the foot."

"What does that mean?"

"See how the toes spread out? Now, my Doberman is a little flatfooted. I didn't get her until she was grown, and she may not have been fed properly as a puppy. Poor nutrition can do that. A poor surface will affect a canine's foot, too. Too hard or slippery, like concrete or tile, and the dog will spread its toes to try to get a grip."

"Sure, horses are like that," Harley said, "only with them it's too soft. A horse that's always in sand, his hooves get kind of big and floppy. You're ashamed to be seen riding a sandfooted horse."

"At least now we know something more about our critter," Christy said. "It's not only got darned big feet, but they're splayed."

The young Navajo called to them from the other side of the pile of lumber. "Over here's where Little Foot was," he said. "Lying down. Looks like Big Foot didn't come all the way."

"Yeah, I saw that," Harley said.

"Any clear prints of Little Foot's tracks?" Christy asked.

"Plenty. There's some next to the pool house, too. You going to take a picture of those tracks?"

Christy took a few, but he was careful to save some film at the end of his roll. It was five o'clock and the sun was uncomfortably hot on his back. Time for a break, and what better place than the State Line Trading Post and its exhibit of imported wolves?

CHAPTER 7

The young Navajo stayed behind as they left. He didn't say why. He just got into his pickup, turned on the radio, and propped his feet on the dashboard. Back in the Bronco, Christy asked Harley, "Who was that kid? A neighbor?"

"Eli Tom? Naw, he and his mother are from around Canyon de Chelly. He just moved over to live near a cousin a few months ago. Wanted to learn silver-smithing. Or that's what he said. He probably really wanted to see his father."

"His father?"

"Old Man Fawkes."

"You mean he's a . . ."

"Halfbreed? Yeah."

"He looks all Navajo."

"Doesn't act it. I guess he tries, though."

Amazing, that the young man was only half Navajo. But even among animals, a first-generation outcross could resemble only the sire or the dam. Dobermans themselves were prime examples, and the buyer of a Dobe with no papers often discovered only upon breeding the animal that its offspring enjoyed such non-Doberman traits as a curly coat or no rust markings.

As they approached the highway, Christy asked, "Would you like to stop at the trading post with me? I'd like to meet those wolves you told us about."

"What are you going to tell Bianca Wilson? That you want to measure their feet? She'll just lie and say they can't get out."

"Maybe we can decide for ourselves after we've looked over their quarters."

"That won't take long," Harley said. "They're in a little bitty cage. No, I won't go there. I need to go on across the highway. That's my sister over there, selling rugs."

Christy spotted a strip of late afternoon shade on the east side of the State Line Trading Post in which he could park Gala. It was near a blue van, out of the way of the serve-yourself gas pumps in front of the building, but a young blond man with a deep tan came to the side window and waved at Christy and Harley as they got out of the Bronco. Harley nodded at the man and trudged across the highway to the brush-roofed stand at which the three Navajo women offered rugs. Christy got his camera and went inside the post.

It was in no way a traditional trading post. No Navajo could be expected to stalk in to sell wool or to buy a saddle. Instead, potted cacti, baskets, and souvenirs were offered to the tourist trade. Behind an old wooden desk by the front door, a young Indian woman with dark brown hair and light brown skin sat making change for a family that had stopped for gas. Two Anglo children fed coins to a Coke machine, while their mother fingered sets of napkins and luncheon cloths brightly printed with figures of masked dancers. The place had a familiar look. Vail was loaded with specialty shops catering to skiers and tourists, and this one, though modest, would have fitted in well enough. Except for its size. It was airy and spacious, and shops in Vail tended to be small, a direct reflection of the high cost of real estate there.

An open door at the rear beckoned. Christy walked toward it, thinking wolves, but the blond man intercepted him.

"Something I could do for you?" the man asked.

"Yes, I understood you have some wolves on display here," Christy said.

The man looked worried, but he smiled. "Since you came with Harley Tsosie, I guess I ought to frisk you first. Are you an animal-control officer or something?"

"No, just a friend."

"Well, you don't look like the kind of person that would shoot a harmless animal anyway. I guess it's all right."

"Did Harley try to shoot your wolves?" Christy asked.

"He threatened. But he'd been drinking. The menagerie is right through this way. Do you mind if I come with you? We had a little trouble with one of the coyotes last week, and Bianca thinks we shouldn't let people wander around by themselves for a while." He nodded toward the handsome young Indian woman. "Bianca's my wife. I'm Brad."

Christy introduced himself. The State Line Trading Post manager was younger than he had expected, although on a closer look maybe he wasn't so young after all. Middle twenties, said the tan, the white teeth, the smiling good looks, but the way the veins stood up on the backs of the man's hands and a certain loss of elasticity in the skin said his age was somewhere in the lower thirties. He looked peculiarly out of place in a little curio shop in the middle of the high desert, but as he escorted Christy from the shop he promptly explained what he was doing there.

"We're kind of proud of what we've done with the menagerie," Brad said. "When Bianca arranged for us to manage the place, there were only three coatis and about a dozen rattlesnakes and an old cougar that decided to die on us the minute we got his new cage finished. Mr. Fawkes didn't want to spend twenty cents improving the place. We've done most of the construction ourselves. Not bad, huh?"

For a roadside zoo, it wasn't bad at all. Christy had seen others that turned the stomach. Roadside zoos were too often the repository of exotic animals caught in the trap of human egotism. Buy a baby lion and amaze your friends, and when it starts growing up and the Humane Society representatives and the cops start coming to call, get rid of it any way you can. Get a jaguar for yourself and get your kids a pair of miniature horses—and sell them to a self-styled zoo when you get tired of them. Buy a monkey and buy an ocelot and buy a bear, and make the inevitable discovery that they don't live comfortably in an American city. That they lived in misery in the crowded, inadequate quarters of a typical roadside zoo was somebody else's problem.

Here, Christy saw no immediate problems. The trading post apparently had only a narrow strip of land between the highway and the cliffs, and a six-foot-high chainlink fence ran from the back of the building to the Painted Cliffs themselves. Outside the fence sat an odd building that looked as if four stucco hogans had been pushed together and called a house. In the compound, a sanded path led to the animal exhibits. A neatly lettered sign stated modestly, ANIMALS OF THE UPPER SONORAN DESERT. No attempt had been made at natural habitat. The different species of animals were in individual chainlink pens. Each pen had a concrete floor, probably to keep the animals from digging out, and sand had been spread on the concrete to give the animals comfortable footing. But the pens were spacious and clean. The trio of leftover coatis—dubious residents of the Upper Sonora, but close enough—had the polished branches of two dead trees, obviously brought in and erected for them, up which to scamper, as they did agilely when Christy started down the path. A tiny kit fox in the next cage looked typically miserable, but foxes were always shy, unwilling exhibits in any menagerie. At a big pen next to the fox, Christy stopped, spotting trouble. One of a pair of coyotes lay in a corner of the pen, repeatedly rubbing a swollen face between outstretched forelegs.

"What happened to this fellow?" Christy asked.

Brad pointed to the next cage, in which a porcupine sat munching a sweet potato. "Last week's emergency," he said. "Except for the wolves and the snakes, it hadn't occurred to us to lock any of the cages, and some damn little kid decided it would be fun to open a few doors. Well, the coyote had been studying that porcupine ever since we bought Porky off a Hopi over at Shungopavi. You know, yum, yum. Coyotes are one of the few predators that will attack a porcupine, but I guess Roberto the Coyote didn't get porcupine lessons when he was a cub. Porky was wandering along the fence, looking for a way out, I guess, and Roberto had a try at him. Porky swatted hell out of poor Roberto with that spiny tail."

"Ouch," Christy said. "That can be painful."

"You know it. But Bianca got all the quills out."

"She did it herself?" Christy said.

Brad shrugged. "We couldn't let the animal suffer," he said.

Bianca sounded like a very tough lady, Christy decided. But he didn't say so out loud. Instead, he said, "That must have taken courage."

"Oh, it isn't that bad," Brad said. "Roberto's real tame with Bianca. All the animals are. She just muzzled him with a stocking and pulled the quills out with pliers. It took a lot of pulling. I couldn't watch. Poor Roberto acted like he was dying."

Christy shuddered. The barbed points on quills made pulling them out a hellish job, and it was hell on an animal, as well. No wonder Roberto had complained. "If you have any more trouble, be sure and tip the butt end of the quills with scissors before you start yanking," he said. "The quills will depressurize, since they're hollow. It makes them easier to get out. Are you sure she got all of them? The coyote is still working pretty hard at his face. I've handled a few dogs that were quilled. I'm a veterinarian when I'm not on vacation. The worst cases are when an animal gets quilled in the mouth."

Brad Wilson looked grateful. He also suddenly looked worried. "I'm not sure if Bianca looked in his mouth," he said. "Listen, let me call her. Would you mind talking to her about it?"

"Not a bit," Christy said. "I'll be over looking at the wolves."

The wolf enclosure was at the end of the path, built right against the cliff. It had not only a concrete floor but a chainlink roof. Christy was glad, because the male wolf that strolled to meet him was formidable. From nose to tail, it looked every bit of five-and-a-half feet long, and Christy guessed it weighed at least a hundred pounds. Maybe a lot more, given the powerfully built shoulders and neck. It stared at Christy with strange, light eyes, in which there was not a single trace of the curiosity and trust that Christy saw in the dogs he met day in, day out. The eyes of the big gray wolf said it knew all about Christy, and it didn't like what it knew. Christy felt his scalp tighten, as fear stabbed him yet again at the sight of a canine. But this was no dog. This was *Canis lupus,* the lobo, the largest, toughest member of the canine family.

Christy stepped backward. The great gray wolf circled slowly, another step, then another, keeping his body between Christy and two females at the back of the cage. Christy backed up six more steps, then wished he hadn't. He had hoped to see footprints, not exercise a newfound phobia. He forced himself to stand his ground and study the enclosure. It certainly looked escape-proof. The fencing was bolted securely against the red rock of the lower cliff layer. A metal door fitted snugly against the rock. Sleeping quarters, he decided, noting that, unlike the other animals in the menagerie, the wolves had no visible sleeping arrangement. The door was closed, probably to keep the animals from disappearing into their den every time a visitor approached. A sliding section of chainlink had been provided so the pen could be divided into two separate areas, but it was open, giving the wolves the run of their artificial empire.

The big gray wolf stopped staring at Christy and gazed past him. The yellowish eyes didn't exactly soften, but they looked less hostile. Christy turned and saw the girl from the trading post strolling toward him, with Brad Wilson at her side.

Christy was glad to have something other than the wolves to look at, and Bianca Wilson was worth more than a glance. Brown hair and brown eyes—nothing spectacular there. But she had high cheekbones and a small nose and a mouth as delicately pouting as a baby's, all of which added up to a charming face. She looked at Christy once, then looked away, as suspicious as the female wolves that the big male was guarding.

Brad introduced her with more than a hint of pride in his voice.

"Hi," Christy said. "Your wolves don't seem to like me very much. Is that male always so wary?"

Bianca's voice sounded wary, too. "I think one of the girl wolves is coming in season," she said carefully. "He doesn't want even me to come near them now. But he's all right, unless you get between him and the girls. Then he turns a little mean." She approached the enclosure. "Come here, Quest," she said. "Here, boy, I brought you a piece of jerky."

Christy watched with horrified fascination as the girl peeled the wrapper from a stick of jerky and poked it through the fence for the big wolf to chew on. He turned his muzzle sideway to take the jerky between his molars, then tugged. Bianca tugged back. Brad watched, smiling. It was apparently a game his wife and the wolf played. After a moment, she let go, and the wolf retired to the back of the enclosure with his jerky. The two female wolves scrambled over to beg a share.

"They seem very well behaved with you," Christy said.

She nodded. "Brad says I think like an animal, so they like me. You had a question about Roberto the Coyote?"

"I wondered about the quills," Christy said. "Did you look in his mouth to see if he got spined there? He was rubbing his face when your husband and I came by a few minutes ago."

She shook her head. "I got them all out. I know I did. I looked inside his mouth and everything, and the only quills were in his cheek and muzzle. I'm giving him tetracycline three times a day, just in case he got an infection from them."

Christy said, "Would you like me to double-check him?"

The girl seemed to turn the matter over slowly in her mind. "No, I'd rather you didn't," she said. "Roberto has been pretty nervous since the episode with the pliers. I don't think he'd hold very still for you."

Brad laughed. "He doesn't even like me in his cage. None of the animals do, really. They'd rather have Bianca. The only time I go in is to clean up on the evenings when Bianca is off visiting. Even with a divided pen, the wolves are the toughest."

"The wolves aren't so difficult," she said. "All you really have to do is be sort of quiet and calm when you go in with them."

Christy said, "I wonder . . ."

"What?"

"No, I'm sorry. After the trouble you and your husband had with Harley, you wouldn't want a stranger poking around your wolves."

"Did you want to go in their cage?" the girl asked.

Christy gulped. "No, thanks," he said. "I guess I was just hoping to get a clear photograph of their tracks. I'd like to prove to Harley that he's wrong."

"God, I wish you could," Brad said. "Harley's a nice guy, but when he gets something in his mind, it's hard to shake it loose. I don't think a picture of tracks would do much to convince him."

"It might," Christy said. "We've been out shooting pictures of tracks, and maybe if he could see them side by side . . ."

"Out at Mr. Fawkes's ranch?" Brad said. "You found some clear tracks out there?"

"Well, not terribly clear," Christy said. "But good enough to get an idea of the size. If I could get a ruler by one of the wolf tracks, it might show us the difference."

"Oh, Jeez, yes," Brad said. "I'd really appreciate that. I know the wolves didn't do it. They were right here the night Mr. Fawkes was killed. I cleaned the cage out myself that night, just before dusk, and there were all three already in bed. Remember, Bianca? That was the night you went to—"

"I don't think it's such a good idea," she interrupted.

"Dr. Christy wouldn't have to go in the cage," Brad said. "You could slip in and smooth out the sand by the fence here. Quest would make pretty good tracks in that. Okay, Dr. Christy?"

It was more than okay with Christy. The wolves didn't seem to mind, either. They looked up alertly when Bianca unlocked the padlock on the gate but made no move as she stepped inside. Reluctantly, she smoothed a patch of sand with her hands and started back out. Brad remembered Christy's ruler and asked her to place it on the sand.

"Will they come if you call them?" Christy said to her when she was back outside the pen.

"Oh, yes. Quest will. He'll think it's for more beef jerky. I kind of hate to disappoint him, though."

"Maybe he'll forgive you this one time," Christy said.

The big wolf named Quest came quickly when the girl clicked her tongue at him. She wriggled her fingers through the chainlink by the smooth patch of sand and led the wolf to the ruler without difficulty. Then she moved over a couple of steps with the wolf following inside the cage.

"Shoot fast," Brad said. "He's seen your ruler. What do you bet he takes it?"

Christy hastily focused and shot, then got another for a safety.

The paw prints looked good and clear. He moved to his right to try for a shot of the back foot, and the wolf suddenly whipped around and lunged at the fencing.

"Oops," Christy said weakly.

"You moved too fast," the girl said. "Quest likes things slow and easy."

Brad laughed and pointed. "There goes your ruler."

The wolf had picked up the ruler with his front teeth. He dropped it, then delicately picked it up again and took it to the back of the enclosure, where all three wolves nosed it.

Christy was afraid his voice would sound shaky. Adrenaline was pumping hard, and the image ran round and round in his brain of the wolf whirling, lunging, whirling, lunging. He cleared his throat, then cleared it again. "I'm glad it's a metal ruler," he tried to say lightly. "They could eat a plastic one." Words came more easily. He added, "It's still not a good thing for them to have. They could gouge themselves. Do you think I should— Christ!"

The male wolf lunged at him again, banging against the chain-link. Christy stumbled backward. He felt Brad's hand quickly catch his elbow.

"Careful," Brad said. "You almost tripped there. Don't worry about the ruler. Bianca will get it when she puts them up for the evening. You hear that, Bianca? We'll be relying on you not to forget."

He apparently relied on her to tend the store, as well. A buzzer rang loudly, and Bianca hurried inside. Christy thought Brad was looking at him curiously. He concentrated on walking away from the wolves in a casual, leisurely manner. Maybe it worked. Brad followed him, saying, "I really appreciate your trying to clear our wolves. I told Harley they couldn't get out, but he wasn't in much of a mood to listen."

"Harley's worried about his in-laws," Christy said.

"His in-laws?" Brad said. "What have his in-laws got to do with it?"

Christy gave himself a mental slap on the wrist for talking out of school and quickly changed the subject. "How did you get the buzzer to ring so loudly? What triggers it?"

"Oh, that," Brad said. "I jury-rigged a burglar-alarm system so it blats every time somebody touches a gas hose or walks in the front door. It got boring, sitting in the trading post waiting for cars to stop."

"Good idea," Christy said.

"Oh, I'm good with my hands." Brad spread them out, as if to demonstrate. "I'm good with everything except my proposed profession. Would you believe I've sat for my bar exams twice without passing them? I know the material, but I keep tripping up on the multiple-choice questions in the multi-state. I'm supposed to be reviewing for them again, but I've gotten to the point that I'm completely stale. If Bianca hadn't lined up this job for us, I'd still be sitting knee-deep in books, going crazy."

Brad's frankness about his failings made Christy feel a little better about his own. His reaction to the sudden charge of the gray wolf was even more alarming to him in retrospect than it had been at the moment it occurred. He couldn't go on in his chosen profession if he was going to act skittish around animals. But, hell, anyone would feel skittish around a wolf.

Wouldn't they? Christy walked past a woman customer in the trading post so he could peer through the window and make sure Gala was okay. She was sitting up in the front seat of his Bronco, guarding the steering wheel. A large tan Ford station wagon was pulled up next to the Bronco. The shadows were longer. The Doberman looked cool enough. Christy glanced back at Brad in time to see a look on Brad's face that matched his own when the wolf had charged him at the fence, only Brad and his wife were facing the woman customer, not a wolf.

Christy himself looked at the woman appreciatively. And that, obviously, was what she expected. He couldn't have guessed at her age, aside from the fact that she was probably older than he, but her trim body, her shoulder-length hair, her tan blazer and black walking shorts all told the world she was as old as she felt, and today she felt young. She wore a necklace made of fine turquoise nuggets, and her eyes were almost an exact match of their shade. But the strongly marked brows above the turquoise eyes were frowning.

"When did Wheatfields leave?" she asked Brad.

"I don't know, Miss Fawkes. He just took off," Brad said. "I went out there right after you phoned, but he and his wife were already gone."

Miss Fawkes? Christy's ears perked.

"Damn," the woman said. "I wanted his wife to clean up the big house. I'll be staying there a while. Well, Bianca will have to clean it."

Brad's face stiffened. "I don't mean to be disrespectful, Miss Fawkes, but Bianca isn't a cleaning woman. She's my wife, and a partner in the trading post here."

"And the trading post is a part of my father's estate," the woman said. "That means I'm your employer now. I'll be taking over for my father."

Bianca said, "That's all right, Brad. I'll clean the house for her."

The woman went on. "There'll be some changes for you, too, Brad. I'll expect my father's share of the proceeds to be paid to his lawyer, Mr. Browning, for the next few weeks. At least until we clear up the estate."

"I was planning to do that anyway," Brad said. "I always kept a good set of books for your father. Nothing's happened to change that." He sounded miffed.

"What about the cattle and the rest of the stock out at the ranch?" the woman said. "Has anyone checked them lately?"

"Sure, I did," Brad said. "There's plenty of water and graze. The horses will do okay, too. I also checked on the generator your father said was acting balky. It looks like it's working okay."

"I can contend with the generator. I've fixed it before," the woman said. "That leaves unboarding the windows. Can you get someone to do it for me?"

"I guess I could come unboard the windows while Bianca cleans things," Brad said.

"No, someone has to stay here and mind the trading post," the woman said. "What about that youngster, George. Can't he do it?"

"Your father fired George over a month ago," Brad said. He glanced at Christy and added, "I guess the kid didn't work out."

Christy's eyebrows rose at the mention of a youngster named George. "Is that George Benally who got fired?" he asked. "My friend Sam Benally's nephew?"

Brad said, "Yeah. His name's George Laughter, not Benally, but it's the same George."

"And you say someone else is missing from the ranch?" Christy asked, pressing.

"Yeah, the ranch hand," Brad said.

Brad looked as though he would be happy to pat Christy on the shoulder and bid him good-bye, but Miss Fawkes turned a turquoise gaze on Christy's jeans and work shirt and the muscular young body that was in them and asked Christy, "So you know the Benally family, do you?"

"That's right," Christy said. "Sam's home for a visit, and I came along for the ride."

"I've been friends with the Benallys for years," Miss Fawkes said. "They're a respectable family. I'll tell you what—why don't you come over to the ranch tomorrow and unboard the windows? I want to move in tomorrow afternoon after my father's funeral. It's going to take a while to sort through his papers and settle his affairs. Now, I want those tiresome boards taken off carefully. No splitting the window frames or anything like that. But I'll pay . . . let's see. How about five dollars an hour?"

Christy looked down at his rough attire and laughed. "That's the best offer I've had all day," he said. "But I'd be taking your money under false pretenses. I don't know the first thing about carpentry. I'm a veterinarian, on holiday. Tell you what, I'd be glad to take your boards off, gratis. But I may leave a few splinters."

Miss Fawkes apologized, and Brad introduced them to each other. She insisted that Christy call her by her first name, which was Eleanor. It was only a polite prelude to more questions. Where did he practice? How long had he known Sam? Did he know her friends the Stones who also lived in Vail? Or the DeMotts in Beaver Creek? She concluded that they had mutual acquaintances upon discovering that Christy and Dr. Potter had a Labrador patient that belonged to a family named DeMott.

Bianca left to attend to a motorist who came in wanting gas and directions to the Angel Peak recreation area. Eli Tom came in on the motorist's heels and stood frowning in the doorway. Miss Fawkes glanced at him, but for the moment she seemed more interested in Christy than in the young man who was apparently her half-brother.

"Perhaps I can make you another proposition," Miss Fawkes said to Christy. "How would you and Sam like to stay in the guest house at the ranch? It'll surely be more comfortable than anything the Benallys can offer you."

"Thanks," Christy said, "but we're all fixed up at the Benally place."

"I wish you'd reconsider," Miss Fawkes said. "I'd like to have someone else nearby at night." She eyed Eli Tom and raised her voice a fraction. "There are too many strange people around. I don't think I'd feel comfortable being at the ranch all by myself. Especially after what happened to my father."

Christy wondered why she was speaking of people and an animal attack in the same breath. Could she have picked up a superstitious belief in Navajo werewolves? She seemed to be waiting for Christy's answer to her invitation, and he looked for a way to stall. Eli Tom saved him the trouble.

He strode up to Miss Fawkes. "I saw your station wagon outside," he said. "I'd about given up on seeing you. I waited almost two hours at the ranch. Don't try to tell me you didn't get my message. They said they'd be sure to let you know I'd be there at three o'clock."

Miss Fawkes calmly turned her turquoise eyes on the young man. "Yes, my fiancé's answering service gave me the message," she said. "Three o'clock wasn't convenient for me. Next time, try leaving a number where you can be reached."

"You know damn well there aren't any phones if you live off the highway," Tom said.

Miss Fawkes looked bored. "Are you becoming a professional Indian, Eli? Don't forget that I probably know more about the reservation than you do."

"I didn't come here to swap insults," Tom said. "I came here to tell you I want my share, and I want it now. The old man probably had a good laugh at the thought of all the trouble he'd cause by not leaving a will, but I've put up with all I'm going to put up with. I can't wait around for the estate to drag through the courts. I need money now."

" 'The estate,' " Miss Fawkes mocked. "You must have run straight to a lawyer the minute you knew my father was dead."

"He was my father, too," Tom said.

"That's open to question," Miss Fawkes said. "Your mother was never legally married to my father. Who knows whose bastard you really are?"

Tom said, "Like hell. I can't vouch for whether the old man legally married his last Navajo wife, but he was legally married to my mother. In fact, there was never a legal divorce. That means my mother could get half the estate as spousal rights to community property, and I'll get an equal share with the other offspring, meaning you. I say that makes it my house and my ranch, not yours." He let his eyes wander around the room. "My trading post, too."

Miss Fawkes's body stiffened, but her voice was still light and mocking. "My, my, aren't we becoming a legal expert? You'd better find yourself a really good lawyer, Eli, not some little jerk who donates a few hours a week to help the poor. You're apt to find this pretty complicated. Are you even aware of the lien my mother had on the estate? It was part of the divorce settlement, and if Father sniggered all these years about depriving Mother and me of the money, Mother surely had a few good laughs, too. All that interest, mounting up and up for more than twenty years. I'm my mother's heir, too. Whatever you care to claim, now that my father is dead, I'm bound to get a large chunk of his assets. Maybe everything."

"T-t-tell that to my lawyer," Tom sputtered.

"Gladly," Miss Fawkes said. "Perhaps I'll also tell him what I really think about my father's death—that he was murdered."

"Murdered?" Tom said. "You're crazy."

"Am I?" she said sweetly. "Then ask your lawyer who's most likely to be suspected if I'm right. The police will probably come looking for some quick-tempered young man who believed he might profit from my father's death. Does that description fit anyone you might know, Eli?"

"It fits you as well as me," Tom said.

"I had no reason to be impatient," Miss Fawkes said. "I'm not broke. My father was old and would have died eventually. You, on the other hand . . . What was it you said a few minutes ago? 'I need the money now'?"

"You'd better watch your mouth," Tom said. "People can get in trouble talking too much. Just remember, I plan to get what's coming to me, one way or the other."

The young man slammed out of the trading post. In passing, he jostled a shelf and set a display of painted pottery vibrating dangerously. Bianca, who had just come through the front door after giving directions to the motorist, rushed to steady it. So did Harley Tsosie. At the sight of the big-bellied Navajo, Brad Wilson and Eleanor Fawkes frowned in unison.

"What are you doing here, Harley?" Brad demanded.

"Waiting for Dr. Christy," Harley said. "Don't act so surprised. You saw us drive up together."

"Yes, but I didn't think you'd have the nerve to come inside after that temper tantrum over our wolves yesterday. Did you get a good earful, listening outside the door?"

"Good enough," Harley said.

"So did I," Miss Fawkes said impatiently to Brad. "Particularly all that talk from Eli about his lawyer. I have a suspicion I'm looking at the lawyer right now. Have you been practicing law without a license, Brad? Have you been giving Eli advice?"

Uneasily, conciliatorily, Brad said, "No, Miss Fawkes. Honestly. Eli talked to me about getting a lawyer. He said he'd heard a rumor that your father hadn't left a will. But I didn't say anything to him. I just listened."

Miss Fawkes thought that over, eyes still angry. "What did Eli tell you about this business of his mother and my father never getting divorced?"

"Nothing," Brad said. "Not a word. I swear it."

Miss Fawkes sighed. "God knows, Father's marital affairs were chronically tangled. What does it take for a Navajo woman to divorce a Navajo man, Harley? Haven't I heard that she just throws his saddle out of the hogan?"

"I don't know what you heard," Harley said. "You about through here, Dr. Christy? I've got to go on to the ruin. Ann Lang has a job for me."

Christy was glad of the opportunity to avoid any renewal of Eleanor Fawkes's invitation to stay at her father's ranch. He waved good-bye to Brad and Miss Fawkes, then reminded Bianca once more of the ruler in the wolf cage and left quickly. Harley didn't say anything until Christy dropped him off at the Painted Cliffs Ruin, and then it was only to tell Christy that he would catch a ride home with a friend.

At a little past six o'clock on a hot July evening, Christy was free to go back to the Benallys' and see if Sam was still occupied, but he decided to make one more sweep of the area. He turned and headed back west, and this time he kept going past the State Line Trading Post.

CHAPTER 8

Christy forced himself to put people and wolves out of his mind and concentrate on dogs. Bianca Wilson's gray wolves were scary, but Christy could see no way they could escape from their compound and roam the country killing people. But Ann Lang's feral dog was still unaccounted for, and dogs had to eat and drink. If a wild dog was a daily visitor to Mrs. Lang's windmill pond her helpers would have seen it, so where else could it be finding water?

Just past the trading post, the dry, winding bed of the Rio Puerco invited a glance and just past that, on the Arizona side of the line, a big roadside park invited closer attention. It had restrooms. That probably meant a supply of water. On impulse, Christy turned in. He parked and put Gala on a leash to go inspect the buildings of the Painted Cliffs Safety Rest Area. Sure enough, it had two drinking fountains, but unless the feral dog knew how to stand on its hind legs and push a button to get water, Christy could see no way it could drink from them. A sign, CLEAN WATER, with an overhead hose for recreation vehicles brought him over for a closer look. It might leak, although he could see no signs of leakage. Cottonwoods and pines had been planted at the roadside park. They would have to be watered periodically, but would they be watered often enough to give a dog a steady supply?

Christy's own dog looked thirsty. He always carried gallon jugs of water for her in the car, and the roadside park had concrete ramadas to provide shade. But the park seemed no place to loiter. Little signs proclaimed POISONOUS SNAKES AND INSECTS

INHABIT THE AREA. Not a hospitable place, this. That went for the entire area, Christy decided. Wolves, violent death, more violence threatening. Christy had a sudden urge to go back to Sam's home. For Gala's sake, he told himself.

He bumped back past the Fawkes ranch and along the dusty track to the Benally spring. No one was outside the Benally houses. Christy felt uncertain as to what sacred or secular affairs they might be engaged in, so he stayed where he was. He fixed two cups of kibble and a little can of meat for Gala and got a reproachful look because she preferred fresh ground beef for her meat ration. She picked at her food while he got out the tent, a self-supporting dome that packed down to the size of an overnight bag. Soon, two little black-and-white forms carefully approached from the house.

The Benally dogs. Small as they were, Christy found himself watching them just as carefully. Little dogs had teeth as sharp as big dogs, just smaller. Gala growled when she saw them. They stopped midway. One dog lay down and crept a few more feet on its belly. Gala began to eat her dinner more rapidly.

"Hi, fellows," Christy said tentatively to the dogs.

They didn't respond to the human voice. Maybe they spoke only Navajo? They were both extremely shy. But the smell of the food kept drawing them closer. Gala gobbled the last of her dinner and licked the bowl clean, then decided she should challenge the pair. She bellowed a deep-throated bark and charged, but she only charged ten feet. Both smaller dogs lay down instantly, looking submissive. Gala circled to approach them one at a time. The first dog lay still, letting the Doberman sniff it, then beat its tail against the ground with faint optimism. Gala gave it a token growl. Behind her back, its partner crept a few feet closer to her empty food bowl.

Their obvious yearning for food made Christy come to his senses. He called to Gala. Instead of strutting and looking pleased with herself for intimidating a prospective enemy, she seemed puzzled by the two Indian dogs. She pretended to lose interest in them, keeping track of them only from the corners of her eyes. Christy found two aluminum plates in the camping supplies. He made two more dinners and set them out for the little dogs.

They ate hungrily. Of course, many dogs on a once-a-day feeding schedule attacked food just as eagerly. Christy unfolded one of the camp chairs and set it up in front of the tent, then mixed himself a Scotch-and-soda without ice and removed the bandage from his arm. Gregory's fang work was healing cleanly. Christy was debating whether to re-bandage it when Sam came walking down the trail to the spring.

"No chair for me?" Sam scolded. "No waiting drink? Get with it, boy. It's already getting dark, and I'm parched."

"I'll light the Coleman lantern," Christy said. "You can make your own drink."

"Later," Sam said. "I just came down to get the dogs. They've got work to do, and so do I. Irene is in the house throwing hysterics. She went off in her mother's car an hour ago to make sure her best friend was coming to the stargazing tonight, and the friend's damned little kids threw a rock and broke out a headlight. It was probably just kid mischief, but Irene is convinced they did it on purpose. To make matters worse, Irene says the friend made a lame excuse and said she and her husband couldn't come. It looks like everybody's busy tonight, damn them all. People are shunning my family, Christy. I don't know what to do."

"Sam, I'm so sorry," Christy said. "We're going to hurry up and catch this so-called werewolf, that's what. That'll show everybody."

Sam sighed. "Yeah, well, speaking of werewolves, Irene doesn't want the kids out after dark any more. Somebody's got to get the sheep in. I told her we'd do it. Come on. They're in a fenced field near the road. Bring Gala. She could use the exercise."

Sam whistled the two little sheep dogs along, and Christy followed with Gala, worrying about his friend. Gala seemed worried about herself. Where were they going, and why were those two odd little dogs going with them? She trotted at Christy's heel, staying close to him.

"If you hear anything rustling in the brush, sic Gala on it, okay?" Sam said.

Christy felt a little coolness along his spine. "Come on, Sam, you don't believe in werewolves," he said. "What would be doing the rustling?"

"I'm darned if I know," Sam said. "Probably Berenice's imagination. She must be feeling left out of the spotlight, since the family's decided to get all hot and bothered about Lois being sick. Berenice was pretty slow coming up with her tale. Says that evening before last, when she was bringing the sheep home from grazing, she heard something walking in the brush parallel to the trail. If she stopped, it stopped. If she turned around to look, she never saw anything, but the rustling would start again the minute she started walking."

Christy's spine felt even cooler. "That was the night Mr. Fawkes got killed?" he said.

"That's right. And the same night Lois claims she heard something moving outside the house late at night. Even Ruthy's beginning to get nervous. But John Klah will fix everything."

"The stargazer?"

"Yeah. Quite a guy. Ninety-two years old and just about blind from cataracts. His son's driving him over. Kenneth is a student stargazer, so he helps his dad. Veer to the right. The field is on the other side of the wash. By the way, I've promised your services to John Klah in return for his diagnosis. The usual payment is sheep or cash, but he said he needs a new shirt and that his Poodle is ailing. You don't mind, do you?"

"A Poodle?" Christy said.

"Grandmother says he's had it for years," Sam said. "What's the matter? You think the *Dinéh* ought to stick to mutts instead of purebreds?"

Christy had given the matter no thought at all. The mental image of a pampered Poodle living in a hogan just struck him as unusual. He ignored Sam's raillery and said, "What's *Dinéh?*"

"The people. The human beings, if you prefer. Darn it, we should have brought a flashlight. It's getting too dark to see the sheep."

It was the time of evening between dusk and dark, when things started losing their form. Regardless of darkness, the two black-and-white dogs knew their job. They slipped under the barbed-wire fence before Christy, veteran of many ranch gates, could nudge Sam aside and undo the chain that held this one closed. He'd worked with more cattle than sheep on the ranches around Vail, but he knew enough to stand aside to avoid spooking the flock as it came out. If sheep were like cattle, they were nervous of strangers. Gala trotted back and forth, torn between the urge to stay with Christy or to go see what business the sheep dogs were conducting as they darted, dropped, darted, dropped, moving the sheep neatly out of the field. When the sheep came pouring forth, Gala could stand it no longer. She darted at the nearest bobbing blob of wool, then leaped back as the sheep lowered its head and threatened to charge.

Sam clicked his tongue, whether at the sheep or the sheep dogs Christy didn't know, and fell in behind the slowly moving flock. He said to Christy, "I finally got in touch with Tully Kee, the Navajo cop. He may come out in the morning to talk to you."

"To me?" Christy said. "Why?"

"I guess I bragged about you. He's got a dog expert, some old boy who works for the McKinley County sheriff. The guy used to be on a police force that used guard dogs. So Tully says the guy's all excited about a theory that someone's guard dog could have killed Mr. Fawkes."

"Who would be using guard dogs around these parts?" Christy said.

"Ranchers," Sam said, "just like you used to drone on about when we were at Fort Collins. The word is a few ranchers in the area have started experimenting with new breeds of dogs to protect their sheep. So I told Tully you were an A-number-one expert on herd dogs."

"Gee, thanks," Christy said. But he thought it over. "I suppose I could tell him a lot of basic things," he said. "Damn you, Sam, I didn't drone, but I was in on that pilot project on herd-guarding dogs at Fort Collins. Why does he think a herd-guarding dog attacked Mr. Fawkes?"

"I guess he doesn't want to miss any bets," Sam said. He pointed his chin at the two black-and-white sheep dogs. "See how they work? Not a peep out of either of them."

Christy watched the two shadowy forms move around the flock. They were doing all the work. They were so experienced with their own flock that a human was apparently useful mainly for opening gates. Ewes bleated as the flock flowed over the dark trail like a white, ragged-edged cloud. The dogs were always on hand to dress the edges, but they worked silently. Not a sound.

"So?" Christy said.

Sam shrugged. "Tully says Mr. Fawkes had a thirty-thirty rifle with him when he was killed. It hadn't been fired. Tully was wondering how a man can stand there with an animal rushing out of the darkness, and he's got a rifle, and he never gets off a single shot at it."

"I'm sorry to sound simplistic," Christy said, "but it was night, wasn't it? Maybe Mr. Fawkes didn't see the animal coming at him."

"That's the point," Sam said. "Mr. Fawkes was a little hard of hearing, but he wasn't deaf. He would have heard it, wouldn't he? You're around animals all the time, so tell me—don't most animals snarl and growl when they attack?"

Christy thought of his arm and of the shaggy black dog who had bitten him. Gregory hadn't growled, but his bite had been basically a snapping reaction, not an all-out attack. He thought of the injured Rottweiler that had spooked him. Probably serious intent, and certainly a growl. He thought of the one occasion he had seen Gala go for someone, and how glad he'd been to see her go. No growl there until she had launched herself, then there had been snarling and growling aplenty.

"I guess," Christy said. "But if it was a herd-guarding dog, that wouldn't necessarily account for an absence of sound. They can be as vocal as any dog. For that matter, a lot of the smaller livestock herders are yappy."

"Are most of the herding dogs big?" Sam asked. "Tully mentioned a Rhodesian Ridgeback, some big dog he was out checking earlier when I tried to get him on the phone. Is that one of those tough herding breeds?"

"They're not herd-guarders, but they can be tough, all right," Christy said. "They were bred in Africa to hunt lions. The herd-guarding breeds are the Great Pyrenees, the Puli, the Komondor, the Shar Planinetz, the Kuvasz, and, let's see, I've heard about the Akbash and the Maremma and the Anatolian Sheepdog. Some of them get pretty big and fierce. They have to be to take on wolves and bears."

Gala watched the two small sheep dogs until jealousy got the better of her. She made a rather timid lunge at a sheep that lagged. It sped up and disappeared into the middle of the flock, and Gala ran to Christy and stared up at him as if to say, "Wow! Did you see how well I did that?"

Sam picked up a rock and chunked it at the darkness. "Tully may want us to ride around with him and take a look at a few dogs. Is that okay with you?"

"Sure," Christy said. "That's what I'm here for."

"Good." Sam whistled to tell the dogs to turn the sheep toward the houses, then asked, "What did you do this afternoon?"

"I just poked around and asked a few questions about tracks and dogs," Christy said. "I met Mr. Fawkes's daughter."

"Eleanor Fawkes? She's good people."

Christy started to take issue with Sam's evaluation, then thought better of it. First impressions were often wrong, and Sam had known her longer. Instead, he said, "She was over at the State Line Trading Post, asking about someone named Wheatfields. It seems he's disappeared."

Sam laughed. "Not disappeared. Just gone. Raymond and his wife did day-work for Old Man Fawkes. They took off for a hurried visit to relatives in Tohatchi right after Fawkes was killed. If you're a Navajo, you don't have any trouble understanding why. A man dies, that's a *chindi* place. Fawkes's house is a death house now. No Navajo would want to stay around one."

Christy had been about to mention Eleanor Fawkes's invitation to him and Sam to stay in her guesthouse, but he decided now wasn't the time. Even if Sam was a thoroughly acculturated city dweller, as sophisticated in his outlook as anyone in an American metropolis, he still had Navajo roots, and he might feel obliged to turn the offer down out of respect for the feelings of his family. Christy certainly had no intention of entertaining the notion without Sam.

Their pace toward the houses became brisk. The air was noticeably cooler, but Christy could feel the back of his shirt getting damp as he jogged in the dust at the rear of the sheep. They poured into the Benally compound, and a figure stepped to the door of the hogan to whistle and hoot the sheep on to the other corral near the spring.

"That's Harley," Sam panted. "He went with you this afternoon, didn't he? Was he any help to you?"

"Yeah, he was," Christy panted back. "I'll fill you in on everything when there's time. Gala! Head that buck off! Get 'em, Gala!"

Timid, out of her depth, Gala rushed to Christy instead of after the buck. At the very mouth of the corral, the whole flock tried to scatter. Two racing black-and-white figures turned the buck, then a half-dozen sheep that tried to follow it, and the front edge of the flock crumbled and passed into the corral. The rest swept in without further rebellion. Christy hopped up to close the gate. He pulled out his handkerchief to wipe his dusty face. He could see a white gleam in the darkness: Sam's teeth as he grinned.

"Pretty good," Sam said. "I'll hire you on as a full-time herder, but it'll take some tall training to turn that dog of yours into a proper sheep dog. We'll have to water the sheep, then we can finally relax and get something to eat. Our diagnostician should be here pretty soon."

The light of a flashlight appeared from the hogan. Harley came at a leisurely pace to a big water drum mounted on a platform next to the corral. He opened a spiggot, and water flowed into a series of watering troughs.

"Great," Sam said. "I thought we'd have to haul water from the spring."

"I filled up the drum this morning," Harley said. "I've got a little pump now that does it in minutes."

"I didn't see a pump at the spring," Sam said.

"I put it away every time I use it," Harley said. "Got to. Things keep disappearing around here."

"What does that mean?" Sam asked.

"Ask your nephew. George won't say anything to me, but I've been wondering, too. It looks like you didn't lose any sheep. How about it? Hear anything moving behind you in the brush, like Berenice?"

"Nothing," Sam said.

"That's what I figured," Harley said. "You two go on now. They're keeping your dinner hot. I'll see to the sheep."

Christy hesitated. What to do with Gala? But Sam whistled to her, and she accompanied them to the smaller Benally house, where light glowed warmly through a screen door. Sam opened it for Christy, then closed it in Gala's face. She blinked, amazed at being left outside, and sat down on the kitchen step.

It was the kitchen they entered. Also the living room, dining room, and somebody's bedroom, from the looks of the furnishings. A small iron stove over which Irene Laughter stood emitted waves of heat and the odor of fried potatoes. In one corner, the two young girls sat on a bed with plates on their laps, while George and the grandmother sat at a wooden table finishing plates of potatoes and what looked like canned corned beef. Two overstuffed chairs, a chest of drawers, and an old-fashioned treadle-type sewing machine vied for space in the room. Navajos didn't decorate their walls with Navajo rugs, Christy noticed. Instead, there was a gas-company calendar and a framed picture of John Kennedy cut from a magazine. Linoleum was the preferred flooring. But the crowded room was clean and surprisingly well lit, given that the light was from two kerosene lamps.

"You want to wash?" Irene said to Sam and Christy. "Look at Mother's new sink. That's where you can wash. Isn't that some sink?"

Entering from another room, Ruthy smiled proudly at her sister's words. "Harley put in that sink," she said to Sam. "He put in a water tank, too, and he fills up all the tanks every morning. He's done all kinds of things around here since he got laid off."

"I didn't know Harley got laid off," Sam said.

"You haven't been home for a while," his sister said. "You lose track of things that way."

Her voice hadn't sounded reproachful, but Sam became very quiet. Nephew George wiped his plate clean with a slice of sandwich bread from a plastic-wrapped loaf on the table, put the whole slice of bread in his mouth, and rose from the table. He turned to the door.

"No, you're not going anywhere!" Irene said shrilly. "You leave that motorcycle alone, and you stay home!"

"I'm going outside to wait for people," he said through his mouthful of bread. "Is that bad? Come on, tell me, what's so bad about that."

Ruthy gave him a little push. "You stay right by the house. Stay in the light where we can see you," she said.

The youngster muttered something inaudibly, then he sucked in his breath so sharply that he coughed. *"Chindi,* it's that damn Doberman," he said. "Can't I walk out of my own house without stumbling over a Doberman?"

"Christy, you let the dog in," Ruthy said. "She can lie under the table. Okay, sit right down. You got their plates ready, Irene?"

Gala gratefully slid into the room. Christy was waved to a place next to the grandmother, and Gala lay down on his feet. The grandmother smiled at Christy while he forked up bites of hash-browned potatoes. Potatoes, bread, and corned beef. The former was plentiful and the latter adequate, but Christy was uncomfortable. Was he taking from the poor the food of the poor? He made a mental note to load the Bronco with groceries the first time he saw a grocery store.

Soon, Mrs. Benally came into the room with face freshly washed and a command to the little girls to go get dressed. The ailing girl, Lois, trailed slowly after her sister, but Christy noticed approvingly that she had polished her plate. As long as any creature ate with good appetite, it was a good sign. Then came the sound of a car and the Benally dogs barking. With an apologetic look at Christy, Ruthy grabbed the loaf of bread from the table and began to tidy the room. No one went to the door. Sam finished his supper and rose. Mrs. Benally bustled into a back room and returned with the girls, both dressed now in velvet tunics with long skirts.

Seeing that the womenfolk were nearly ready, Sam motioned to Christy and stepped outside to greet the stargazer.

CHAPTER 9

Gala didn't bark a single bark. Unheard of. She always barked at strangers. Even seeing a large Standard Poodle in the back seat of the visitors' car didn't get a sound out of her. To be on the safe side, Christy slid his fingers under Gala's collar and held her. She had been around all kinds of dogs at the clinic, but Dobermans were notorious for not liking shaggy dogs, and this Poodle, which looked as if it had never seen a clipper in its life, was definitely on the shaggy side.

The visitors had opened a car door, but they had politely refrained from getting out until the Benally family indicated it was ready to receive them. A middle-aged Navajo man in jeans and a flannel shirt sat smoking a cigarette behind the steering wheel, and next to him was a very old man with white wispy hair and filmed eyes. He wore a blue cowboy shirt that looked as though it hadn't left his body for years. Time for a new shirt, indeed. Sam greeted them in Navajo, and the old man answered in English, "Yes, a pretty night. A good night. This is your doctor friend? I brought my dog like Sam said. I hope you can make my dog feel better."

"I'll surely try," Christy said. "What seems to be the trouble, Mr. Klah?"

The old man nodded approvingly. "You know my name," he said. "My dog's name is Lady. Now you know her name. Lady's got a swelling in her ankles. She says ouch, those ankles hurt. That's Lady's trouble. Now, I've been to white people-doctors, but I've never been to a dog-doctor. How do you go about finding out things about a sick dog? Lady can't tell you." He smiled, showing more teeth than Christy would have expected from his apparent age. "Me, I look at stars."

Sam and the stargazer's son laughed, so Christy knew it was all right for him to laugh, too. He said to the oldster, "I wish I knew how to diagnose illnesses by looking at stars. Sometimes we need all the help we can get."

"Yes, everyone can use help," Klah said. Slowly, he lifted one leg out of the car and began a painful process of trying to get both feet on the ground.

To Sam, Christy said, "I'll get my bag. Is there somewhere with pretty good light where I can go over Lady? Your mother's kitchen would be fine, if she wouldn't mind."

"I'll bring enough lamps into the hogan," Sam said. "Mr. Klah will feel more comfortable there." He lowered his voice and added, "Listen, Christy, even if there isn't much you can do for the dog, give the old fellow some kind of liniment or ointment he can rub on her. Old-time Navajos are accustomed to ointments. It'll make him feel better."

"It could be a heart condition," Christy warned. "Sometimes you get swelling of the legs and other fluid accumulation."

"Make him happy. Give him an ointment anyway. You can take your time. Mr. Klah has to be offered food, and I've never known a Navajo to turn down a meal."

It took ten minutes, largely because Christy couldn't remember where he had packed his flashlight. With its help, he found the satchel that contained the jumbled leftovers from old house calls. He felt like a heel when he coaxed Gala into the Bronco and, as an afterthought, locked her in. If things were disappearing around the Benally place, Christy didn't want his car and his dog to be among the missing. He left Gala whining unhappily in the car. While hanging around with Indian dogs had seemed to give her culture shock, she still preferred going with Christy to staying behind.

Christy could see light through the cracks around the ill-fitting wooden door of the hogan. He knocked hesitantly, and the door was opened by Sam. A small fire burned in the center of the hogan, and behind it, seated on sheepskins, the Klahs were eating bowls of stewed peaches with enjoyment. Klah's big Poodle lay beside him chewing a mutton bone from their empty plates. The Benally family hadn't yet come from the house.

The cedar logs that made up the sides of the six-sided building were heavily smoke-stained from past fires, but the hogan looked as if it wasn't used much now. The only sign of occupancy was a pile of sheepskins on the dirt floor. Sam held a kerosene lamp, and he lit a second one after Christy came in. Mr. Klah put down his bowl of peaches. He spoke to his son, who jumped to his feet and helped the old man rise. Lady sniffed the peaches but didn't go for them. She was busy looking apprehensively at Christy. He wondered how animals always knew it was a vet approaching them.

"Hello, Lady," Christy said. "We're going to be friends, aren't we?"

He spoke to the dog reassuringly. If he moved toward the dog more carefully than usual, he had Gregory's toothmarks on his arm to thank for it. Young Mr. Klah knelt beside the dog to hold her, and old Mr. Klah roughly patted her head, then moved out of Christy's way. Christy stroked the animal soothingly for a few moments before motioning Sam closer with the lamp.

"Do you know how old Lady is, Mr. Klah?" Christy asked.

"She's eight. I got her when she was two years old from a man in Albuquerque. He said he'd always had her, so I guess he knew. He said he was going to go work in Idaho, and he couldn't take her there."

Lady had all the earmarks of a purebred Standard Poodle. Deep chest. Intelligent eyes. Aristocratic. The white coat was matted, but the texture was good, not dry or brittle, and her skin was supple and in good condition. Without realizing that he was doing it, Christy began to hum tunelessly while he examined the animal. Overweight. Old Mr. Klah had been feeding her all too well. No obvious accumulation of fluid in the abdomen.

"You've never taken her to a vet before?" Christy asked the aged man. "No annual shots? No heartworm pills? But maybe you don't have mosquitoes around here."

The old man laughed comfortably. "What does Lady need pills

and shots for?" he said. "She does what I do, and I don't get shots. She eats what I eat, and she sleeps where I sleep. I've never been sick much, and she's never been sick at all."

Christy marveled at how a dog could even survive, much less be in apparent good condition, without basic care. He decided that he would at least pop rabies and DHLP shots into her rump, to give her protection against the more infectious dog diseases. He made a mental note to do the same for the Benally dogs and asked more questions.

Did Lady's lameness and the swelling come and go, or did they stay? They stayed. Did Lady lose her appetite from time to time, maybe act as if she had a fever? Her appetite never flagged, and Mr. Klah didn't know how you decided if a dog had fever. Did she seem lamer in cold or wet weather? Yes. Did she seem lamer after strenuous exercise? Well, yes, she limped more if she chased after Mr. Klah when he went somewhere on his horse.

The thought of Mr. Klah, at his age, trekking off on horseback distracted Christy, and he almost forgot to ask if Lady had exhibited swelling in other joints. Mr. Klah answered negatively as Christy fished into his bag for his stethoscope.

The sight of the dangling stethoscope alarmed Lady. She tried to back away, but the old man spoke to her in Navajo, and she steadied. Her heart was steady, as well. Christy heard a firm, regular double thump as he went over her chest. He put away the stethoscope and felt more cheerful. No obvious signs of heart disease. Now for the problem of actually checking the swelling of her carpals. Metacarpals, too? The carpals especially looked baggy, like housemaid's knee, but with so much hair and no clippers, he would have to palpate thoroughly, and that would hurt.

Christy asked the son to hold the big Poodle securely, and he started at the hips, then the back legs, feeling the joints carefully. Lady didn't seem to mind, but the front legs were a different story. Shoulders and elbow joints were normal. Carpals distinctly swollen and painful, though not hot. Metacarpals normal. Christy sat back on his heels and wished for high-quality, high-detailed radiographs. He wished for analysis of the synovial fluid around the involved joints. He wished for a clinic instead of a hogan.

The old man said, "You're stumped. I see enough, blind, to see that. You got the wrong things in your bundle. I ought to loan you my medicine bundle." He turned his head, listening. To Sam, he said, "You got more people coming? Friends? Relatives?"

"Yes, two or three," Sam said.

"People won't come?" Mr. Klah said. "Don't feel bad. Nobody really believes what they're saying about your mother. She's on the council, and she speaks right out in front of all the people, but she's a woman, so they say, 'How come that woman's got that power? She's taken power from bad stuff.' I want you to know, I don't believe that. A lot of people don't believe that."

The lamp in Sam's hands trembled slightly. In a flat voice, he said, "I didn't know people were singling out my mother for their stupid talk."

"Don't you worry about that. You want to think good thoughts now. Those two or three people you got coming, that's better than none. That's good. That's the right way." Mr. Klah asked his son to get his ceremonial bundle from their car, then kneeled painfully beside the dog and said to Christy, "Okay, so what's Lady got?"

Christy said, "It's pretty certain that Lady has arthritis."

Mr. Klah shook his head. "Lady's not old. She's too young for arthritis. I know about arthritis."

"It can happen even to a younger dog," Christy said. "Arthritis just means an inflammation of a joint. Or Lady might have a sort of general breakdown of the joint. Osteoarthrosis. It's the most common form of arthritis in dogs."

"Does it get worse?"

"Not necessarily. There are several things we can do. The most important thing is that she has to lose some weight. Fifteen pounds, by preference, but at least ten. That'll relieve some of the stress her ankles are having to put up with."

"No more mutton fat?" the old man said. He put his arm around Lady's neck commiseratingly.

"No more mutton fat," Christy said. "Now, she needs exercise, but it should be in the form of easy walking, not wild running about. If she starts limping anyway, like in cold weather, hot-packing her ankles with a hot, moist towel could make her feel better. Do you think you could do that?"

"Sure," said Mr. Klah. "What else?"

Christy dug into his bag for a bottle of buffered aspirin. "An aspirin twice a day for a couple of days at a time would ease her pain, but don't overdo the aspirin. They could cause other troubles."

"Okay, what else?" Mr. Klah said.

The oldster looked so hopeful that Christy dug deeper into his bag for a jar of DMSO gel he thought he'd remembered seeing. "The last thing we'll try is Dimethyl Sulfoxide, DMSO. It isn't approved yet for humans, but I understand that some people have been trying it already for their arthritis, and we've had some good luck with it on dogs. Here, I've got some surgeon's gloves in here somewhere."

The son reentered the hogan, and Christy turned his head to address both of them. "DMSO penetrates so rapidly that you should wear rubber gloves when you apply it. Otherwise, it'll penetrate your own skin before you can wash it off. Dip a bare finger in it, and in a few minutes you'll get a nice garlicky taste in the back of your mouth. It probably does no greater harm than that, but it's one of the many mystery medications. We're not sure how all of them work. But it's excellent for reducing swelling. I want you to try rubbing it onto Lady's ankles twice a day for two weeks. If you want, you can forget the rubber gloves and paint it on with a paintbrush."

"Not me," old Mr. Klah said. "I'll put it on with my bare hands. I got arthritis, too. Maybe it'll help my hands while it helps Lady's ankles."

"Then be sure to wash your hands very carefully both before and after you use it," Christy said worriedly. "DMSO could carry anything on the surface of the skin right into the body."

"It's strong," the old man said admiringly. He took the chunky jar from Christy with hands that looked as if they hadn't seen soap and water for days, if not weeks. For a moment, Christy had severe misgivings.

"Mind you," Christy warned, "it's only a good bet that Lady has arthritis. Given a chance, I'd take a few X-rays and be sure."

"X-rays?" Mr. Klah questioned.

"Yes, to take a picture of the bone so you can see the degree of any joint deterioration."

Mr. Klah unwrapped a buckskin bundle that his son had put beside him. It was filled with smaller bundles. He carefully put in the aspirin and the jar and the thin rubber gloves. Christy dug into his own bag and handed over a handful of cotton balls. Mr. Klah looked them over and added them. "That seeing inside the body to look at a bone sounds like what I do," he said. "Maybe you're not guessing about Lady and arthritis. Maybe you're 'seeing,' like me."

Christy glanced at Sam. His friend looked interested but not apprehensive at the turn of the conversation, and Christy was dying of curiosity. "How do you 'see,' Mr. Klah?" Christy asked. "How does gazing at stars help tell you what illness a person is suffering from?"

"I don't know," Mr. Klah said simply. He struggled to stand. The son and Christy both jumped to assist him, then the son moved the ceremonial bundle to one of the sheepskins. "You say you don't know how the medicine in the jar works, and I don't know how stargazing works. Pretty soon here, all the people will come to the hogan. I'll talk to the girl who's sick, and then I'll talk to the others, and we'll all talk about how she's sick. We put the fire out. I eat a pinch of pollen, and I chant a little, and I do a little prayer. Everybody has to close his eyes. Everybody can't move or speak. We all think about the sick person and try to see something. Then I go away from the hogan. I look at some star. I hold my hand out to it. Well, I better tell you all of it. You're a doctor, so you need to know things. I have this special stone you can see through. It's like a star stone. I hold that stone in my hand in line with the star, and I do a prayer to Gila Monster, and then I get a white shining, something white and bright. When you get the white shining, you see things in the star stone. You come back pretty soon, and you bring some answers back with you. Yes, that's what happens."

The stargazer let out a long sigh. His middle-aged son sighed along with him, sounding a little wistful. Christy felt wistful, too. A white shining sounded like a handy thing to have when you were faced with a tricky diagnosis.

"Shall I get everyone now?" Sam asked. He looked meaningfully at Christy, and Christy realized it was time for him to depart. Old Mr. Klah acted as if he wouldn't have minded having Christy around for a stargazing session, but the Benally family had acted otherwise.

Christy held them up long enough to tell Mr. Klah that after he had been into Gallup to pick up vaccines, he would like to drop by and vaccinate Lady. He would also be able to check her again to see how she was progressing on the DMSO.

"Okay, but don't charge me a big fee," Mr. Klah said. "Stargazers don't get rich the way singers do."

"It'll be on the house," Christy assured him.

"Maybe we can trade," Mr. Klah said. "I can find things that are lost sometimes."

"Dad finds lost things for people all the time," the younger Klah said proudly.

Christy said good night to the pair and backtracked to the spring. It was time, at last, to light the lantern for the night. Time to set up the gasoline stove and spread the sleeping bags and get the coffee pot set for the morning. But before Christy reached for a match, he stood for a moment and gazed upward at a gibbous moon hanging in the blackness of the sky and at the white shining of the stars.

If stars anywhere could talk, these could. No, not talk. Shout. Scream. With no haze to dim them, no city lights to compete with them, they stabbed down fiercely from the black bowl of the heavens, shining so brightly, so whitely, that Christy could see the shadow of Gala's head thrown against the side of the tent.

Back at the hogan, old Mr. Klah might be talking now to the little girl whose family thought she had been poisoned by a Navajo wolf. Maybe Mr. Klah was eating his pinch of pollen, preparing to pray, preparing to consult the stars. Would he look for Sirius, the Greater Dog? Or would any star tell him what he needed to know? There was mystery here. Mystery in old Mr. Klah and mystery in the night.

Something rustled in the brush on the other side of the spring. Instantly, Christy's imagination provided it with huge paws and feral red eyes and clashing teeth. He glanced quickly at Gala. She was sniffing the grub box and only flicked an ear toward the rustling sound. Perhaps a ground squirrel, coming to the spring to drink. The flickering beast of his imagination faded, leaving behind only a subtle fear. Christy stood for a moment and decided that some fear was only sensible. Out there somewhere was a dark reality. He would be on his guard. But Christy moved closer to his dog, and he didn't waste any more time lighting the lantern.

CHAPTER 10

The Navajo police officer arrived the next morning while Sam was still asleep. Sam had come to the tent long after Christy went to bed, but Gala thought daybreak was a good time to start a day. Thanks to her, Christy had been up for an hour—plenty of time to wash in the chilly water of the spring, make coffee, and produce breakfast for Gala and the two Benally dogs, who had appeared at the first clack of a can opener.

Christy was sitting in the Bronco shaving when he saw a white Suburban pull in by the Benally houses, followed by a McKinley County sheriff's car. He unplugged the shaver from the cigarette-lighter socket and watched as young George, looking apprehensive, came out to speak to a uniformed Navajo in the Suburban. With apparent relief, the youngster pointed to the spring, and the Navajo officer and two sheriff's deputies climbed out of their cars and walked toward Christy. He closed Gala into the Bronco and went to meet them.

"Morning," the Navajo officer said. "I'm Tully Kee, and this is Deputy Bob Turland and Deputy Jack Martin. You'd be Dr. Christy. Sam told me he'd brought you down with him. He kind of gave me the idea you were here to find the animal that killed Mr. Fawkes and get rid of it."

"Sam exaggerates," Christy said. "I hope I can lend a hand, of course, but I had no intention of interfering in any police investigation."

"There's no problem with interfering," Kee said. "We all want to catch the dog before it causes more trouble. The deputies here would welcome your help. Sam says you know all about the breeds of dogs that guard sheep."

"I know a little," Christy said. "Sheep ranchers up in Colorado have been using a few new breeds. New to the United States, that is."

"These sheep-guarding dogs," Deputy Turland said. "They can be pretty mean?"

"Well, they can be formidable," Christy said. "For that matter, any big dog that's allowed to roam around loose in the area could be a problem."

Kee said, "I thought I had a line on a likely sounding dog yesterday. You might say I interviewed him. He's a Rhodesian Ridgeback, and Deputy Martin here told me they can be mean. He belongs to a family up toward Ganado. But he's so fat and lazy and spoiled that he barely looked up when I went in their house. Just stretched out on the couch he was lying on and went back to sleep. The family laughed when I asked them if he ever left the place. They can't get him to exercise enough. I guess he spends his life snoozing. But now I've turned up some big white herd dogs only five or six miles from the Fawkes ranch, near Manuelito. Shaggy dogs. Commanders, they called them. You know anything about Commanders?"

The older deputy's mouth quirked, as though he was suppressing a smile. "Komondor," Martin corrected. "Komondorok when there's more than one. It's a Hungarian breed, so the plural is funny."

Kee's expression didn't change. "Right," he said. "All these guard dogs for sheep, are they mostly big and fierce, Dr. Christy?"

"Most are pretty good size, and they can easily run over a hundred pounds in weight," Christy said. "The breeds have varying degrees of aggressiveness, but they all have to be pretty aggressive to be able to do their jobs. And a lot of them are as shaggy as the sheep they guard. Your Komondor is especially shaggy."

"And white?" Kee repeated.

"Yes."

Turland, the younger of the two deputies, said, "We were told you and Sam Benally could maybe come along with us and look at the dogs, Dr. Christy. We'd sure like to have your opinion. I followed up on a lead on some Pulis that a Mexican rancher is using, but Jack says they're too small to attack a man with much success. So it looks like the Komondors are our best bet."

Which odd Hungarian plural would the older deputy correct this time? Christy waited for Deputy Martin to correct Pulis to Pulik and insist on Komondorok for Komondors, but the dog expert said nothing this time. Christy assured the younger deputy he'd be glad to accompany them. He offered them coffee and called Sam, and while a fresh pot of coffee was perking on the little gasoline stove he mentioned the hint he'd gotten from Ann Lang's helper about the large feral dog that had been seen in the area. Tully Kee and Deputy Turland pondered together as to where they might start looking for it.

"It could be some Navajo's dog," Turland pointed out to Kee. "I've yet to see an Indian dog on a leash or in a fenced yard. What if it's not wild at all? Just wandered off from somebody's place and attacked Mr. Fawkes and then went home again?"

"Yes, there's always that possibility," Kee said. "Don't worry. I've already been asking around all over the place. But it could also be an abandoned dog. There are plenty around, from time to time. Town people bring them out to the country to dump them."

"Yeah, and if one survived, it would have to be a crafty, quick kind of animal," Turland said.

Sam listened sleepily. He was never very talkative in the mornings. The older deputy, after his one correction of Kee's dog terminology, said nothing at all. He gazed idly at Gala in her car. The deputy's mouth continued to quirk occasionally as he listened to his fellow officers talk dogs, causing Christy to look at him more closely. Deputy Martin was a lean, tidy man with a weathered look about him. He also had the look of a veteran. Veteran of what? Probably of at least one war. Korea, probably, given a guess at his age. He had a queer air of weary tension dashed with desperation, but tightly controlled.

"For a feral dog, it comes down to food and water," Christy

said, in answer to another question from Turland. "A dog can go for a long time without food. Ten days, twelve days. But about five days without water is the maximum."

"The Fawkes ranch sounds like the best bet to me," Turland said. "There's always water available for stock, and we saw some tracks out there that I keep wondering about."

Christy nodded. "Harley Tsosie showed me what was left of the tracks yesterday afternoon. Two sizes. That could mean two dogs running together. Something happens to an animal when you get a pack syndrome going. They reinforce each other. I don't know if it's worth much, but I took some pictures of the tracks. I was thinking I could run into Gallup later today and leave the film to be developed."

"Give the film to Turland," Kee suggested. "He can take it in and send the prints back out with the first patrol car that comes this way. Save you the trouble. That okay with you, Deputy Turland?"

"Sure," Turland said. "First-rate service for our animal advisor. It's only fair. Considering the county budget this year, it's the only payment he's apt to receive."

Christy said, "Thanks, I'd appreciate that." He went to the Bronco to unload the film from his camera. When he got back, they were talking about herd-guarding dogs again.

"The man that's using the Komondorok near Manuelito is Ed Lee," Kee said. "He's about your age, Sam. Do you know him?"

"Not that I recall," Sam said. "I've got an errand to run north of Wide Ruin, but it can wait until we look at the dogs. Just give me a chance to get dressed."

"Fine," Kee said. "Sam can be translator if the deputies need one. I've got to go back to the substation. Turland, you stop by later and tell me what you find out, all right?"

Within a few minutes, Kee waved and drove away. The two deputies got into their car and waited patiently enough until Sam was ready. Christy stopped the Bronco at the Benally house while Sam ran in to speak to his mother. She came to the door looking none too happy. As Christy followed the deputies' car to a blacktop road on the other side of the Benally place, he asked

Sam, "Is anything wrong? Your mother seems worried. What did Mr. Klah say last night, anyway?"

"Not much of anything," Sam said. "That's the trouble. In effect, he said there was nothing wrong with Lois."

"She's not ill? No ghost-sickness?"

"So said the stars. Mr. Klah said just do a Blessingway. At least Grandmother thought up a hotshot singer. I hope I've got the directions straight. If he's home, we'll find him in the boonies north of Wide Ruin. But the family was really disappointed."

"Of course," Christy said. "I understand perfectly."

Sam interrupted a yawn with a grin. "I guess it sounds a little complicated. What it amounts to is that now the family can't do its rooting-tooting anti-witch act. Blessingway isn't a fancy, dramatic affair. All your friends and relatives and neighbors don't have to come. A family just has in a singer and has the ceremony, and that's that. Not much public relations value there."

"How did the little girl take it?"

"Lois looked pretty relieved, actually. It was Mother and Grandmother who got indignant. The minute Mr. Klah left, Grandmother started saying he was a witch himself. Of course, all old people are suspected of being witches, but Grandmother didn't seem to think of that."

"Since Mr. Fawkes was pretty old, did people suspect him of being a witch?" Christy asked.

"I don't know," Sam said. "Maybe. I guess, given the perils of living on a starvation diet with little medical aid, Navajos figure anyone who lives to a ripe age gets supernatural help in doing it. You know—'Take my neighbor, oh, chief of witches, and let me live longer instead.' But Blessingway doesn't have anything specific to do with witches. It's like taking vitamins: it guards you from disease instead of curing something."

"Then it can't hurt," Christy said.

"Blessingway could never hurt. That's what Ruthy claims. So I get the job of finding the Blessingway singer and making the appointment. I hope you don't bust an axle driving me around the reservation this morning."

The blacktop road took them smoothly to the crossroad village of Lupton. As they passed it en route to an east turn on I-40, Tully Kee's Suburban was already parked in front of a small building with a big name: NAVAJO DIVISION OF PUBLIC SAFETY, WINDOW ROCK DISTRICT, LUPTON SUBSTATION.

"Why didn't Officer Kee come with us?" Christy wondered aloud.

"Jurisdiction, probably. Manuelito is in McKinley County, and while a lot of the *Dinéh* have land around there, it's privately owned, not reservation land. Tully likes to stick to the rules when he can. It makes it easier to keep the *bilagáana* cops off the reservation."

The cliffs they followed back toward Gallup became buff-colored rather than blood red, and the mesas to the south receded, leaving a zone of grazing land. Manuelito was much like Lupton—a tiny settlement with a store that doubled as a post office and a dirt crossroad that they took to the south. It was well graded but dusty, and Christy lagged so far back to avoid the dust thrown up by the deputies' car that he almost missed the turn they made to a ranch house off the road. Like Harley Tsosie's house, it was of concrete blocks, but like the Benally house, it had a log hogan beside it for ceremonial purposes. Two dark-faced children ran to the door of the big house and looked at the cars, and there was the inevitable pause before a young Navajo woman in slacks came to the door. The slacks seemed to be a signal that this was a modern, English-speaking family. Deputy Turland went to speak to her.

Gala was getting tired of her beloved car. She gave her "walk time" bark, but Christy shushed her. "Wait until we know where the dogs are," he said.

The dogs were almost three miles back the way they had come, off a wagon road that made Christy glad he drove a four-wheeler. The road drifted behind a mesa, and Christy was surprised to see a thick growth of spindly aspens. Aspens in this waterless country? But, if not thriving, the trees were at least alive and there.

So were the animals that the dogs guarded. Some four hundred Angora goats grazed among the aspens. A youngish Navajo man on horseback frowned when he saw the cars and rode toward them. Sam got out of the Bronco. Deputy Martin started to get out of the sheriff's car, but the younger officer held him back, giving Sam a chance to smooth the way for them. After a few minutes, Sam beckoned to the deputies. Christy told Gala to stop nagging for a walk and went to join them.

A puzzled look had replaced the frown on the young Navajo's face. "You want to see my dogs work?" he said. He nodded toward a sunny slope. "Well, there they are. Working."

Christy shaded his eyes. What he had taken for another goat, plodding along next to a nanny, turned out to be a big white dog with a heavy coat that was, for a Komondor, properly hanging in a thousand tightly kinked strings from the top of its head to its floppy feet. Christy could see a black nose and a pink tongue but no eyes; the hair covered them.

"That's Ace," the Navajo rancher said. "The female's around here somewhere. She's Queenie."

Deputy Turland said, "Are you sure the female isn't missing?"

The frown reappeared. "Why should she be? She never leaves the goats." He whistled sharply, a good blast that on a city street would have produced a taxi in nothing flat. Sure enough, taking her time, a slightly smaller Komondor meandered out of the aspens. She refused to come all the way to the rancher, but she at least turned her head in his direction.

Deputy Martin, the quiet one, had lagged behind with Christy, and now he opened his mouth for the first time to ask a question. "Who trains herd dogs, Dr. Christy? The people who work with them?"

"Nobody does," Christy said. "People just take advantage of what they call a 'following instinct,' meaning the dogs follow along with the sheep or goats."

Deputy Martin was insistent. "They have to be trained," he said. "They're guard dogs, aren't they?"

"Well, some people call them livestock guard dogs," Christy said. "Most people call them herd-guarding dogs. I guess it comes out to the same thing."

"I've worked with plenty of guard dogs, mostly German Shepherds," Martin argued. "So, all right, if you're talking about show rings, German Shepherds are classed now as herding dogs, but no breed makes a better guard dog. Either way, you have to start with basic obedience training and go on from there. So I ask you again, who trains these dogs?"

Understanding lighted up in Christy's mind. "Oh, I see the problem," he said. "We're talking about different types of herders. There are your bite-and-chase herders, like your Collies and Shelties, and then there are the herd-guarding dogs, like your Komondorok out there."

"So what's the difference?" Martin demanded.

Turland, the younger deputy, grinned. Christy didn't know why, but he explained, "Herding dogs have a natural instinct to run after sheep and nip them. You train them in line with their instincts, then you can direct them while you're moving herds."

"Of course," Martin said. "I've seen Border Collies work. Voice command. Arm signals. Whistles. The same stuff you use in training guard dogs."

"That's right," Christy said patiently, "but the herd-guarding dogs aren't guard dogs in the sense that they guard people or buildings. They don't move livestock, either. All they do is guard herds. Their training hasn't changed for centuries. Ranchers just raise the dogs with their flocks. They put the puppies in to nurse a ewe or nanny when they're three or four weeks old. The dogs grow up identifying with the rest of a flock of sheep or goats, only they've got sharp teeth, and they'll use them to defend their buddies."

"The owner doesn't train them to attack?" Martin said insistently.

"No. There's no reason to. I saw a bunch of Great Pyrenees last winter in Colorado guarding about five thousand sheep in South Park. According to the rancher, the dogs ran off everything from coyotes to bears. They just do it naturally."

Stuck in the Bronco, frustrated at not being able to go for a walk, Gala the Doberman chose to bark a challenge at the furry dogs. The effect was instantaneous. Queenie backed up, barking, and the goat flock closed ranks behind her. The male Komondor trotted forward in a businesslike manner. He detoured around

Christy and the other men, but not before Christy found himself taking two steps backward. He cursed himself silently, hoping no one had noticed, especially that touchy deputy, Martin. The Komondor was making straight for Gala in the Bronco, but she was safely locked in.

The young rancher whistled. Ace ignored him and kept trotting. Deputy Turland said, "They don't pay much attention, do they?"

"Only if they're in the mood," the Navajo rancher said.

Martin nudged Christy. "Why don't you let your Dobe out of the car," he said. "Let's see what the Komondor does."

"Not on your life," Christy said.

Martin shrugged. "Queenie's occupied, and Ace won't attack her. Dogs never go for bitches."

Christy said, "Maybe most don't, but I treated three bitches in Vail that got chewed on by a male Saint Bernard."

"Oh, Saint Bernards," Martin said with a grimace. "Most of them are nuts."

The male Komondor trotted the rest of the way to the Bronco. While Gala raged, ricocheting from side to side within the vehicle, the Komondor lifted his leg on a tire and strolled back to the goats. He lay down, as if ready for a nap after his exertion.

Martin had a defensive look as Turland questioned the Navajo rancher quietly about the roaming habits, if any, of his dogs. But Ed Lee ran a tight operation, checking the goats and, in the process, the dogs, twice a day.

"That's my year's profit on the hoof, right there," Lee said. "I've got a hundred and fifty head of cattle, and I used to graze sheep, too, but the wool sold from a ewe's fleece barely paid for her keep. Oh, some sheep men make a few dollars shipping slaughtered lambs to meat markets back East, but Angora goats, there's been a market boom in mohair. Upholstery velours mostly. There's no oversupply of mohair. All my people, they're still raising sheep, sheep, sheep, and maybe Spanish goats, but what's a Spanish goat good for? Roast kid, nothing else."

Deputy Turland asked, "And the dogs are always with your goats, every day when you check them?"

Lee said, "Yes, morning and evening. Goats are a little tricky. They're not as dumb as sheep, but the nannies aren't very protective of the kids. If you don't watch them, they wander off and let the kids get into trouble. Queenie's good about helping out, though. I've seen her shouldering many a nanny along, pushing it back to its kid."

Sam seemed to like the rancher. He asked several questions about water supply, and they walked off together, gesturing. Turland asked Christy, "What do you think? Just because Lee checks the flock twice a day doesn't mean one of the dogs couldn't have made a little overnight journey to the Fawkes ranch, killed Fawkes, and got back for breakfast the next day, does it?"

"No, but it seems unlikely," Christy said. "I can't see any reason why the dogs would want to hike off and kill a stranger. They seem very content with the goats."

Martin started to walk slowly toward the flock. Ace, the shaggy male Komondor, decided to wake up. He rose and shook himself lazily. He ambled slowly on an angle that would intercept the deputy if the man kept coming.

"Watch it," Christy called to Martin.

Martin kept walking. So did the dog. Ace didn't bark or growl. He just ambled onward until Martin was some fifty yards from the nearest goat. At that point, Ace lowered his tail and turned his head directly to watch Martin. His ears went forward and slightly up.

"Holy Christ, your deputy friend is going to get bitten," Christy said. Not wanting to in the least, he jogged toward Martin, calling, "Hey, that's close enough!"

Martin turned back. "I just wanted to see how close I could get to one of his goats. He's protective, all right, but I don't know how aggressive he is. Not very, I guess, if it came to training him for man-work. He's big enough, but he's too slow to be much good."

"Do you really think one of the Komondorok went over and attacked Mr. Fawkes?" Christy said tactlessly. "Face it, the only way you could get an attack out of that dog is the way you tried —to come to his flock and try to steal a goat."

Deputy Turland chuckled. "Hear that, Jack?" he said to Martin. "There goes your pet theory." To Christy, he explained, "Jack's been trying to convince us for two days now that someone could have trained the animal that attacked Old Man Fawkes. That's the way it goes with these old canine cops. They got dogs on the brain."

Christy stared at Martin. "You think the attack was premeditated?"

"I didn't say that," Martin said. "I just said a dog can be trained to kill. Maybe one got loose, and Fawkes got in the way."

Christy was silent for a moment, then said, "I met Mr. Fawkes's daughter yesterday. She said her father was murdered."

Turland said, "Yeah, she told us that, too. But the sheriff doesn't buy it. Neither does Tully Kee. They both saw the body. Thank God, I didn't. They said it was definitely an animal attack, and definitely very messy. That rules out premeditation and murder."

"Damn it, one doesn't necessarily rule out the other," Martin said stubbornly. "That's all I'm trying to tell you. I could take any dog, if he's big enough and isn't too damned dumb, and train him to tear into a man. If you know what you're doing, you can get an animal to do anything."

"The training methods can be pretty ugly, though," Christy said. "Don't you have to beat dogs to make them aggressive?"

"That's the stupid way to do it," Martin said. "Clucks that hire out attack dogs, they figure they have to mistreat a dog before it's willing to go after a person. Teach it to be afraid, then teach it to hate. The clucks that do Schutzhund work are just as bad. They've always got some guy with a stick, slashing away at the dogs to get them to attack. That's as silly as beating a dog for making errors when you're teaching it simple obedience work. No, if you want a dog to do something useful, I guess it's the same business of going along with its natural impulses. You want a dog to attack when you say so? You tease it. That helps it get mad. And when the dog finally goes for you, you've got the padded sleeve on, and once the dog gets to bite down, boy, does that feel good. The dogs like it. They want to keep on doing it. A trained attack dog can get real nervous if you don't let it work. They have to be taken out for regular tune-ups. Workouts. You only have to think of things from a dog's point of view, in all the training. Some strange tough dog comes onto their territory, what do they think of just naturally? Attack, bite. We teach them as puppies that they can't do that to people, but if you want an attack dog, all you have to do is retrain it."

"I don't think it's as simple as all that," Christy said.

"Maybe not for the sickies of the world," Martin admitted. "Face it, some people just plain enjoy cruelty. But teaching a dog to fight at your side, that's what he was born for."

Christy didn't agree at all. In his opinion, teaching a dog aggression toward humans was a risky business, and it was especially risky for the dog. One bite, and the dog could be subject to legal action to have it destroyed. On an even deeper level, Christy was opposed to tampering with a dog's own good judgment. He knew from past experience that Gala was capable of deciding if real danger threatened her master or herself. If she'd been trained to be aggressive toward anyone and everyone, deliberately keyed up and kept on edge, her judgment would be muddied, maybe ruined. But Christy didn't waste time arguing with Martin. He said, "If it was an attack dog that killed Mr. Fawkes, then what's your best guess? Do you think he was killed by a dog on command or a dog without anyone around to command it?"

Martin hedged. "It would depend on the dog and the kind of training. Sure, you can train an animal to attack without command. No command, that's what a lot of the attack-dog companies use. They just want a tough dog to guard some used-car lot, so they keep the dog in solitary, depriving it of all human or canine companionship until it goes half nuts, and when they do let it out, they encourage it to go for anything that moves."

"To kill?" Christy said.

Martin nodded. "Maim. Kill. Just like I've been saying."

"Could you train a wolf to kill?"

Martin looked surprised and not entirely displeased at the new thought. "Why not?" he said. "But the trick would be to start with a tame wolf, not a wild one. Animals need basic socializa-

tion with humans, at some early point in their lives, so you can
train them at all."

Christy said slowly, "If you're right about all this, maybe we
should be looking for a motive behind Mr. Fawkes's death, instead of only looking for dogs and wild animals."

"Sure, I agree," Martin said. "But I can't get any of the others
to go along with me."

He sounded bitter, and he seemed upset that they had made
little progress that morning. Deputy Turland murmured something about getting back to Gallup, now that they had looked
over the Komondorok. Christy decided he would ask Officer Kee
later if he had an autopsy report. After talking to Martin, he
found the whole idea of an animal attack was beginning to sound
unlikely. What if they were all wrong about how Mr. Fawkes had
died?

Sam was still deep in conversation with the young rancher.
After the deputies drove away, Christy pushed himself to call to
the female Komondor. Queenie came slowly and warily, but she
came, stopping three feet from him. Christy studied her for a
moment, then studied himself. Afraid? Or only afraid that he
might be afraid? There were butterflies in his stomach, but he
stretched out his hand to Queenie and chatted to her coaxingly.
Queenie came all the way. Doglike, she used her nose to get
acquainted with Christy, then seemed perfectly happy to have her
throat scratched.

Christy was feeling elated when Sam returned to the Bronco.
The butterflies were still there, but he had had a pleasant meeting
with a strange dog. Gala was predictably jealous. To make it up
to her, Christy demanded that they stop in some unpopulated
area so Gala could stretch her legs.

"We'll stop at the Puerco," Sam said. "I had a good chat with
Lee once we were alone. He swears his nice teddy-bear dogs
haven't left his property, and I believe him."

"I think the deputies were convinced, too," Christy said.
"We'll have to think up a new suspect." He was silent for a
moment, then said, "We seem to have a new option."

"Oh?" Sam said.

"Yes. So far we've been looking for a wild dog, or maybe herding dogs running in a pack. Deputy Martin thinks it could be a trained attack animal, maybe even with someone using it like a weapon. That would change everything."

Sam whistled low between his teeth. "It sure would," he said. "I picked up something, too. Something Lee told me while we were out with his goats."

"What's that?" Christy said.

"There's talk about a big white wolf," Sam said. "Not just any wolf, either. This was 'a white wolf floating across the sky.' They say some kid saw it the night Old Man Fawkes was killed, and he warned a Navajo family about it, and they warned somebody else. It's got everybody scared spitless."

"A big white wolf," Christy mused.

" 'Floating across the sky,' " Sam repeated. "I asked Lee where we could find the kid, but he didn't know. He said he'd ask around and tell us if he found out anything. Like it or not, Christy, we may have to put another option back on your list. One we'd almost forgotten."

Christy stared at him. "Are you saying what I think you're saying?"

"That's right," Sam said. He made an eerie sound while sweeping his hand in an arc over the dashboard of the Bronco in imitation of a floating form. "There may still be something supernatural out there."

CHAPTER 11

Peter Madman, member in good standing of the Navajo Medicinemen's Association, was willing to begin a two-night Blessingway on Saturday night. When Christy and Sam returned that Thursday afternoon with the news and a carload of groceries, Sam's mother and grandmother immediately started preparations. Harley and George were set to work hauling clean arroyo sand to cover the floor of the medicine hogan. Sam was assigned the shelling of blue, gray, and white Indian corn. The women, with mano and metate, began grinding a small mountain of the corn to feed what the grandmother stubbornly insisted would be a large gathering for the ceremony.

Christy would willingly have helped Sam shell corn, but Sam suggested he keep his appointment with Eleanor Fawkes instead and help her with her windows. Again, Christy had that feeling that he was in the way at the Benally place. At two o'clock he set off with Gala for the Fawkes ranch. "On the whole, I think I'd rather haul sand," Christy confided to Gala as they bounced along the ruts. "Miss Fawkes strikes me as a touchy woman. If she growls at me, Gala, I hope you'll growl back."

But Miss Fawkes was smiling as she came through the big front door of the ranch house to greet Christy. She was also looking rather chic for a woman engaged in opening a big, dusty house. She wore a black cotton shirt and black-and-white shorts, and her hair was tied back with a green silk scarf matching eyes that today were green, Christy saw, not turquoise. Colored lenses, he realized.

"You came," the woman said. "How nice of you. The way I acted yesterday, I was afraid you wouldn't."

"Oh, no, I'm glad to help out," Christy said. He reached back into the Bronco for tools borrowed from Harley Tsosie. "I feel like a fraud, Miss Fawkes. I'm not much of a carpenter."

"Call me Eleanor," she said. "I'll help you with unboarding the windows. We can muddle along together. Bianca Wilson is already here vacuuming, and I've got the washer and dryer going. I don't dare turn on any other lights. The generator used to blow if you asked it for too much electricity. With the windows open, we'll at least be able to see the rest of the dirt. Don't you want to bring your dog in? He'll be cooler in the house."

"You don't mind?" Christy asked.

"Of course not. I like dogs. And Bianca seems to be a fellow spirit with all animals."

Christy opened the car door for Gala. "She's a she," he said. "Her name is Gala. And everybody calls me Christy."

Eleanor Fawkes seemed experienced with dogs. She gave Gala her hand to sniff, then ignored the Doberman, letting her take her time in getting acquainted. "Just let her wander wherever she wants," Eleanor said. She gazed across the circular driveway at a big barn on the far side. "Well, not the barn," she said. "We have to be especially careful to keep Gala away from it. My father stored his coyote poisons there. He was absolutely fanatical on the subject of coyotes. But, then, he was fanatical about nearly everything you could imagine."

Eleanor had little sympathy to waste on a father she had buried only that morning, Christy thought, as he followed her through dark rooms to start on windows at the top of the house. She produced another hammer and pried energetically. Light flooded in as, one by one, they wrestled the rough boards off the windows in three bedrooms and started on yet another bedroom, the largest. Like the others, it was furnished not in heavy Spanish colonial furniture but with chairs, chests, and a writing table that looked handmade of a bleached wood, pretty but simple. Christy saw that a suitcase was open on the bed, with two other suitcases sitting beside it. Eleanor was obviously settling in for more than an overnight stay.

A lizard ran up a drape at the next-to-last window as Christy approached it. Gala saw it and barked.

"That's it, Gala," Eleanor said. "Protect your master from that nasty old lizard. I can't imagine how they get in. My father lived in the smaller house, but he kept this one closed up tight. Afraid someone would get in and steal his treasures, I guess."

"Did he keep valuables here?" Christy asked.

"Yes, he did," Eleanor said. "I'll show you when we get downstairs. Of course, he was always right over in the guesthouse, lurking about with his favorite rifle. He was an excellent shot. Rats! I just split the hell out of the window frame. I'd better demote myself. You're a much better carpenter than I am. I'll start hauling the boards outside. Donkey's work, that's what I'm best at. I think I'll stack them by the swimming pool. We'll set them on fire tonight. No marshmallows, but we'll at least be able to enjoy a heck of a bonfire."

"Uh—I doubt that Sam and I can come back over tonight," Christy said.

"What a shame," she said. She sounded genuinely disappointed. "Bianca and I cleaned the guesthouse first thing, so you'd be comfortable there. It's got two little bedrooms and a good-sized living room and a little kitchen. Don't you want to change your mind? Really, you'll love it."

"Yes, well, but Sam's mother seems to have a thousand things for him to do to get ready for a Blessingway ceremony Saturday night. So I offered to cook dinner for everyone since they're so busy. Why don't you join us? It'll be steak and all the trimmings. I'm getting to be a pretty good campfire cook."

"Thanks for asking, but I'd better spend the evening working on my father's papers. His lawyer is anxious to see everything I can find relating to his assets. So am I."

Eleanor went downstairs with an armload of boards. Gala followed her. Christy finished the windows, then took his tools into the living room. Bianca Wilson was there, cleaning red floor tiles with a noisy canister vacuum. Christy shouted over its buzz, "Hi, Mrs. Wilson. How's Roberto the Coyote today?"

The handsome Indian girl said, "Fine." She kept vacuuming. Taken aback by her curtness, Christy applied himself to the front windows and decided to keep his questions to himself.

As Christy worked, light began to play on whitewashed walls hung with old Navajo rugs. Out of the gloom appeared a traditionally rounded corner fireplace, flanked by two walls of white floor-to-ceiling shelves reminiscent of Ann Lang's bookshelves. Christy looked over his shoulder at the shelves, then turned to take in their contents more fully. One wall was filled with baskets, most of them with time-chewed edges. On the other wall, a white olla with a black collar led off a parade of big pots and little pots, plain pots and more black-on-white pots decorated with geometric swirls. On the higher shelves there were arrowheads and spearheads, and there were crudely carved dolls wearing molting feathers and elaborately painted dolls decked out in new feathers. More Navajo rugs, these folded, were stacked on the lower shelves.

Eleanor came in for the next armload of boards. She looked to see what Christy was gazing at. Bianca's back was turned. Eleanor put an index finger against her lips in a shushing motion to Christy. Aloud, she said, "Almost finished with the living room? Let's stop and take a beer break." She tapped Bianca on the shoulder to get her attention. "Time for a break," she said. "Would you like a beer, Bianca?"

"No, thanks," Bianca said. "I'd rather finish here."

Outside by the empty swimming pool, Eleanor said to Christy, "I didn't want you to say anything about Father's Anasazi pots and baskets while Bianca could hear. I'm afraid it's a sore point with her. He had quite a fight with Bianca and Ann Lang about pot-hunting on his property. Not that he hadn't dabbled in pot-hunting himself, but he took it badly when Bianca and that husband of hers tried to tote off a few tons of petrographs from one of the canyons on the east side of the ranch."

"Isn't pot-hunting illegal?" Christy said.

"Of course, but it's been going on for at least a hundred years, and it shows no sign of stopping. Actually, the Navajo blankets that Mother collected used to be far more valuable than any of Father's hodgepodge of artifacts. But the hot items on the black market these days are apparently ancient pots and kachinas. Fads. Everything's a fad. Do you mind light beer? I love beer, but I'm a calorie-counter."

She left him to go to the kitchen. Christy found two lawn chairs in the pool house and dusted them off. Gala preceded Eleanor when she returned with two icy beer mugs. But for once, Christy paid little attention to his dog. Instead he looked at Eleanor Fawkes. Her crisp shirt and shorts were streaked with dust. A lock of hair had escaped her green scarf and fallen over a cheek that was similarly smudged. Her arms were scratched and reddened from carrying the boards. Despite or because of her disarray, Christy experienced one of those moments when a person of the opposite sex suddenly rivets one's attention, and he found it ridiculously hard not to stare at her bare tanned legs. If Eleanor Fawkes had to fight calories, she was winning the battle, he concluded. For a woman of uncertain years, she looked more than fit. She looked downright alluring.

Today's green gaze inspected Christy with similar approval. But she broached an impersonal subject. "Do you know anything about Anasazi artifacts, Christy?" she asked.

"Not even what Anasazi means," Christy said.

" 'The ancient ones,' " Eleanor said. "They occupied the plateau country from about the first century A.D. until they fizzled out in about A.D. 1300. Most of their ruins are over in Canyon de Chelly, but there are little scraps all over the place. They usually built in shallow caves. The original ruin on Ann Lang's property was probably Developmental Period Anasazi, but, of course, her predecessor dug out anything interesting a half-century ago."

"You seem to know a lot about it," Christy said.

Eleanor sipped her beer. "It's the reservation syndrome," she said. "It's really peculiar how just about all the kids I went to school with have ended up back near here. After Mother divorced Father, we lived in Philadelphia for years. I thought I'd changed my stripes, but here I am, too. The country gets to you.

When you're away from it, you think about it and read about it. Navajos who move away nearly always come back to the reservation. So do the Anglo kids who got exposed to it."

"Does that include Mrs. Lang?" Christy asked.

"No, she's an outsider. She's only been around six or eight years. Father bought a number of Early Basketmaker cooking baskets from her when she first started staking pot-hunters around here. You might call it her little cottage industry. But being what he was, Father had to start digging for artifacts himself. I don't think he found much more than some Modified Basketmaker pots. That's probably what made him so mad when he found out Mrs. Lang was financing diggers on his own property. Then Bianca started. Can you imagine, trying to chisel a petrograph off a huge slab of rock? Father knew it was there. I'll bet Mrs. Lang did, too. I've seen it myself. It has considerable charm. A troop of eight or ten Spanish soldiers on horses. If you could get it out in one piece, it might really be worth something to a collector."

"It sounds like it would be worth more than a pot."

"I'll really have to make a few inquiries," Eleanor said. "With all the money coming from Father's estate, I suppose I needn't be interested in selling it off, but there's no point in letting someone else take it." She smiled happily at Christy. "I think I'm going to just love being rich. You know what I mean."

"Not me," Christy said. He laughed.

"But you do," she said. "You own a Doberman. Having Gala with you must make you feel so safe and protected. Like being a millionaire. I tell you, I'm going to rejoice in every dollar of it. And I'm not going to be like Father, just sitting on all that money. I'm going to enjoy spending a lot of it."

"But . . . I thought your father was a rancher," Christy said. Then he added, "Pardon me. What a dumb thing to say. I guess a lot of ranchers could sell out for a real bundle."

"No, I'll keep this place," Eleanor said. "I can't think of anyone else who would want it, except Mrs. Lang, and she can't afford it. But, heavens, Father's money all came from Grandfather. He was in petrochemicals. Two of the plants have had to be closed, but Father had enough business sense to see that coming. He cashed out over five years ago for two and a half million dollars."

"That *is* rich," Christy said.

"Yes, and if Eli Tom thinks he's got a claim to it, he's got another think coming," Eleanor said. "Do you know, I'd actually planned to help that boy out once Father was gone. I wouldn't have given Eli a big chunk of money all at one time. He would have spent it within a month. But some tidy trust fund, to give him enough to live on decently. He wanted to become a silver-smith. That was touching, somehow. Or maybe I enjoyed the idea of being a patroness of the arts. But after what Eli may have done to Father, I wouldn't give him a cent."

"Eleanor, the law doesn't think Eli Tom or anyone else killed Mr. Fawkes," Christy said. "It's pretty certain it was an acciden-tal attack by an animal. Maybe a feral dog."

"I don't know how anyone could make it look that way, but I know someone did. Feral dog, pooh. Although . . ."

"What?"

"Father did complain about a month ago about a dog he'd seen. He was determined to shoot it. For all I know, he did."

Christy's dog, who had stretched herself on the grass for a sunbath, raised her head and stared behind him. Her eyes were benign and welcoming, and Christy was unsurprised to hear Bianca Wilson speak.

"I've finished mopping the downstairs, Miss Fawkes," Bianca said. "Do you want those blankets of your mother's hung up outside? The wind's coming up. It might knock some of the dust out of them."

"I'd be afraid of fading them," Eleanor said. "The Ganado Reds and the chief blankets are really first-rate, you know."

"Yes, I know," the Indian girl said quietly. "A couple of those old kachinas would easily bring you two or three thousand apiece in Phoenix, too. Or a whole lot more, if they're from Shungopavi."

"Father bought those from a Hopi medicine man twenty years ago," Eleanor said firmly. "There's no 'if' about it. They've been gathering dust on that shelf for just about as long as you've been alive."

"You're sure?" Bianca said.

Bianca had previously been so quiet that Christy was surprised by her aggressive tone. He turned to look at her. Bianca stood with her arms folded, staring at Eleanor with a steady gaze.

"I know what you're implying, Bianca," Eleanor said. "Go take a closer look at the kachinas. The Shungopavi *talaotsumsime* were much older. Besides, only their faces were carved, and these are carved all over. Now, don't stand there pouting. Are you sure you don't want to get yourself a beer and join us?"

"No, I'm going to have to get back to the trading post," Bianca said. "I'll just vacuum and mop your bedroom today, and maybe we can finish up tomorrow."

She left. Eleanor sighed and stood up. "Stupid girl," she said. "Father may have messed around with pot-hunting, but he would have drawn the line at stealing idols out of the Hopi kivas. There was a really terrible theft earlier this summer. The Hopi have these underground chambers that are so sacred and secret that only one Anglo ever managed to bull his way into one. That was a preacher in the early 1900s, and the Hopi are still furious about it. The tribal leaders think it's young Hopi men who have raided the kivas this time. They took four extraordinarily sacred figures at Shungopavi in the late seventies, then they hit another village on Second Mesa in 1983 and took two other stick deities, *aloosaka*. Now they've hit Shungopavi again. Only one of the figures has ever been recovered. The others are probably in Germany or Japan by now."

"Second Mesa, is that far from here?" Christy said.

"Maybe fifty miles. That's a stone's throw around here. But if you're wondering whether Bianca or Ann Lang are busily stealing Hopi gods, I doubt it. Mrs. Lang is brazen about digging artifacts, but I don't think she'd out-and-out steal the Hopi's religious figures, any more than my father would. The Hopi depend utterly on their rituals to make the rain fall and the crops grow, and people like Mrs. Lang and Father would respect that. But I wonder . . . I'm not at all sure how Bianca Wilson would regard somebody else's religion, if there were enough money involved."

"Is there?" Christy asked.

"Who knows? To the Hopi, the *talaotsumsime* are of divine origin, so they're priceless. To a collector in West Germany who doesn't ask the wrong questions about provenance, well, there was talk that the first stolen set could be worth up to two hundred thousand dollars. Of course, that's probably an exaggeration. Say fifty thousand dollars. That's still a lot of money for some old stick figures made out of cottonwood roots, isn't it?"

"Too much not to be tempting," Christy said.

Later, he couldn't resist a long look at the rough wooden figures in the living-room shelves. There were five of them, about a foot tall and boldly carved. Christy had no idea if they were made of cottonwood roots, but they drew the eye. The gaily painted modern kachinas that stood next to them were far brighter and prettier, but the old kachinas had power. Christy went to look for Eleanor. Finding her in the kitchen, he suggested that the figures be packed up and put in some safe place.

"You're right," she said. "I will. They've attracted a little too much attention." She took a box from which she had been unpacking groceries. "This should be big enough," she said. "Come with me. I want you to see one of the rugs."

The folded rug she selected from a bottom shelf was much smaller than those on the walls. About three feet square, it had a sand-colored background, and when Eleanor spread it flat on the floor Christy saw with delight that a fat round face, with straight black lines for eyes and mouth, stared up at him.

"It's a sandpainting rug," Eleanor said. The green of her lenses danced in the soft light of the now gracious room. "That's the sun."

Christy knelt to examine the little rug. The Navajo sun god had a white forehead and an ochre chin. Seven thin bands of color radiated from its face in the four directions, and eight black-and-white feathers glorified the deity, filling in the rest of the design.

"It's a real beauty," Christy said. "No wonder your mother collected them."

"She just bought this on a whim. I want you to have it, as a thank-you present for helping me."

"Eleanor, I couldn't accept a gift like that."

"You can. You will. It's a little unusual, but it's not at all old or valuable. It'll make a pretty wall hanging for you. Think of it as a bribe, if you want to. Because I hope you'll do me one last heavy-duty favor before I let you get away. Father has moved all of the dishes out of the top kitchen shelves and stuffed them with accordion files full of God-knows-what. Maybe you can help me move them into the study. That's where I'll be all evening, digging through dusty papers. I hope you'll at least think of me while you're all eating your delicious steaks."

Christy's outdoor dinner party began earlier than he had planned for two of the Benally family. Well before sunset, Harley Tsosie and Sam's young nephew brought the sheep to the corral by the spring. The Benally dogs reported to Christy the minute they finished work, and Harley and George came to the campfire almost on their heels. For once, George had a few words to spare for Christy. He said, "Those dogs bothering you? Throw a rock at them. They'll clear out."

Christy looked at the youngster with surprise. The idea of chunking a rock at the shy little dogs seemed criminal. He said, "The dogs are no bother. They've been dropping by at dinner time. I'll fix them something in a minute."

Harley said, "They're not so dumb. How about people-dinner? Is it anywhere near ready? I got something I got to do tonight. I thought maybe you were serving up stuff early."

"The potatoes aren't done yet, but if you'll settle for beans and salad on the side, I can grill you up a steak in no time," Christy said.

"Sounds good," Harley said. He seated himself in Sam's folding chair and grinned at young George, who hung back, much like the little dogs, but with something of their same hungry look.

Christy saw it. He said to George, "Want me to slap a steak on for you, too? Although you'll be missing my famous campfire stuffed baked potatoes."

"Yeah, I could go ahead and eat now," George said. As usual, he sounded sullen. "I got something I got to do tonight, too."

"Pour yourselves a glass of wine," Christy said. "Sam got some sweet stuff he thought his grandmother would like, but I stuck in a jug of burgundy, too. It's in that box next to the tree."

"George is too young to drink," Harley said. "I keep hearing he buys vodka by the gallon, but he's sure too young to drink it."

"Crap," George snorted. He opened the burgundy and found plastic glasses and poured for himself and Harley. As a more gracious afterthought, he poured a glass for Christy and brought it to him.

Christy had built a real campfire after returning from the Fawkes ranch. He edged the Dutch oven in which the potatoes were baking to the side of the grill and forked two big T-bones onto it for Sam's kinsmen, then dug in the grocery box and produced cheese and crackers for them as an appetizer.

George stuffed his mouth with cheese. He was no less backward about the burgundy. "Good wine," he said.

Harley said, "You know all about it, don't you?"

"I'm nineteen and out of high school," George said. "That's old enough."

George seemed far more approachable than usual. Christy asked, "What are your career plans, George? Are you going to go on to college?"

"College," George said contemptuously. "That's all I hear, go to college, go to college. I got better things to do."

"Sure he does," Harley said. "He's so smart he couldn't even keep a filling-station job in Gallup. Then Old Man Fawkes fired him, too."

"Bastard," George said. It was hard to tell whether he was referring to Harley or to Mr. Fawkes. He added to Harley, "You think you know everything, but you got fired, too. Couldn't even keep a well-digger's job."

Christy said, "Well-digging? Is that your specialty, Harley?"

Harley took his time answering. "I did that for the last three years," he finally said. "Couldn't find anything else to do around here, and Ruthy didn't want me working up on the Defiance Plateau any more. Lumbering, that's what I did there, but then I dug wells and helped build stock tanks and dug irrigation ditches. Until the man who owns all the equipment hired his nephew instead."

George snickered and reached for more cheese.

"That's too bad," Christy said.

"No, that's how people here do things," Harley said. "They look after their kin and their clan members first. It's not a bad way. A man's got a nephew, the son of one of his sisters, that man's got to look after that nephew. He's got to help raise him. That's the way it's done. But your friend Sam doesn't seem to know that. Does he, George?"

"I don't need any more raising," George said. "Listen, I've really got to hurry. How are those steaks doing?"

The coals were hot. The steaks cooked quickly. Christy piled hot beans and cold fruit salad on two plates, then served the T-bones sizzling. His guests ate enthusiastically. Christy refilled their wine glasses and made dinner for Gala and the other dogs. Harley's fork finally slowed down and he started talking again, this time not to needle George but to talk well-digging.

"That's what I got to do tonight, start a well. It'll be slow, hand-digging. But that's what this family wants. They don't want anyone to know they've got a well, see. They're real traditional. Like this outfit's gotten to be. Real traditional people think you got to drink from just springs and rivers. Natural water. They think when the Holy People first came up from under the earth, everything was covered with water, and that water had some kind of beings or animals in it, and it all had to be drained off. So they think no water in the ocean and from under the ground, like you get from wells, is any good for the people to use. Are you listening, George?"

"I'm eating," George said. "I don't care about stuff like that."

"You ought to care. The beginnings, that's what old Peter Madman's going to start with when he sings over your sister

Saturday night. That's Blessingway. That's what it's about. Dr. Christy, what's this you're smiling about?"

"The singer's name," Christy said. "It's a great name."

"Maybe a lot of people would think Dr. Christy was a pretty silly name. But yeah, Madman, that's a funny-sounding name. It's a funny world we live in. Especially when you got to go out and hand-dig a well by night so nobody will know this family doesn't want to walk a half-mile to the spring any more. So that's what I'm going to do tonight, and George says he's got to hurry and do something tonight, but he hasn't said what. George? You don't want to go out tonight. You ought to stay here where it's safe. George! Do you ever pay any attention when I tell you something?"

"I didn't hear you," George said. "I just heard your mouth running." He gnawed the last morsels from his steak bone and stood. Rather awkwardly, he said, "That was good, Dr. Christy. Does your dog want this bone?"

"No, T-bones aren't too good for dogs," Christy said. "Splintery. I'll bury the bones later so the dogs can't get them."

"Hear that, George?" Harley said. "You don't want to listen to good things from me, that's okay. So maybe you want to learn about bad things. Dr. Christy just gave you a warning about how not to treat dogs. You treat a dog bad, and you know what can happen. That dog can get even with you. You torment a dog bad enough, he can do witchcraft on you. You're a dumb kid. A smart kid would know something about witchcraft and stop going out by himself at night when a witch can get him, but you don't really know anything, do you?"

"I know the dogs will dig up those T-bones tonight after Dr. Christy buries them," George said. "They'll eat them up, splinters and all, that's what I know."

The youngster stalked off to his motorcycle. He wheeled it toward the back road, perhaps unwilling for his mother to hear the noisy motor and know that he was leaving. Harley looked after him. "Dumb kid," he said. "I try to help him, but he thinks he's too grown up to listen. Hear that wind, Dr. Christy? It's gonna be blowy tonight. There's not a person anywhere that would want to be out on the reservation by himself tonight."

"You're going to be out by yourself," Christy pointed out.

Harley chuckled and poured himself another glass of wine. "Not me," he said. "We'll be digging right in back of that family's hogan, with lanterns, and all the men will be digging with me. Maybe I'm a little bit like George and I don't believe everything I used to believe, but that doesn't mean I'm crazy enough to be all by myself. At night. When the wind blows. And after all that's gone on around here."

Christy sat down with his own plastic glass of jug burgundy. "Harley, just what else has been happening?" he asked. "Yesterday in Gallup you said something about some witch talk a few months ago. If it had anything to do with an animal, I'd sure like to know about it."

"I'm not sure it was anything," Harley said after some deliberation. "Just talk. It was that sister of mine that started it. That woman selling rugs on the highway? Well, she's a clan sister, not a blood sister, but what she said was a coyote followed her early one morning. She was looking for wood, and she forgot to put turquoise in the coyote's tracks, so it witched her. How she knew was, after a couple of weeks she fell off a truck and broke her ankle."

"The coyote didn't attack her? Bite her?"

"Naw, they don't have to do anything for people to start saying there's witch-people around. The people here, they'll talk about anything. The way they'll talk about me if they hear I've gone digging that well. You don't say anything to anybody about that, okay?"

"Of course not," Christy said.

"I want you to be careful, too, Dr. Christy. You've been asking questions about a lot of things. People that believe in witches, they say witches go looking for a man that knows about them. They don't like for someone to know. That someone, he's maybe going to get got by that witch."

Christy put down his glass. He couldn't tell if Harley was being malicious again or if he was trying to be helpful. "What are you trying to say, Harley?" he asked.

"Nothing. I just say be careful."

"Good advice," Christy said. "I'll take it."

"That's good. Listen, you do one other thing. When Ruthy and Irene and everybody asks where's George, you don't say anything. Maybe they'll think he's gone off with me instead of off on that damned motorcycle. Okay?"

"Count on me," Christy said. "I'll be as quiet as the grave."

It was the wrong simile, he thought later. The dinner party was a success. Sounding slightly tipsy after her glass of sweet wine, the little grandmother had a long conversation with Christy, completely in Navajo, while the others finished off their meal with coffee and chocolate-chip cookies. Irene did fret aloud about her son's disappearance, but only Sam remarked on Harley's absence, and that was quietly to Christy alone.

"Mother-in-law avoidance," he said. "Ruthy said Ma revived the tradition. It must make life pretty awkward for them, but as customs go, I suppose it has its uses. You can't quarrel with your in-laws if you never get close enough to talk to them."

Christy had drunk just enough wine to find the idea charming. After all, he had been happy to avoid a prospective father-in-law by refusing Karen's invitation to visit her wealthy father in Houston. The thought of Karen's father reminded him of Eleanor Fawkes's revelation of her own father's net worth, and Christy scolded Sam.

"What do you mean telling me old Mr. Fawkes didn't have any serious money?" he asked his friend. "Eleanor puts his assets at two and a half million dollars. Reason enough for a murder, I'd say."

Sam said, "I wouldn't have guessed more than a million or so. Two or three million? That's a sum I might be happy to murder somebody for, too. But I guess I misled you by thinking in oil jargon. If you're in oil, serious wealth is two or three billion, not a few million." He stretched his feet to the warmth of the campfire and smiled across it at his mother. "Let's not wash up tonight," he said lazily to Christy. He raised his voice to include the others in the conversation. "You can do the dishes in the morning, Christy, while I work my poor sore fingers to the bone shelling more corn."

"Go to the grocery and buy cornmeal," Christy said callously.

"Nope. It's got to be Indian corn, and if it's home-grown, all the better. Ma says they'll need a lot more to grind after the first night's singing. Little Lois gets herself washed with soapweed, then dried with cornmeal. Isn't that right, Ma?"

"That's right," Mrs. Benally said. "But it's wrong to leave dirty dishes overnight. They'll be stuck too hard to wash. You two boys get out of my way, and I'll do the dishes."

"No, you won't," Christy said. He swung a borrowed metal bucket filled with water to the grill to begin warming. "It's only your lazy son who wanted to put them off. I'll have them done in no time."

They quarreled without heat as they gathered the empty plates. Its own dinner long forgotten, one of the small Benally dogs pushed Gala out of the way in an enthusiastic charge at the plates, and they were all laughing at the Doberman's amazed expression when car lights flashed, turning in off the blacktop road.

"Harley's home," Irene Laughter said.

Ruthy Tsosie said, "That's not Harley. The headlights are shaped wrong."

Sam questioned his mother with a look. She nodded, and he rose and went to see who it was. He didn't take a flashlight. The moon was rising, a misshapen yellow eye above the dark mesa. The headlights flicked off after Sam reached the car. Staring after him, Christy became aware of the loud sighs of the three pines under which they were camped. Only three trees moving in the night wind, but they were as noisy as a whole forest.

Just then, Sam called, "Christy? Can you come here for a minute?"

There was urgency in Sam's voice. Christy rose, suddenly alarmed by the dark car.

"What is it, Dr. Christy?" Mrs. Benally said. She sounded worried, too.

"I'll just trot over and see," Christy said. He called Gala and started off, careful not to run.

As Christy neared the car, someone opened a door and the inside lights came on. Christy breathed easier to see a familiar face, that of Deputy Bob Turland from the McKinley County sheriff's office.

Relief came too soon. Christy knew something was seriously wrong the moment he saw Sam's expression. But it was Deputy Turland who spoke.

"We've got another favor to ask you, Dr. Christy," Turland said. "Tully Kee sent me to get you. A young man's been killed, and Kee wants you to look at the body."

"Why me?" Christy asked softly.

"You know him. A fellow named Eli Tom. He's a bloody mess, just like Mr. Fawkes. Kee wants you to decide for sure if it was an animal, but, hell, any fool can see that much. Something ripped his throat clean out."

CHAPTER 12

The dead man lay flat on his back, as though he had tripped and fallen. Christy took one look at Eli Tom's throat and called for more light. He wasn't stalling. The Navajo police officer seemed to think so, but Christy didn't worry about what Kee thought. He felt a great coolness fill his mind. Eli's face was the stark face of death, austere and quiet, despite staring eyes and distorted mouth. But Christy wasn't there to think about a dead man's face. He was there to examine torn tissue and cartilage. The wound was clotted with black blood instead of fresh, pumping blood. That was the main difference, just then, between the mangled throat and all the other wounds Christy had explored and treated, most successfully, after his canine patients got into a fight. When it came to bite wounds, Christy was in a known element with a simple job to do.

A second Navajo officer and Deputy Jack Martin went outside with Deputy Turland to set up an additional light. Christy and Officer Kee were left alone for a moment in the primitive brush shelter in which Eli Tom had died. Two hazard lights had already been stretched from the officers' cars. Christy looked around the shelter. Hugh Fawkes's dead son had had few possessions. An iron skillet and a pot hung from pegs in the support poles, and a sleeping bag, a footlocker, and a heavy old leather suitcase made up the rest of Eli's gear. Maybe he kept the rest of his belongings in his pickup. Christy hoped so. So barren a life. So bloody a death. Christy looked at walls made of stacked brush and at the open doorway. No door panel. No blanket stretched across. No barrier whatever to close against a marauding animal.

The deputies and the new Navajo officer came back, unwinding another hazard light on a long extension cord. Deputy Martin hung it directly above the body. The others stood aside, but Martin squatted over the body and said to Christy, "Look at his right arm."

Christy kneeled, then glanced up at Kee. "Is it okay to touch the body?" he asked.

"Yes. We've got everything we need."

So Christy looked.

Blood had already been wiped away from the puncture wounds on the forearm. Upper and lower canine teeth had clamped once, then torn downward through the flesh, as if the animal had leaped for the arm that tried to ward it off, then swung its weight off the ground. Even in the brighter light, the throat presented a less certain picture. There was too little of it left.

"It got him more than once," Deputy Martin said. He pointed to the right of the throat. "I'd say it went for him here, then it went for him again."

"Probably more than twice," Christy said. He was glad his voice sounded calm and steady. He looked up to be sure he had Kee's attention. "It'll take a pathologist to be really sure, but I'd say the animal kept working on the throat after it had Eli down. It's a pretty organized job. First forearm, then throat, then Eli fell, and the animal went for the throat again and probably kept it up until there was no more movement in the body."

"Sonofabitch," the other Navajo officer said.

"Okay," Kee said, "two questions. First, what should the pathologist look for?"

"He'll know," Christy said. "He'll probably start by looking at the striations in a scope. Double-check the obvious and be sure they were made by big sharp teeth. And I'd check for animal hair, of course. It could tell us a lot."

"Tell them animal saliva, too," Deputy Martin said. "Tell them to check these flecks around the boy's chin and ears."

Reluctantly, Kee said, "Okay, now my second question. Did the animal chew? Does it look like it tore off any chunks? Goddamn it, what I'm saying is, did it just kill Eli, or was it hungry and did it make him into dinner?"

Christy and Martin looked at each other. Then Christy said quickly, "No, no, it killed him. There's no question of anything else."

Deputy Turland said, "Thank God for small favors."

Christy busied himself with looking at blood on the left hand. There were no bite marks on this arm. The blood probably came from the animal's mouth as, struggling, Eli tried to shove the animal away from him. Until he was too weak. Until it was too late. Christy checked over the rest of the body. There were no other marks. He stood and gave the opinion Kee had asked for: "Definitely the work of an animal. The spacing of the puncture wounds on the right arm suggests it was a large animal."

"Dogs?" Kee asked. "Wolves?"

"I don't know. Conceivably, it could even be a bear. But it's probably a canine. *Canis familiaris. Canis lupus.* Dog or wolf, the dental formula is the same. There's one thing we can tell with greater certainty. This was an attack by a single animal. It wasn't a pack or even a pair. One animal did it all."

Deputy Martin frowned. "I wouldn't be so sure of that. I've seen what a dog can do to a man, but I've never seen this kind of mess."

"Look at the pattern," Christy said. "In a dog fight, if you've got more than two combatants, the other dog or dogs all rush in and try for a bite. You'll get a bite wound on the shoulder or the foot or the rump. Wherever. One dog wouldn't calmly hold onto the arm while a second dog worked on the throat." He looked up at Kee. "Any tracks?"

"None," Kee said. "It's too dry, and the ground around here is packed down. We'll look again when it's light, of course." He glanced at the other Navajo officer. "Maybe I'll call in some volunteers. What do you think, Chee? Aren't the Nakai brothers about the best trackers around? Maybe they can tell us more about our wild animal."

Deputy Martin said, "This wasn't done by a wild animal. You should look for a motive, not tracks."

"Shut up, Jack," Deputy Turland said sharply. As he had explained to Christy on the six-mile drive north from the Benally home, the death had definitely occurred on reservation land. He and Martin had been sent out only to observe and to be helpful around the edges.

Kee left the brush shelter in which Eli Tom had lived and so recently died. Poor young man, Christy thought. Such great expectations, but so poor that his possessions didn't even include an extra blanket to spread over the body. The two deputies began winding up the hazard lights, leaving the body in the dark. Christy took one last look at the wound on Eli Tom's throat, and suddenly he couldn't get out of the shelter fast enough. He had felt steady enough while working, but his work was done. Now his hands began to shake. He put them in his pockets to hide the shaking as he joined Kee outside.

The gibbous moon, its hunchback more pronounced, spread stark light across the desert. Kee stood staring at a hogan sixty yards away. Farther off the road, there was a second hogan. Light shone from both, but both were tightly closed. Christy remembered being told that Eli Tom had moved to the area to be near relatives. But if the people in the closed hogans were his kin, they weren't exactly lamenting over his corpse.

Kee said, "Thanks, Dr. Christy. I've got to wait for the ambulance. They're sending one from the hospital at Fort Defiance. Deputy Turland will take you back to the Benally camp." He hooked his thumbs in his belt and dropped his eyes. After an awkward pause, he said, "About the Benallys . . ."

"Yes?" Christy said.

"Damn it, it was an animal. I know that. I'd rather think it was a wild animal. Because if I don't, people around here are going to say *maicoh,* witch-wolf. People like you and Turland and Martin don't understand. You're not Navajo. You think maybe murder, with trained animals and ordinary motives. Okay. Maybe you're right. Things are getting screwier and screwier. Why would some wild animal go for Hugh Fawkes, then a few days later go for his son? Why not chew up a half-dozen other people that weren't related to Fawkes? So okay, maybe I go looking for someone who was mad at Fawkes and who was mad at Eli. You know where it leads me? To a family that's already got a bad reputation in this witchery business. Harley Tsosie, he's only related by marriage, but he had a big argument with Old Man Fawkes after that kid, George Laughter, got himself fired. And Harley Tsosie had a big argument with Eli Tom not more than two weeks ago. But if I go looking at Harley, people are going to say it was him or one of the Benallys, using the old way. *Maicoh.* You could make things a lot easier for me. You could tell me that Harley and George and all the others were with you at the Benally place tonight. If it's the truth. Was Harley with you?"

Christy didn't want to answer. Finally, he said, "No, Harley had to go out. But he said he would be with a lot of other people. If you're thinking alibis, he should be in the clear."

"Who was he with?"

"I guess you'll have to put your question to Harley," Christy said.

"I will tomorrow. Right now I've already got more questions than I know what to do with. We went through that poor damned kid's stuff. You saw it. Next to nothing. But you know what we found in his footlocker? Seventeen hundred dollars. Nice crisp hundred-dollar bills. Eli never had any money before. Mr. Fawkes may have given him a few bucks from time to time, but not real money. So where did Eli get seventeen hundred dollars?"

Christy said, "Did his relatives know about the money?"

Kee sighed. "I haven't asked them yet. They're too scared to think."

"I can sure understand that. The women in Sam's family are all holed up together in Mrs. Benally's house, with Sam and my Doberman on guard duty. That's why Sam didn't come with me. After Turland came with the news, Sam's family went into shock."

Kee said, "Yeah, I won't be able to get any information out of Eli's kinfolk until it's light. They used up the last of their courage coming to the substation to tell me Eli was dead. Five of them, all jammed together in the front seat of Eli's pickup."

"Who found the body?"

"One of the kids. A fifteen-year-old boy. He wanted Eli to come play hearts. He got enough of an eyeful to give him bad dreams the rest of his life."

"Poor kid," Christy said.

"Yeah, and that's the screwiest part," Kee said. "Screwier than dog or wolf. Maybe screwier than *maicoh.*"

"What?" Christy said.

Kee nodded to the nearby hogans. "There are nine people living out here. That's eighteen ears. None of them heard a single sound before the kid found Eli's body."

"Nothing?"

"Nothing. Some . . . *thing* . . . is going around killing people in my jurisdiction, and nobody has heard nothing. If it's a real animal, I want to hear about howling or snarling or growling. If it's *maicoh,* I'll settle for pebbles rattling down a smoke hole or something moving outside a hogan. But nobody heard any kind of sound. An animal attacks a man and does one hell of a thorough job of killing him, and there's all those ears not sixty yards away, and no one hears anything at all." He hesitated. "Look, Dr. Christy, will you do me a big favor? We've got to hunt this animal down. Two men dead. God knows who it will kill next. And it's playing hell with the lives of all the people for miles around, including the Benallys. Especially the Benallys. There's already been some muttering about them. There'll be even more when word of this gets out. People get scared enough, they can get dangerous. We've got to catch this animal. Will you help us?"

"I'll damn well try," Christy said.

"I checked with Ann Lang. She flatly denied she'd seen any wild dog. Said you must have misheard the girl that helps her. Her pond's no good for tracks, either. So now where do we start looking?"

"I think you're doing just right by starting with water. Eleanor Fawkes told me her dad had seen a stray dog. It could be drinking at one of his stock tanks."

"Did she describe the dog?"

"No. I don't think she even saw it herself. But it's a lead." Christy paused, worrying about Sam and his family. "Listen,

Sam and I could go out tonight and hide and see if anything comes along about dawn to drink. And I'm still not convinced that nothing is coming to Mrs. Lang's windmill pond. Maybe Sam and I could split up, watch them both."

"No," the Navajo officer said firmly, "I don't want you or anybody else running around while it's still dark. I'll finish up here first thing in the morning, then I'll come by. We can plan the hunt together."

"We might be wasting a day," Christy said. "I've heard enough hunter's gab to know that wild animals move around most at dawn and dusk and stay in hiding during the day."

"Better to lose a day than lose another man," Kee said. "Just remember what it did to Eli Tom, and remember that it didn't make any sound. So you stay home tonight. You don't do anything until it gets light tomorrow. Got it?"

"Yes, I see what you mean," Christy said. He said it sincerely. His enthusiasm about staking out water holes sifted away quicker than sand through an hourglass. A silent, unknown beast, leaping suddenly out of the darkness? No, Christy thought, the local Navajo families were right. Only a fool would go out on the reservation. When the wind blew. In the dark.

Harley was home in bed before Christy got back, and he took off again early the next morning before the rest of the Benally family was awake. Off to Ann Lang's ruin to handle some work for her, Harley's wife said. Sam growled and muttered. He had wanted to talk to Harley before Tully Kee could, and he kept muttering irritably as he worked with Christy Friday morning to mark an area map for Kee's animal hunt.

They drew in all the springs, water holes, and stock tanks that the family knew of, but Sam wasn't satisfied. At midmorning, the wind finally died. Sam threw down his pencil. "Damn it, do the McCreas still haul water, or did they get a well dug?" he demanded of Christy. "Harley would know. I tell you, we've got to talk to Harley."

Christy looked at Sam. He saw tension and temper in his friend's face, and he knew what was causing it. Desperation.

Sam's mother and the rest of the Benally womenfolk hadn't left the premises since the stargazing, but Sam didn't seem to think that avoiding neighbors would keep them safe. The idea that they could be harmed by some intruder was pushing Sam hard. Worry about him was making Christy feel desperate himself. He looked for even a small way to help.

"We could run up to the ruin and talk to Harley there," Christy said. "If you leave word with one of your sisters, Officer Kee wouldn't have any trouble finding us when he's ready to organize the hunt."

"I'd better stay here," Sam said morosely. He didn't say why, but Christy had seen an old shotgun propped against the front of Mrs. Benally's house that morning, and it was still there.

"George is home," Christy pointed out. "We could wake him up. Tell him to make himself useful."

It was something. Better than nothing. Sam called to his sister, then hurried Gala and Christy to the Bronco, his face brightening. It brightened still further when they turned in at the ruin and saw Harley's pickup parked to the side of several vehicles with out-of-state licenses. Christy started for the entrance, but Sam charged toward the windmill. Looking up, Christy saw Harley's bulky figure at the very top of the tower. Sam called to him to come down.

Christy's most immediate interest was the perimeter of the windmill pond. He walked around it. There was no natural run-off, no wet ground in which animals might leave tracks. Evaporation apparently kept the water level constant. As for the edges of the pond, the thick growth of reeds left no clear surface for prints. But movement caught Christy's eye, and he saw that the pond was populated by salamanders. Where a salamander could live, other animals would surely drink.

Sam was already jawing at Harley. "When the hell did you get here? Before dawn?"

"Your brain's asleep," Harley said. "It was good and light. Why would I try to lube a windmill in the dark?"

Sam said, "And why would you dig a well for somebody in the dark? I don't believe that story for a minute, Harley. Where did you really go last night? Damn it, if you're mixed up in something, I'll help you any way I can, but you've got to make sense."

Harley turned reproachful eyes to Christy. "I thought I asked you not to talk about that well," he said.

"Christy didn't tell me," Sam said. "George told me when he finally came dragging home last night. His story was as lame as yours. Some crap about going to see a friend in Sanders. Well, he won't be roaming around at night any more. You'd have thought he was going to die on the spot when we told him what happened to Eli Tom. It was a bad night to be away from home, Harley. You try to tell Kee you were off digging some damn well—"

"That's not Kee's business," Harley said. "That's not your business, either."

"Harley, you're in trouble," Sam said. "Don't you realize that? Kee says the two dead men are both men you argued with. He's going to come around asking you why. Can't you confide in me? We can at least help you make up some decent-sounding story."

Harley's chin jutted. "Hold on," he said. "I don't have to make up some story. Everybody knows the truth. Ruthy knows. I bet your mother knows. Me and Fawkes had a few words about the way he fired George. Fawkes told everybody who'd listen that George stole four head of cattle off him. How do you think that sounds to people? So I told off Fawkes for telling lies, but maybe I told him wrong. Because I found out some more things about those cows, and that's when I had a few words with Eli. I think Eli Tom and George stole those cows together. They wouldn't admit it, but that's what I think. I think that's not the only thing they stole. My rotary saw's gone, Sam. Gone. Remember that ring Ruthy had with the big Villa Grove turquoise? Gone, too. No telling how much stuff of your mother's and grandmother's is gone. Stuff just kept walking off, right up until those four cows of Fawkes's got themselves slaughtered and trucked off. Eli was a bad influence on George. That's what I told Eli, and I told him I never wanted to see George hanging around him again. You and Tully Kee call that an argument, okay, that's an argument. But if you think I'm gonna tell Tully anything about your nephew, you're crazy."

"Christ, I didn't know George was hanging around Eli," Sam said.

"You don't know nothin' about George," Harley said bitterly. "Somebody had to try and look after your nephew. You weren't here, the way you should have been."

"I'm sorry you felt that way," Sam said. "I come when I can, but I can't get away from my job all that often. My job helps the family, too, Harley."

"Sure. You buy your mother a new car. You buy George that damned motorcycle. You send a nice little check to Irene, and you send a nice little check to Ruthy. Well, Ruthy don't need your damned checks. I gave up a good job because she wanted me close to home, so maybe now I have to take whatever work I can get, but I still can make enough to help look out for the rest of your family, and what do you do? You say you can't get off from that big-shot job of yours, but you get off plenty to go fishing with Dr. Christy all the time, instead of coming home to look after your nephew when he's set on getting in trouble. Maybe big trouble."

Sam looked shaken. "God, Harley, I didn't know. I'll talk to George. I promise. I'll straighten the little bum out."

"I guess you can try," Harley muttered.

A car pulled in from the highway, and Sam looked around. He said, "Oh, hell, here comes Tully now. What can we tell him? Christy, go keep him occupied for a few minutes."

The two men began hurriedly to discuss what Harley could say to Officer Kee without bringing up George's misdeeds. Christy left them. Kee disappeared into the stockade, so Christy followed the officer inside. Both of Mrs. Lang's helpers were in the ruin, escorting tourists, and no one was on duty at the gate. Christy headed for the shop, thinking Kee might be there. He quickly blundered into another argument between Officer Kee and Ann Lang in the shop.

". . . and I'll call the American Humane Society, and by God, I'll tell the Animal Liberation Front, and they'll come bomb you," Mrs. Lang said fiercely to Kee. "You shoot that dog, and I'll raise so much hell for you that you'll wish you met a grizzly instead of me. Don't think I won't do it, Tully. I've got the names of two dozen Humane Society reps in my files. I used to meet them all the time. They were always on any set where animals were used."

Christy made the further mistake of letting alert interest show on his face. Black eyebrows lowering, Mrs. Lang went for him.

"You," she said to Christy. "You louse. You started all this. I told you and I told Tully, I haven't seen that dog for weeks."

Kee said, "I know what you told me, Ann, but I don't think you're telling the truth."

"So what if I'm not?" she said. "That animal couldn't have hurt anyone. He ran away every time he saw me. I scared him to death. He wouldn't have gone anywhere near a human." She frowned again at Christy. "You want to help Tully hunt dogs, Dr. Christy? Let him take a few potshots at that Doberman of yours. Let her out of your car. Tell her to run to and fro a while and make sport."

Kee said calmly, "We're not going to shoot any dog unless it tries to attack someone in the search party, Ann. Even then, it would be only as a last resort. Remember, we're looking for a dog that's killed two people. That's some tough customer. And it's still out there. This wild dog of yours is about the only dog that fits what we're looking for."

"The dog I saw couldn't have killed my cat," Mrs. Lang said contemptuously. "It was too busy starving to death."

"If it's survived this long, it's getting food somewhere," Kee said. "That's what Dr. Christy says." The face he turned to Christy was tired, but his red-rimmed eyes crinkled a little as he threw Christy to the lion.

"Dr. Know-it-all," Mrs. Lang scoffed at Christy. "Can't you do anything useful? Something besides setting up a damned trigger-happy posse? What about tranquilizer darts? At least give the dog a sporting chance."

"That's a good idea," Christy said. "Tully, do you think we could lay our hands on tranquilizer guns?"

Kee looked both thoughtful and grateful at the suggestion. Anything to keep Ann Lang off his back. He said, "I'll ask Deputy Martin as soon as I can get him on the radio. He and Turland were going to cruise and see if they could find the repair crew that's been working the highway. Martin says they're usually out early and working all day. He thought they might have spotted this wild dog of ours."

Mrs. Lang seemed slightly mollified. She looked at her watch. "It's nearly ten-thirty. If you want to find the road crew, you should try down by the rest stop. The road people are usually there by eleven for an early lunch. I guess if the McKinley County boys can bring you tranquilizer guns, maybe I won't make such a fuss."

"I'll do my best," Kee promised. "I don't want to go killing any animals until we're sure. But I need help. *Have* you seen the wild dog since Mr. Fawkes was killed?"

"No," she said.

"The truth, now."

"I haven't seen it," she said stubbornly. "But then, I don't spend all my time staring at the windmill pond. At best, I only see the dog occasionally."

With a cautious glance at Mrs. Lang, Christy produced his map. "Sam and I put this together for you this morning," he told Kee. "There are lots of places where the dog could drink. We've marked all the available water with blue ink, but so far the animal has been seen only here at the ruin and at the Fawkes ranch."

"Yeah, Chee Day is out at the ranch now, double-checking that with Eleanor Fawkes," Kee said.

"Good," Christy said. He fished out his fountain pen and drew a black line between the ranch and the ruin. "Since water and food are the dog's two essentials, that leaves food." He marked an X on the map just west of the state line. "Here," he said. "The roadside park. Mrs. Lang says the highway repair crew eats there. A lot of other people must eat there, too. Tourists. Truckers. It's got picnic tables. And it's got trash barrels. An animal could find food on a fairly regular basis."

"Maybe it catches prairie dogs," Mrs. Lang said.

"Maybe," Christy agreed. "But the trash barrels could be inviting. Bread crusts and chicken bones don't run away." He made a triangle on the map by running lines from the ranch to the roadside park, and from Ann Lang's ruin to the roadside park. "Frankly, I think your best shot is inside this triangle. Water here and here, occasional food here."

Tully Kee bent over the map, then raised his eyes in dismay. "Do you know how much territory you've got in that triangle? You've marked six or eight square miles of hills and arroyos."

"More than that," Christy said. "We can't stick inside the triangle. We'll have to add an apron on the outside as a safeguard. Say a quarter-mile or so outside the triangle. And we'll probably have to comb every yard of it. I never said it would be easy."

Mrs. Lang said, "What about Eli Tom's place? Aren't you going to mark it?"

"Hey, no," Kee objected. "That's a good ten miles away from the triangle."

"But you think the dog was there," Mrs. Lang said. She didn't look at all unhappy at their discouraged expressions.

Christy shook his head. "There's no way I can explain why a feral dog living in one area would go as far as Eli Tom's place," he said. "Any wild canine tends to have a set territory, and just making its living is pretty much a full-time occupation."

Kee said, "That's good enough for me. I'm going to see if the road crew is at the roadside park, and then I'll radio the deputies and Chee Day. So stand by. I'll send for you when we're ready. I'm going to start right in the middle of the triangle and work my way out."

"Not without a tranquilizer gun, you aren't," Mrs. Lang said.

The Navajo officer dodged a reprise. Murmuring that he needed a word with Harley Tsosie, he left, taking Christy's map with him. Christy started to follow, but Mrs. Lang said, "What's with you and Sam? I thought you were going to be coming by to use the phone, but I haven't seen Sam since he got in."

"Sam sort of fell into the middle of a family crisis," Christy said. "One of his nieces was ill."

"The girl they're having the Blessingway for Saturday night?"

Mrs. Lang said. "Well, tell him he could at least stop by once in a while to speak to an old friend."

"He's here right now, talking with Harley. He'll probably come join us when Tully Kee is finished."

Mrs. Lang said, "You've had a couple of phone calls. A girl named Karen Hamilton called you Wednesday night, but she said there was no message. And a Dr. Potter called yesterday from Colorado. He said something about lab reports on a cat named Callie, wondering if you knew where they were, but he found them on his desk while we were talking. He said to tell you he's sick and tired of losing medical records and that he's going to put in a computer. I told him to be sure and hire someone temporarily to feed all your old records into the database. A little expert help at the beginning can save you endless trouble later."

"Thanks, Mrs. Lang," Christy said. "That was nice of you."

"What are you thanking me for? It was no trouble. Besides, Dr. Potter sounds like a nice man. I'll bet if he were here, he wouldn't be wanting to kill a starving dog."

Christy felt his ears turn red. It wasn't embarrassment. It was anger. "You might be wrong, Mrs. Lang," he said. "Slow starvation is a miserable way to die, and Dr. Potter doesn't like to see animals suffer any more than I do. But we don't shoot abandoned dogs in our practice. We try to help them. So do a lot of people. If you feel truly sorry for a stray dog, you can do more than just talk about it. You can feed it and take care of it. If you can't give it a home yourself, you can try your best to find it a good home somewhere else. At the very least you can see that any abandoned animal is taken to an animal shelter."

Mrs. Lang looked defensive. "They kill the unwanted dogs at animal shelters," she said. "Or they sell them for some blood-thirsty bit of so-called medical research."

"That's true. I think selling them is an abomination. But to be put painlessly to sleep and never wake up is a better fate than many animals have to endure. You haven't seen the things I've seen, Mrs. Lang. The people who abandon their dogs probably think the animal will find another home, but damned few do. The dog gets a last car ride to another part of town and gets turned out on the street, and it gets hit by another car and takes a week to die, suffering, in a ditch. Or people dump their dog on a country road to get gut-shot by some farmer who doesn't want a stray dog around his stock. That's not a painless death, either. Even if an abandoned dog doesn't get injured, it can go through hell. Up our way, we found two dogs that froze to the ground after they got too weak to move. Well, those two are fine now, and they have a good home, thanks to people who did more than worry about them. And I treat a half-dozen happy dogs that people have adopted from animal shelters. For that matter, my own dog came from a pound."

"Please," Mrs. Lang said. "That's enough."

"Sorry," Christy said.

"No, I'm the one who's sorry," Mrs. Lang said. She brushed her short black hair out of her eyes. "Maybe it's not too late to make amends. I'll put food out by the windmill pond this evening. Maybe the dog will find it. Have one square meal before you catch him." She smiled tentatively. "Thanks for the lecture. I deserved it. I'll do better the next time I see an animal in trouble. Meanwhile, I want to tell you that my cat hasn't vomited since I got her some Petromalt, thanks to your free advice. So I thank you, and Margery Kempe thanks you, too."

Christy relaxed a little. "I'm glad Margery feels better," he said.

Mrs. Lang relaxed, too. "Yes, and I'll get on the ball and line up a vet for her in Gallup so I'll have someone to take her to in the future. Driving thirty miles with a squalling cat in the car isn't my idea of pleasure, but I suppose it's a small penalty to pay for the privilege of living out here."

"Why do you live here, Mrs. Lang?" Christy asked.

She gazed at him with surprise. "Why, because it's the most beautiful place I've ever seen in my life," she said. "I've been to a lot of places. My movie work took me everywhere. But this is the one that speaks to me. You're staring at me like you think I'm nuts. For heaven's sake, just look around you. Watch the way the cliffs change color as the sun changes. Watch the clouds. Look at a sunset sometime."

Ann Lang gestured to the windows in her shop as she spoke. Christy obediently looked out. Instead of clouds and blue sky, his eyes were drawn to movement at his Bronco, where a girl and Sam leaned in the window to greet an excited Gala. The girl reached through the window and took Gala's leash from the top of the dashboard, then hooked it to Gala's collar and opened the door. Gala bounded out and the three of them started toward the stockade. As the girl turned toward him, Christy saw her clearly for the first time, face framed by long wheat-colored hair. His eyes widened, and he smiled. Because coming through the stockade gate with a prancing Gala and Sam, walking with her usual long stride as though she was walking against a light wind, was the girl Christy saw every night in Vail. Karen Hamilton.

CHAPTER 13

Karen had a quick kiss for Christy, an approving look for Ann Lang, and a cool glance for Mrs. Lang's two young helpers. Karen also had an uncertain look in her eyes that didn't fade until Christy kissed her properly in Mrs. Lang's kitchen.

"If you don't let me go," she finally said, "we'll never find the Bloody Mary fixings."

"I don't want to let you go," Christy said. But he did, mainly in order to look at her admiringly. Karen's high, healthy coloring was not quite concealed by a golden tan, and her hair had new sun streaks in it. "What did you do in Houston?" he said. "Spend all your time in a swimming pool?"

Karen laughed and hugged him again. "Mostly," she said. "Christy, are you really glad to see me?"

"Glad? I'm delirious."

"It's not that I didn't trust you with so many women around," Karen said.

"The thought never occurred to me," Christy said.

"And I really was stuck with driving the new car back to Vail, so once I was in West Texas I just floorboarded it and drove over to pay you and Sam a visit."

"It's great," Christy said. "Not a smidge more than four or five hundred miles out of your way."

"Well, you didn't sound at all sure when you'd make it back to Vail."

"Maybe soon," Christy said. "We'll ask Sam to drive the Bronco back, and I'll go with you in your new car." Karen stepped away and began peering into the liquor cabinet to which

Mrs. Lang had directed them. Idly, Christy said, "An Olds sedan is quite a departure for you, isn't it? What will you do with your sports car?"

"Sell it to some kid, I guess," Karen said. "Daddy wanted to buy me something more sedate. He says it's time for me to settle down— Christy, I've got a wonderful surprise for you!"

"Another surprise? Having you turn up is all the surprise I need."

"Then I'll tell you about it later. There. Vodka, tomato juice, Worcestershire sauce. What else do we need for Mrs. Lang's Bloody Marys?"

"Tabasco sauce and lemon juice," Christy said. "Want me to mix them?"

Christy had a hunch Karen's second surprise was connected to Daddy, and he was anxious not to ruin the joy of the moment. They busied themselves in the white kitchen at the back of Mrs. Lang's house, where, surprisingly to Christy, she had sent them to mix everybody a drink with which to welcome Karen. More tourists had pulled in at the ruin, so only Mrs. Lang's cat accompanied Christy and Karen. Intrigued by the strangers but suspicious, the gray tabby appeared at one door of the kitchen, ran madly through, then disappeared through another door. In a minute, she made another mad dash through the kitchen.

On the cat's third run-through, Sam followed behind with the Doberman on her leash. Knowing she was a visitor, Gala was on good behavior, but Margery Kempe immediately leaped to the top of the refrigerator, where she crouched, hissing at the dog. Gala jerked forward, ready to chase, then remembered where she was and was quiet.

"Good girl, Gala," Karen said. She patted the dog before turning to the cat. "Shouldn't we help the kitty down from there?" she asked.

"No, she'd scratch. She'll jump down by way of the cabinet when we leave," Christy said.

"What are you smiling at?" Karen asked.

"You. Remembering when you were afraid of big dogs. Now I'll have to teach you to be cautious of frightened cats."

Sam had come to tell them to wait a few minutes before bringing the drinks. "A bunch of the tourists have wandered into the shop, and Ann's busy talking them out of buying anything," he said.

"Mrs. Lang's squash-blossom necklaces are lovely," Karen said. "Are they authentic, Sam? I need a thank-you gift for my stepmother."

"All of Ann's jewelry is top quality," Sam assured her. "She wouldn't handle anything that wasn't authentic. I think she likes to look at it herself."

"The State Line Trading Post has lots of jewelry, too," Christy said.

"Yeah, made in Taiwan," Sam said. "Old Man Fawkes always went for the cheap stuff. Brad Wilson gets it in California. Two-dollar lighter cases with an eagle on them. Belt buckles with 'End of the Trail' horses and riders. You don't want anything like that."

"For my stepmother, never," Karen said. "She might like a good necklace, though."

"Good squash blossoms are a major investment," Sam said.

"Maybe I could afford one. Daddy gave me a nice check."

Karen gave Christy another hug and went back to the shop to look at jewelry. Sam and Christy followed more slowly with the tray of drinks. They found Mrs. Lang looking happily harried. One helper was showing bracelets to a quartet of tourists, and Karen was looking at two magnificent necklaces of heavy silver beads alternating with the traditional Navajo design of delicate squash flowers crafted in silver, with fine turquoise adorning the base of each blossom. "Sure, I could have it restrung on a silver chain, but you wanted authentic," Mrs. Lang was saying to Karen. "Authentic squash blossoms are strung with plain old string."

Karen lifted one of the necklaces to show to Christy and Sam, but they had no chance to admire it. Deputy Bob Turland rushed into the shop. He cried, "Kee's spotted the dog, Dr. Christy! Right where you said. He wants us to bring everyone who can help."

"What dog?" Karen said.

"Damn your eyes," Mrs. Lang said.

"Where are we going?" Sam said.

"You're not going anywhere without me," Karen said.

"Come back here! Leave the dog alone! I haven't had a chance to feed it yet," Mrs. Lang roared after them.

Deputy Turland obviously thought he had an emergency on his hands. Tires squealing, he tore out before they could scramble into Christy's car. The chase was short. Turland pulled in at the roadside park, with Christy right behind him. Kee's white Suburban was already there beside two empty pickups, and within seconds the new Navajo officer drove up in another Suburban, with Eleanor Fawkes sitting beside him. They both jumped out. Tully Kee came puffing over a hill in back of the rest stop. Gala leaped out of Christy's car with Sam, and Karen took Christy's hand as they all joined Officer Kee.

Kee looked unhappily at Karen and Eleanor, then turned the same unhappy look skyward. Following his glance, Christy saw a huge cloud mass drifting toward them from the northwest. The towering tops of the clouds were white, but the bottoms were black.

"Bad timing," Kee said. "We might get some of that rain. Look, I've got men on both ends of the big arroyo. That's where the dog ran when I spotted him near the east edge of the triangle. Sam, you and Chée circle out on the west side of the arroyo, and Deputy Turland and I will go back east. Dr. Christy, you'll have to stay here with these women."

"We can help," Eleanor objected.

"Somebody has to patrol around the rest stop," Kee said. "You can do that with Dr. Christy's Doberman."

Panting, he jogged back over the hill. Karen and Eleanor muttered together, a mutual disapproval of Kee's sexism making them instant allies, but Christy felt a guilty sense of relief at being excluded from the hunt. He gratefully let the idea of coming face to face with a frantic feral dog sink back below the surface of his mind. He leashed Gala, and they climbed the hill to get an idea of the terrain.

"Why are we looking for a dog?" Karen asked. "It's not the animal that killed the man, is it?"

"It could be," Eleanor said.

"It's not a great big dog, is it?" Karen asked.

Big dogs had been a bugaboo for Karen until she had gotten acquainted with Gala and got over her fear. Nowadays, Christy could sympathize even more. He admitted, "It's a possibility. Maybe you should go back to the car. You can keep your eyes peeled for a strange dog and honk like crazy if you see one. Gala and I will come running. Or would you rather keep Gala with you?"

"Where you go, I go," Karen said.

Looking at the tall blond girl, Christy felt a warm sensation within him. He had heard her whisper she loved him. He had heard her sigh it. But he had never heard it said more clearly than this. Christy squeezed her hand, then tried to pay attention to the business before them.

East of the roadside park, he could see Kee's big arroyo, a deeply eroded cut that wound down out of higher land to join the Rio Puerco's sandy bed. A sign by the arroyo said NO DUMPING. Next to the sign, a flood of rusted cans littered the bank, while old cars had been junked farther along. Low junipers and brush grew on the banks, and members of the search crew were walking from both ends, watching the bottom of the arroyo and probing the brush. A gust of wind brought the smell of water and dust. That was all the warning they had before a sheet of cold rain suddenly enveloped them.

Christy could barely see for the raindrops in his eyes. Karen grabbed his arm, and they ran for the roadside park. They took shelter under one of the concrete ramadas. Sam and the two McKinley County deputies came soon after, and the Navajo officers and their trackers came a few minutes after that.

"Nothing?" Deputy Martin asked Kee.

"No."

"I didn't even see the damned thing," Martin said. "Are you sure it was a dog?"

"Dead sure," Kee said.

"What did it look like?"

"Sort of black and brown all mixed up," Kee said.

He looked hopefully at Christy, and Christy supplied, "Brindle?"

"Yes, brindle. White chest markings. Short hair. He was tall. He'd make a dog-and-a-half compared with Dr. Christy's Doberman. Awful thin. He had a German Shepherd look to him. And he's mixed with hound. A lot of hound. But big as he was, he just sort of materialized out from under a little bitty greasewood."

Martin asked, "Did he growl? Bark?"

"He growled a little," Kee said, "but mostly he was busy getting out of there. I know he ran into the arroyo. But I don't know where the hell he went after that. He just disappeared. Dematerialized."

Eleanor asked Kee, "Are you going to try for the dog again this afternoon, Tully?"

Kee regarded the rain. "No, I think I'd better do it right and get a full search party together. It's too late today. We'll do it tomorrow morning. With wet ground, we ought to have good tracking. And I'm not going to wait for daylight. This time we'll start before dawn."

"Can I join the hunt, or are you just generally boycotting women?" Eleanor said.

Kee looked her in the eye. "I'm not ruling out women," he said. "A lot of women I know can do most anything a man can do. But, then, they're not like you and Dr. Christy's friend. They're not so pretty. If a dog got 'em in the face and left a big scar, well, even if they could afford it they probably wouldn't go through a couple of years doing plastic surgery. It wouldn't matter so much to them."

Kee's tact was admirable. Christy saw that Eleanor touched her wet hair and Karen casually rubbed a hand over her smooth throat. Eleanor shrugged. "Let's get out of this rain," she said. "Christy, I've already imposed on you so much, I might as well ask another favor and get you to run me out to the ranch."

They dashed back to the Bronco through rain that showed

little sign of slackening. Karen said, "We're soaked. I need to change. Where are we staying, Christy?"

"In a tent at Sam's place," Christy said.

"It's not good enough for Karen," Sam said. "We'd better fix her up with a motel room. There's a Best Western not too far down the road."

"Nonsense, use my place," Eleanor said. "I've already invited Christy to stay there."

Karen turned to eye Eleanor. "With Sam," Christy said hastily. "But Sam has to be close to home. They're making preparations for a special ceremony."

"Yes," Sam said. "Do you really mean it, Eleanor? Would it be all right if Karen moved into the ranch house with you?"

"I'd love it," Eleanor said. "I've felt downright spooky being alone in that house."

The downpour lasted only a half-hour, but the afternoon remained cloudy and noticeably cooler. Karen took Eleanor to the ranch and parked her car in the garage with Eleanor's station wagon. Sam and Christy followed in the Bronco. Sam needed the Bronco to run some family errands, so Christy grabbed a sweater before Sam dropped him and Gala to join Karen at the ranch house. There, firewood was in order, and Christy and Karen volunteered to fetch dry juniper logs from a woodshed in back of the guesthouse. Gala followed them.

"What a darling guesthouse," Karen said. "It has its own veranda. Come on, Gala, let's go peek at it. I wonder why they did it in stone instead of adobe?"

The answer seemed evident when Christy walked behind it. The little house was so near the mesa wall that, despite the recent rain, he could feel stored heat still radiating from the towering rock. All along its base, sandstone had crumbled and tumbled, and rock was more than plentiful.

While Karen peered through the windows of the guesthouse, Christy peered into the shed, thinking of rattlesnakes and black widows. The guesthouse had its own gas-powered generator, he saw, and it obviously had a fireplace of which Mr. Fawkes had made use, for there were two cords or more of logs. He gingerly threw a load out the door, log by log, and loaded Karen's arms before taking the bulk of them for himself.

Gala barked, staring toward the big house with her ears pricked so tightly that her forehead wrinkled. They rounded the guesthouse in time to see a big blue van receding down the drive with Brad Wilson at the wheel, and at the kitchen door they met Bianca Wilson. She seemed so startled to see them that she dropped a mop she was carrying.

"Oh!" Bianca said. "Miss Fawkes didn't tell me anyone else was here."

Gala trotted forward to greet Bianca, and Christy juggled his load long enough to introduce Bianca to Karen.

"What a beautiful name," Karen said to Bianca. "Bianca, Blanca, Blanche. The white one. The fair one. Were you named that because you're so fair-skinned?"

"N-no," Bianca stammered. "My mother just liked the name."

Karen rested her chin on her armload of firewood. "Sam Benally told me about old Navajo call names once," she said. "He said before everyone was just named Fred or Hortense, he would have been called School Boy, for obvious reasons. And if a man was gabby, he might be Man Who Speaks Often, and if you're fair-skinned, you might be Pale Girl. That's nice. Almost as nice as Bianca."

Bianca smiled, showing her white, square teeth. She petted Gala and allowed herself to be thoroughly sniffed, but she had nothing further to say to Christy and Karen. They took their logs to the living room just as Eleanor bustled in with newspaper and matches. She bustled out again, saying she needed to get Bianca started. Gala gave Christy a guilty look and pattered out after this interesting new friend.

"Christy, move out of the way," Karen said. "You'll never learn how to build a good fire."

Christy stood back and watched as Karen efficiently arranged kindling and logs teepee-fashion in the fireplace. He watched Karen rather than the logs. Her heavy hair was not quite dry, and it fluffed about her face like spun sugar.

"Pretty," Christy said softly.

"My fire?"

"You."

"Flatterer. Hand me a match. Gracious, you've got resin all over your sweater. How wonderful."

"Why?"

"Just wait right here. I've brought gifts for you and Gala, and I almost forgot to give them to you."

Karen rushed upstairs to the bedroom Eleanor had assigned her. Christy grinned happily at the thought of Karen's gifts. So this was the surprise she had mentioned. Her presents were always too extravagant, and she wouldn't allow him to protest, but he would have a fine time getting even with her by choosing a surprise present of his own from Mrs. Lang's shop.

She clattered back down the stairs, already talking. "Joyce took me to this wonderful place in Houston that specializes in silk," she said. "I got me a lovely white crepe de chine kimono, and I got you some underwear. See? I couldn't decide between silk and polypropylene. They're both so good for ski johns. So I got you one set of each."

She produced a red-, white-, and blue-striped polypropylene union suit and a blue turtleneck of heavy knitted silk with matching long johns.

Christy laughed. "That's underwear? I'd want to wear it on the outside and show it off."

"Then you like it?"

"I love it. Thank you, Karen."

"Try on the turtleneck," she said. "You can wear it anywhere you want. It'll look gorgeous with a sport coat. And, look, I didn't forget Gala. Here's a red silk scarf for her. She can snoot all the dogs that just wear bandanas."

Christy thanked her again and claimed a kiss before stripping off his shirt to put on the silk turtleneck. Karen gasped. She gently touched his forearm.

"Good God, Christy, what happened to you?" she said. "Your arm is absolutely mangled."

Christy had left his bite wound unbandaged. It was healing well from beneath, but the outer surface still looked ugly.

"I got nipped by a patient in Durango," he said. "It's not half as bad as it looks."

"It looks awful," Karen said. "A dog did that? That's terrible. Oh, Christy, and I had such a wonderful surprise for you. Daddy has offered to set you up in practice at your own clinic in Houston. But, good God, a dog bite. Daddy must be psychic. Instead of 'Christy Animal Hospital,' it can be 'Christy Dermatology Clinic.' Daddy already said why don't you take more course work and specialize. He's talked to all kinds of people, and since Houston fairly bristles with fleas and fungi and all kinds of things that cause allergies, it's a perfect place to practice veterinary dermatology. Dermatologists never have emergency calls at all. And you'd make tons of money. I told Daddy we'd insist on paying him back, and he said whatever we want to do would be fine, and it can be strictly business."

Karen's rush of words dropped on Christy like dirt on a coffin lid. He said carefully, "That's very generous of your dad, Karen. I hope you'll thank him for me."

"You can thank him yourself, you know. Daddy's really keen on meeting you. Don't you still have time for just a tiny little one-day trip to Houston?"

Christy sought compromise. He didn't want to hurt her. He said, "Karen, I can't take your father up on his offer. But let's plan a visit for me to meet him, anyway. I can take off four or five days later this summer, and we'll fly down together."

She tightened her lips. "I knew it," she said. "All you want to do is putter around in Vail with Dr. Potter. Monitoring hormone levels on infertile bitches. Putting cats on reducing diets. I thought you might want to do . . . something different with your life. Something more."

Christy shrugged helplessly. "I'm just where I want to be, doing what I want to do. The only thing I want more of is you."

Gala trotted into the living room. She stopped and looked from Christy to Karen, who were standing stiffly on either side of the fireplace. Like all dogs, she loved people's laughter and hated their quarrels, and she could scent a quarrel as quickly as smoke from the fireplace. Eleanor Fawkes saved the situation by coming in with an ice bucket and Bianca Wilson.

"Sunset," Eleanor announced. "Time for a drink. No, Bianca, I won't take no for an answer. You look decidedly off-color this evening. I prescribe for everyone a Jack Daniels on the rocks with a twist. My fiancé is an M.D., Christy. He practices in Gallup. Jeff says alcohol taken in moderation is excellent for the nerves, high blood pressure, and just about everything that ails you. I'm sure you agree. Get some glasses, will you?" She gestured to the wall of shelves next to the fireplace. Where the old kachinas had stood there was now a collection of liquor bottles and a tray of glasses.

Christy took the ice bucket from Eleanor, who said, "Rats, I forgot the lemon peel. Bianca, sit down. I'll be back in a moment."

Bianca and the Doberman both came uncertainly into the living room. The dog seemed to say, "No quarrel? Is everything okay?" Bianca's problem was different.

The Navajo girl picked up a sofa cushion and plumped it nervously. She turned to Karen. "I can't make Miss Fawkes listen," she said. "She doesn't understand that some people can't drink. I did once. Brad helped me stop."

Karen unbent. "Why, bless your heart," she said. "Then of course you don't want anything alcoholic. My mother had a drinking problem once. When she stopped, the worst thing was sitting around staring at her hands when everyone else decided it was cocktail hour. So she and I started having tea. It's every bit as good. Tea and toast dripping with butter. We always cheated and had Texas sheet cake, too, all gooey with chocolate and pecans. I'll bet the kitchen can at least rise to tea and toast. I'll go make us some right now."

Eleanor accepted the substitution casually, seeming determined only that the trio of strangers in her house accept her hospitality. Bianca didn't stay long. She refused a refill of her teacup with shy thanks to Karen, and shortly they heard the vacuum cleaner begin to whine upstairs. Gala begged the last of

Karen's buttered toast, then modeled her new scarf, but only the dog and Eleanor were at ease. Finally, Eleanor said, "Is everyone jumpy this evening, or is it just my imagination? Christy, you've been acting funny ever since our dog hunt. What's wrong?"

It wasn't something Christy wanted to talk about, but there were other topics he liked even less. He said, "I suppose I have a ridiculous problem. Veterinarians can't be afraid of animals, but after I got bitten a few days ago by a big shaggy dog that didn't like his medicine, the very next dog I met spooked me a little. Well, to tell the truth, he scared the socks off me. Now I keep feeling uneasy around strange dogs."

He couldn't have chosen a better ploy. It was his turn to be called a poor baby by Karen, although less solicitously than she had spoken to Bianca. There was a reserve in Karen's voice that made Christy nervous as she asked, "Does your heart start to race and your palms go all sweaty? Feel short of breath? Legs rubbery?"

"All of the above," Christy admitted.

"My poor Christy, you've become a phobiac," she said more warmly. "What's the word for fearing dogs? Cynophobia. Now, don't go calling it ridiculous. Just because fear is irrational doesn't make you any less afraid."

"My, yes," Eleanor said. "I'm afraid to drive over high bridges, but I found out that half the world is, too."

"Of course. It's common," Karen said enthusiastically. "There's nothing that someone isn't afraid of. Public speaking. Shopping malls. Cats, flowers, lightning, elevators, mayonnaise, flutes. I love some of those. Imagine having a phobia about mayonnaise. But, Christy, a lot of phobias can be cured, and the cure is basically a simple one. It's the old business of getting back on the horse once it's thrown you. You have to keep exposing yourself to your fear."

"I guess I'll have plenty of opportunity to do that," Christy said. He laughed awkwardly. "So, great, it's nothing. It'll go away."

"It'll go away even faster if you help it along," Karen said. "I tried what they're calling 'in vivo desensitization.' I imagined dogs, then I looked at pictures of dogs, and finally I could touch Gala and learn that big dogs can be darlings, not monsters. But now everybody is talking about 'flooding.' You confront whatever you fear, and it scares you, but you stick it out, and eventually the body gets tired of feeling the anxiety attack, and you just kind of burn it out. Then you're cured."

Eleanor said, "If you're not dead of a heart attack."

Karen raised her eyebrows. "I think that only happens in horror stories."

Christy was grateful that Karen took no advantage of his admission of fear to suggest again that he swap the general practice of veterinary medicine for dermatology. He had never wanted to be a specialist. He was glad others did and doubly glad to send patients to specialists when his own skills were insufficient, but he had wanted to be a general practitioner since he was an eleven-year-old kid cleaning out cages in a basement clinic on Ninth Street. However, there were Karen's hopes and desires to think about, too. She seemed to be considering changes in her life, and Christy devoutly hoped the changes wouldn't exclude him. Damn Daddy and his bright ideas. What would Christy's refusal of Daddy's offer do to his relationship with Karen?

Christy's senses were alert for any danger signals in her attitude, and maybe she did seem a little arbitrary when she volunteered their services again to help Eleanor and Bianca with the house. Nor did she have much to say as they dusted light fixtures and replaced light bulbs that would be needed for the fast-falling night.

While Christy teetered on a stepladder in the dining room, there was a movement of fresh air in the house. It smelled of wet sage, though Christy could have sworn there was no sage in the area. He reached for another bulb in the wrought-iron chandelier, and the bulbs dimmed. They brightened again for a moment, then went out.

"Don't move," Karen said. "You'll fall."

"I'm all right," Christy said. "What did I do wrong? Did we turn on too many lights?"

"Hey in there," Eleanor called from the back of the house. "What happened?"

"I'm afraid we blew a fuse," Christy called back.

"No, you didn't. It's that ratty generator again," Eleanor said. They could hear shuffling movements as she felt her way through the kitchen to the back door. Christy climbed off his ladder. They played their own game of blindman's bluff, making their way to the living room and the flickering light of the fire.

Eleanor called to them from outside. "It's out of gas. I'll have to go get a fresh can."

The Doberman began to growl nervously. She went to the front door.

"What is it, Gala?" Karen said. "Do you need out?"

Gala looked to Christy, then back to the door.

"I'd better see what it is," Christy said. He was worried, but only a little. Gala was naturally fussy about strange people and strange noises, but her growl was different from a signal that she thought there was someone around.

As Karen followed them out, Gala's head swung toward the cliff. Christy thought he could see movement in back of the guesthouse. Then he saw that it was Eleanor, going toward the shed where the firewood was stored. He started to turn back to the house, intending to look for a candle or a flashlight, but Gala began to bark wildly. Near the cliff, he saw Eleanor Fawkes lift her head and stare at the rocks above her.

"Something's moving up in the rocks," Karen said.

"Where?" Christy said.

Karen pointed. Christy could see nothing, but, ears alert and body tense, Gala stared upward at the cliff. Her head turned fractionally, then a fraction more, as if she was tracking the movement of something only she could see clearly. Then Gala jerked as though she had been hit by a stone or a bullet. Christy jerked, too, but his brain belatedly told him there had been no sound of a shot, no thud of an impact, no sound of any kind.

"Eleanor!" Karen called. "Eleanor, get away! Run!"

Christy hesitated, then sprinted toward the cliff. Gala followed him tentatively, as if she feared she would be scolded. Karen hurried after them both. They ran past the chainlink fence surrounding the empty swimming pool. Beyond the pool house another running figure hurled itself toward them. Karen pushed past Christy and took the figure into her arms.

"Eleanor," she said, "are you all right?"

"Oh, my God," Eleanor said. "Oh, thank God you were here."

"Let's get into the house," Karen said.

"It's all right. It's gone now."

"What was it?" Christy said.

"I couldn't see," Eleanor said. "But there was something breathing up there. I could almost feel its hot breath."

"I saw something," Karen said. "I think. Or maybe I heard it. Rocks sliding. Didn't you hear rocks sliding, Christy?"

He had only heard his heartbeat thundering in his ears, and he wasn't about to admit that. "No," he said, "but Gala heard something."

"She must have heard the breathing," Eleanor said. "It was loud. Snorting, almost. Or chuffing. The sounds a horse makes." She laughed shrilly. "That's probably all it was. A horse wandering around."

"Horses don't climb around on sheer cliffs," Karen said.

A flashlight bobbed rapidly toward them from the house. Bianca. They heard her voice calling, "Miss Fawkes? Karen? Dr. Christy?"

"We're by the pool house," Karen called back.

The flashlight swept across them, pausing briefly on each face, then swept on to Gala. "What was it?" Bianca asked.

"We don't know," Karen said.

"Are you all right?"

Eleanor said, "Yes, yes, nothing happened. Gala barked like a maniac and scared it away. At least I hope she scared it away. I still have to get the auxiliary gas tank."

"Christy will do it," Karen said promptly.

Christy said, "Uh . . ."

"Let's get you back to the house," Karen said to Eleanor. "Bianca, give Christy the flashlight. He might need it. We'll light some candles. And, Eleanor, I'm going to make you another drink. Come, Gala. You can protect us."

Gala plastered her ears meekly to her head and trotted rapidly toward the ranch house with Karen and Eleanor. Bianca hesitated, then handed the flashlight to Christy and followed the others.

Left alone in the darkness, Christy stared wistfully after them before turning toward the cliff. He went slowly, mentally damning society and particularly all those members of it who had slowed the push for equal rights for women. If women were truly equal with men, would he be out here all by himself? Sure, let old Christy do it. Let old Christy walk through the dark night, his scalp crawling. Lucky me, he thought. I'm a protector. I'm a man.

Christy played the flashlight beam over the tumbled scree at the foot of the cliff. Nothing there but rock. The door of the shed was open, and Christy approached the yawning blackness of the shed even more carefully than he had done earlier. He stood for a moment, the light picking out stacked logs and the guesthouse generator but nothing more. Two five-gallon tanks of gas stood by the generator. He set both of them outside the shed and closed the door behind him. If Eleanor ran a full load of lights from the big generator at the ranch house, she would get only about three hours of light from each tank. And after her scare, she'd probably want plenty of light tonight.

Still holding the flashlight, Christy looked for another moment at the cliff. Faint warmth still radiated from it, but now there was a current of cooler air flowing down from the top of the mesa. Like water, the current flowed strongest at points of least resistance, and here the sandstone was falling slowly, slab by slab, to meet the tumbled rock at the bottom. Was the downdraft audible? Had it sounded to Eleanor like something breathing?

A bank of cloud shifted, exposing the ripening moon. It was almost full. Christy turned off the flashlight and stuck it in his hip pocket. He reached for the gas tanks. Above, on the steepening rock wall, a pebble tumbled. Christy jerked his head and stared at the slabs of sandstone.

Silently, softly, something moved in the moonlight. Something white. It poured itself down a rock slab that had separated far enough from the cliff for a young tree to grow atop it. Poured. Or floated.

Christy felt a surge of pressure behind his eyes. Frozen, he watched as a huge white shape blotted out the tree.

It flowed again, a half-foot downward, a half-foot closer, then stood poised on the slab of rock above him.

Christy yelled. Or he thought he did. He opened his mouth, threw his left forearm across his throat, and grabbed for the flashlight in his right hip pocket. It caught, and he ripped it loose, his heart beginning to race.

Damn the flashlight. There. There was the switch. Light on now. Right hand trembling. Body stooping. Left hand reaching for a rock to throw. Scalp cold, anticipating a great weight hurtling itself downward. Feet knocking against one another scrambling backward. Rock in hand. Flashlight beam unsteady. There. Trained now on the slab. Trained on the white floating. Trained on . . .

Nothing at all. The white shape was gone. It disappeared before the beam of light could hit it. Christy swept the flashlight beam frantically across the rocks overhead, but there was no movement, no white form, nothing.

The flashlight became unsteady again. He realized his hands were slippery with sweat. He started to back up farther, then remembered the auxiliary gas tanks and grabbed one of them. Only one. He had to have a free hand for the flashlight, and he had to get the hell out of there before . . .

Before what? Before the great white shape could come back? Christy turned and lumbered toward the house, the gas tank banging heavily against his leg, but his brain ran on before him.

What white shape? A goat? Christ, it was probably only a goat. Goats could climb rocks. Goats could climb anything. Yes, it must have been only a goat. Never a spectral white hound. Hound? Dog? A white Dog of Death?

Christy slowed to a walk and forced himself to face his fear. He didn't want to know, but he had to sift the sighting of a floating

white form and look for the muddy tracks of fear left in his mind
and wonder when the form had turned itself into a dog. There,
then, dog. And now the mind in question had to question itself
again. Fearing that he would see a dog, had he seen a dog? Was it
only a trick of the mind? A trick of the moon? Had he seen
anything at all?

Right now he could see candlelight in the kitchen. Christy
hurried, steadying the gas tank so it wouldn't bang his leg so
hard. He tried to grin at himself. He was being foolish. He hadn't
really seen anything. Just nerves gone crazy and imagination
working overtime. Nevertheless, he was eager to get the gasoline
tank changed over and the lights back on.

The generator had its own small shed a few feet from the
kitchen door. He smelled gasoline as he approached it. Fumes
from a spill. He took a careful look with the flashlight. A small
trace of gasoline seeped rapidly into the dirt beneath the concrete
pod on which the generator sat. The coupler hose on the old gas
tank was disconnected.

Christy squatted and studied the hose to the fuel tank and its
quick-disconnect coupler. He thumped the old tank. It sounded
half-full or more. He reconnected the hose. In a minute the generator began to hum. Lights came on in the house.

"That was quick," Karen called through the kitchen window.

"When in doubt, punch the restart button," Christy said.

Karen stepped to the door. "Is everything okay, Christy? Gala
has been wanting back out. Can I let her?"

Christy cleared his throat. "Sure," he said. "Glad to have her."

Gala's black form rushed out the kitchen door. The dog hurried to Christy, then sat down quickly and precisely at his left
side. She rolled her head up at him, anxiety fairly bristling from
her, and Christy kneeled beside her, petting her, reassuring her,
and gaining assurance from her presence.

"Good Gala," he crooned. "My good Gala girl."

Karen stepped outside. "What are you two talking about?" she
said. "Gala hasn't been very good. She kept pattering around like
a nervous ant. Looking for you, I guess. But something stung her
a couple of minutes ago. She jumped like everything. Just like she

did when we were watching Eleanor out by the cliff. Do they have scorpions here?"

"I don't think it was a scorpion," Christy said. "I think she heard something."

"What? Pebbles bouncing on the cliff? Eleanor's breathing sound?"

"No, something none of us could hear. An ultrasonic whistle, maybe. One of those things that are too high in range for the human ear. A signal."

Karen looked at him oddly. "What on earth would make you think a thing like that?"

Christy showed her the gas line. "This was disconnected," he said. "Someone loosened it so the gas couldn't get to the generator. Our blackout wasn't accidental."

Karen drew in a quick breath. "Are you sure? That's a terrible thing to say. How do you know it didn't just vibrate loose?"

"I tried it," he said. "It's a pretty secure connection."

"Still, to suggest that someone disconnected it on purpose . . . All kinds of queer things can happen with machinery. I'd rather think it just popped loose on its own."

Christy began to feel foolish. Sure, machinery did nutty things. And he wasn't thinking logically after his scare out by the cliff. White shapes that didn't exist. Heavy breathing that no one else could hear. Gas lines that shook loose by themselves. It was enough to jar anyone's grasp on the rational.

"You're probably right," he said.

"I hope I am," she said. "But come back in the house. It's too dark out here."

"Sure, coming," Christy said. He groped for his handkerchief in his torn hip pocket. His palms were sweating again.

There was movement at the kitchen door. Christy looked up. It was Eleanor.

"Did you see anything out there?"

"Monsters galore," Christy said. "But they were probably all in my imagination."

She gave him a sour look. "I did hear something breathing."

"I'm sure you did," Christy said. Then, with a quick look at Karen, he amended it. "Almost sure, anyway. Didn't someone say something about another drink?"

CHAPTER 14

After rain in the night and rain in the black hour before dawn, muddy water flowed sullenly in the Rio Puerco on Saturday morning, and Sam had unkind words for Officer Kee about the station to which he, Christy, and his nephew were assigned for the dog hunt. They were at the juncture of the Puerco and the arroyo in which the dog had disappeared the day before. Sam warned Christy strongly to stay away from the river bottom.

"Give the Puerco a little water and it can be instant quicksand," Sam said. "Cars sink in it. Horses disappear. Disobedient little boys who wade in it can take a wrong step and get pulled under. Isn't that right, George?"

George hunched his neck into his slicker. "That's what everybody says," he said vaguely. He looked to the east. "Sun'll be up soon." For the first time that morning, he left Sam's side, wandering off across the arroyo, which apparently served as everyone's trash heap. George could choose between an old refrigerator half-buried in sand or a rusted bucket on which to seat himself. He chose the refrigerator.

George hadn't seemed at all enthusiastic about coming on the hunt. Christy thought he had been stampeded into it by Harley and Sam, who had busily divided the available weapons without even asking the boy if he wanted to volunteer. Harley, however, had stayed home with the Benally women, and Christy had noticed that Harley kept with him the best rifle, a Remington .721 that looked old but beautifully maintained.

Christy asked Sam softly, "Is George all right?"

Sam shifted his own Marlin .22 to his left shoulder. George

was armed with the old shotgun, and Christy had been issued a borrowed tranquilizer gun by Officer Kee.

"No, the kid isn't all right," Sam said. "I can't figure out what's bothering him. Unless it's me. Maybe I raked him over too hard yesterday. I can't stand being lied to. I really let him have it after he all but swore he didn't even know Eli Tom and had never seen a steer in his life, much less rustled four of them. But what's there to do? I can't just dump George on the mercy of the law, and he knows it."

"George isn't acting like he's mad at you," Christy said. "He's acting . . . oh, I don't know. Edgy. Apprehensive."

Sam looked at Christy silently. The look said that his troubled nephew wasn't the only one who had been behaving peculiarly.

Christy took a deep breath, trying to release the tightness in his chest. It had been there since midnight, as he awakened repeatedly at the camp site on the Benally place, thinking not only of the white figure of his last night's imagining but of the big dog they would be hunting this morning. He felt especially vulnerable without Gala. Eleanor had told Sam all about her own scare when he came to pick up Christy. Although she had ended by laughing it off nervously, Eleanor had looked every bit as happy as Karen when Sam suggested that the Doberman should stay with them overnight at the ranch house.

Hopping puddles, George moved to their side of the arroyo. In his haste, he stepped noisily on a caved-in plastic milk bottle. "Someone's coming," he said. He edged close to Sam, clutching his shotgun.

"Someone or something?" Sam whispered.

"Christ, don't talk like that," George said. He shuddered. "It's people. I saw two people."

It was Ann Lang and Bianca Wilson's husband, Brad. They came silently along the Puerco's north bank. Brad waved. Mrs. Lang trudged along with her hands in her blue jean pockets and the collar of a windbreaker turned up.

"We're reinforcements," Brad said cheerfully when they scrambled into the arroyo. "That deputy, Turland, said the trackers are about ready to move now, so they figure the dog could be spotted any time."

"If it's still here," Mrs. Lang said. "I don't see why any animal in its right mind would just sit around and wait for people to come hunt it. Christy, is that the tranquilizer gun? Turland said they managed to get two from the Forest Service. It looks like a real rifle. Are you sure it doesn't have bullets in it?"

Christy hefted the gun. Shorter than a rifle, it looked more like a light shotgun. "No, it's dart-loaded," he said.

"Then what in hell are the darts loaded with?"

"A combination of tranquilizers. Ketamine and xylazine. They're safe. Honestly."

Mrs. Lang said to the others, "Okay, if the dog comes our way, the rest of you get out of the way and let Christy do the shooting. Do you hear? Hell, the roadside park looks like a National Rifle Association convention. Every fool on the state line has turned up with a cannon. Some guy named Ed Lee was asking for you, Sam. He's got a gun big enough to kill an elephant. As big as Brad's."

Brad smiled at her. Held in the crook of his arm was a .30–.06. "I just brought a gun to protect you with," he said. "Of course, that doesn't mean you're entirely safe. It's not too late to turn around and go home. I probably couldn't hit anything I aimed at."

"Don't play the fool with me," she said. "I hear that you're out in the boonies killing rabbits all the time. They say you don't miss much."

"Bianca needs rabbits for her wolves and the coyotes," Brad said. "I just try to oblige."

Obligingly, Brad reported to them the latest instructions from Deputy Turland, who was acting as hunt coordinator. Christy had already seen a gratifying number of volunteers beginning to gather. They came in twos and threes, as if no one wanted to be alone, even in daylight. According to Turland's message, even more volunteers had shown up. They were taking position all along the apron of the triangle. Kee and Deputy Martin were ready at the head of the arroyo with the other tranquilizer gun.

The two most experienced trackers planned to enter the triangle from the east side, where the dog had first been spotted the previous day. Anyone who sighted the animal was to fire three shots in the air as a signal for all hunters to start carefully closing in, checking brush and other hiding places, moving toward the arroyo, where Kee and Martin figured the dog would run again. Guns were to be used only in self-defense.

Christy clutched the tranquilizer gun and stared up the arroyo, breathing rapidly as he waited for the signal. It was only a dog. Just a dog. A lost, starving dog. He had brought a supply of Gala's food for it and even remembered a can opener and a dish. They waited in his car. It was just a dog that needed help—if somebody didn't shoot it first—and he had loaded the pockets of his light parka with emergency gear. He had checked his bag and made sure he had the basics he might need for shock therapy, and he had put Gala's blanket in the car with the bag, and he was as ready as he could be for first aid in the field on a wounded dog. What he still wasn't ready for were the waves of apprehension that filled him at the thought of an unwounded dog.

The first sound that the hunt was on wasn't a three-shot signal. It was a yell, then a single shot. Christy clutched the tranquilizer gun even tighter. "What the hell?" he said shakily.

Brad laughed. "I'll give two to one that somebody stepped on a rattler," he said. "There's plenty of them around."

Two more distant shots blasted. After a moment, a third shot blasted out.

"Is that the signal?" Sam said.

"I don't know," Christy said. "It could be. I guess it's time to move."

Mrs. Lang moved first, and she moved neither slowly nor carefully. She ran up the arroyo. George held back. Christy saw it, and realized that he was holding back, too. He broke into a trot, following the others.

"There he goes!" a distant voice cried.

Mrs. Lang slowed down. Christy breathed more evenly. The shout sounded far away. More voices yelled and hooted. Northwest, Christy thought. He slogged on. The red sand in the bottom of the arroyo was damp, but no water ran here. Brad Wilson was far ahead. The blond man jogged past the tumble of cans by the NO DUMPING sign and stopped for a moment at the junked cars farther up. A trio of strange Navajo men came down a rise and hailed Brad. They spoke briefly, then slid down the eroded bank to join him, and they all walked on up the arroyo.

"Maybe I'd better see what's going on," Sam said. He looked around. "Where's George?"

"Somebody had to watch the mouth of the arroyo, so he stayed back," Christy said. Perhaps he didn't lie. He only knew that George had not come with them.

"Keep an eye on Ann," Sam said. He began to run after Brad and the others, stretching out, obviously enjoying the chance to get in a little exercise.

Christy caught up with Mrs. Lang at the flood of tin cans. She gestured ahead at the junked cars and started to speak. Then she froze.

A dog crept out from under a rusted Ford that Sam had cleared moments before. The dog stood and gazed up the arroyo after Sam. Big, dark brindle, gaunt, it was the feral dog they had all been seeking.

The dog wheeled and started to run out of the arroyo, but it saw Christy and Mrs. Lang and stopped in mid-stride. Its head snapped up. The hair on its back rose rigidly. It crouched, tail low, hollow flanks and stomach low to the ground.

For a second, the brindle dog presented a perfect target, immobile, too big to miss. Ann Lang saw it. "Shoot," she hissed at Christy. "Shoot!"

The dog growled menacingly and backed up to the junked Ford. It bumped a dented front fender and jerked in surprise. Its tail went between its legs, but it burst into a spate of loud barking so fierce that its body heaved with each bark.

"Jesus help us," Mrs. Lang said.

Christy saw bared fangs and red gums spotted with black. He was close enough to see tartar on the dog's fangs. He saw Sam running hard back down the arroyo toward the sound of barking, his light rifle ready. Far behind Sam, he could see Brad Wilson and the trio of strange Navajos trying to close the distance. Spellbound, he saw the brindle dog back up even closer to the car, its rump pressed tight against the rusted metal.

Three shots blasted the air. Then a fourth shot roared, closer and louder. The hood of the dog's car pinged. The dog trembled violently, then his legs slowly crumpled, and he rolled to his side.

"Stop!" Mrs. Lang screamed. "Oh, Jesus Christ, the bastard's shot him!"

She ran straight toward the dog. Christy came back to life and shouted, "Get back. He's hit."

"Then come help him, you dumb sonofabitch," Mrs. Lang sobbed. She halted and stared helplessly at the animal.

Christy got his feet moving. He reached Mrs. Lang before Sam did, but Sam had plenty of time to circle wide of the dog. Sam put his arms around Mrs. Lang. She sobbed, "He's dead, he's dead, and I never gave him anything to eat."

Christy leaned the tranquilizer gun carefully against the car before edging closer to the animal. He dragged out a handkerchief to wipe his hands, and he spilled his car keys and a syringe in the process. He stooped for them, eyes on the dog. The big brindle male was breathing rapidly. His lips were drawn back, and his eyes were open and glassy. Christy checked his watch and eyed the dog's ribs, automatically counting the respiratory rate. Almost two hundred and forty times a minute. Four breaths a second. Not good. Shuddering, Christy stepped closer, but he still couldn't bring himself to get close enough to touch the dog. He looked for other signs of the acute trauma of a gunshot wound. No visible blood on the body. No blood from the nose and mouth. He tentatively ruled out hemorrhage. That left shock and potential respiratory complications as the immediate threats to life.

Brad Wilson thudded down the arroyo. He looked red-faced and upset. He stared at the dog and at Christy, then turned to Mrs. Lang. "I didn't mean to hit it," he said. "I saw it coming at you. I was trying to scare it away."

Mrs. Lang jerked away from the hand Brad tried to lay on her arm. "He wasn't coming at us," she said. "All he did was growl."

"I'm sorry, Ann," Brad said.

She gulped and said to Christy, "Is he in a great deal of pain? God, I don't want him to suffer any more. Could you . . . I mean . . . do you have anything that would make it easier for him?"

"Let me look at him first," Christy said. Galvanized, he finally crouched close to the dog. He shielded the dog's eyes for a moment with his hand, then removed it. The pupils responded to the change of light. He didn't yet dare try to manipulate the dog's body. There could always be spinal injury, and moving the dog could cause further complications. But the rule-outs were mounting. Airway seemed clear. The rapid breathing? Maybe just hyperventilation increasing the intracranial pressure. He had been hyperventilating himself.

Christy thought of three dozen other things he should check to be sure, but he looked up at Brad. "This dog isn't dying," he said. "I don't think you even winged him."

Mrs. Lang crouched beside Christy. "Then what's wrong with him?" she said.

"It may sound nutty, but I think we can more or less say he's fainted," Christy said.

"Fainted?" Sam said incredulously.

"Faint. Swoon. A syncope due to cerebral anemia."

"But he dropped like a stone when Brad fired at him," Mrs. Lang said.

"Maybe the shooting scared him badly," Christy said. "He's got a fairly new scar on his face. Looks like a bullet wound. And some dogs are gun-shy from birth."

"So what do we do now?" Sam said. "Muzzle him? Tie him up? If he's just scared, he's going to come back to life, isn't he?"

A little crowd was gathering. The three Navajos who had been with Brad called to a man at the rim of the arroyo and told him the dog had been caught. George Laughter and another stranger approached cautiously from below. Christy had to make a quick decision. Muzzling a dog that still exhibited respiratory difficulties was risky, but letting the dog get shot was riskier by far.

Christy grabbed for the packets of sterile bandages in his pockets. He impatiently threw out a packet of pads and ripped open one of gauze. He chose a clean-looking stick from the floor of the arroyo. Lifting the dog's muzzle, he put the stick between the teeth and hastily began wrapping strips of gauze around the muzzle. Two hands reached to help him, lifting the dog's head carefully clear of the ground. Christy gazed for a moment into Mrs. Lang's clear hazel eyes, then went back to the job of adjusting the gauze tightly enough to keep the dog from biting, but not so tight that it would hurt him. He cross-looped the last strips under the dog's neck and tied them, then fished for more gauze and began tying the dog's forepaws together. One of the Navajos realized what Christy was doing and bent to help. Another stripped the laces out of his boots and handed them over when Christy and the first man ran out of gauze. The dog lay limply, letting Christy move his paws, but Christy saw that the animal's eyes had begun to follow his movements. Brown eyes, the black pupil dilated, the dark brown of the iris muddying the white slightly at the outside corners. Eyes that were terrified and hopeless. Christy paused and stroked the dog's brindle head, wishing he could reassure it. Then he felt a surge of intense self-disgust. Sure, now he could stroke it. Now his fear was gone, and he could feel pity for the dog. It was safely trussed.

Christy made as thorough an examination as he could on the damp and sandy bottom of a desert arroyo. He ignored the voices that began to question and buzz over his head. No flesh at all over the ribs. No breakfast bulge in the hollow stomach. The dog began to gulp. Christy rechecked the gauze, but it wasn't constricting badly. The gulping came from fear. But fear, long neglect, and starvation were the only things he could find wrong with the animal. The dog began to struggle and jerk as Christy's fingers carefully palpated. He sighed and stood up. One last thing to examine. By the rusted car, he studied the tracks the dog had left in the sand. Then he raised his eyes, seeking Officer Kee. When he found Kee, he said, "This isn't the right dog."

"Hallelujah!" Mrs. Lang sang out.

The McKinley County dog expert pushed up. "Sure it's the right dog," he said. "It's the only feral dog around here."

Mrs. Lang said, "He may be wild now, but he had a home once. He has a worn spot from a collar buckle under his throat."

Brad Wilson broke in. "Wild or not, he was sure ready to go for you when I shot at him, Ann."

"The dog wasn't trying to attack us," Mrs. Lang said fiercely. "He was defending the only thing he possessed—a damned old broken-down car."

"He's been sleeping in it," a Navajo man put in. "There's dog hair all over the floorboards."

"That's how we lost him yesterday," Kee said. "He must have ducked in there to hide."

Deputy Martin raised his voice over the increasing hubbub. "It doesn't matter where he was hiding," he said. "This is the dog that attacked Mr. Fawkes and Eli Tom. We've got him, and that's that."

Officer Kee shot a troubled look from Christy to Martin. To Martin, he said, "You're kind of changing your tune, aren't you? Are you trying to tell me this starving hound is a trained attack dog that somebody set on Mr. Fawkes and Eli?"

Martin looked tired. "When you've been a cop as long as I have, Kee, maybe you'll know that when you've caught a suspect in the act, it's time to discard other hypotheses," he said.

"You didn't catch this poor dog in any act," Mrs. Lang said. "He was just hiding. I'll bet he was in his car this morning when we heard the first shots. They were way the hell to the east. What did you do, spot the real dog there and let it get away?"

Kee said, "No, that was a dumb accident. Somebody flushed a coyote and took a potshot at it."

The dog struggled against the makeshift bonds as more and more people crowded around. Officer Kee raised his voice. "All right, everybody get back. Go on back to your cars. The hunt's over, and I appreciate everybody's help. Let's get back now."

One Navajo man stayed where he was. Christy realized that it was the young rancher who owned the Komondorok. Lee, that was his name. Ed Lee.

"What's going to happen with this dog?" Lee asked quietly.

Kee said, "I guess we'll send him to Gallup with Turland and

Martin. We don't exactly have facilities for dogs here on the reservation, and they can make sure the dog is locked up good and tight at the animal control center."

Mrs. Lang said, "And what will they do to him there? Kill him?"

Deputy Turland said, "We'll probably run some tests. We can't interrogate and fingerprint a dog, but the sheriff might want to take pawprints or something. Dr. Christy, we've got those pictures you shot of the tracks. I'd planned to bring them by to you, but it looks like we'd better keep them awhile."

"Sure, keep them," Christy said, "but there's one thing I can tell you right now. This dog's feet aren't nearly big enough to have made the tracks I saw."

"He's a hell of a big dog," Turland said.

"In body, maybe, but a big body doesn't always mean big paws," Christy said. "His feet aren't much bigger than my female Doberman's feet. Besides, the toes aren't splayed. The pictures of the tracks at the ranch ought to show a definite splaying."

"We'll take that into consideration, Dr. Christy," Turland said politely. "Meanwhile, I guess we'd better get the dog into Gallup. Uh, Jack, how do we do it? Shall I take his front half and you take the rear?"

"You take the rear," Martin said. He wrinkled his nose. "He's emptied his anal glands. That's going to make a nice stink in the patrol car. Maybe we ought to stuff him in the trunk."

Christy said stiffly, "I'll get you a blanket to put him on. If that isn't good enough, I'll drive him into Gallup for you."

Turland said, "Oh, heck, we can take him in the back seat."

"All right," Christy said. "But first I'm going to give him a tranquilizer shot. He's terrified. There's no point in letting him suffer if he doesn't have to. I just have to run back to my car for it. I won't be a minute. Tully, maybe you can stay here with Mrs. Lang. Don't try to talk to the dog or anything. It just scares him."

Mrs. Lang followed Christy as he started to climb out of the arroyo. "Are you really going to give him a tranquilizer, or are you going to put him to sleep?" she whispered.

Christy felt bitterly sorry for the dog. He also felt bitterly ashamed of himself for having been afraid to approach the growling creature. He was confused, and he asked Mrs. Lang, "What do you think?"

"Isn't it like you told me?" she said. "It's better to go to sleep painlessly and forever than to get knocked around and scared so badly?"

Christy looked back at the trembling dog. Tail curled tightly under belly. Breathing too rapidly again. "Damn it, no," Christy said, as much to the dog as to Mrs. Lang. "We caught the wrong animal for them, and maybe we can prove it."

"In God's name, how?" Mrs. Lang said.

"By catching the right one," Christy said. "Now go back and make sure nobody does anything stupid. If I can find the right vial, our dog friend isn't going to mind anything that happens to him until tomorrow. He's not going to be out cold, but he's going to be so calm that he won't care one way or the other."

Christy hurried up to the roadside park. There he saw Karen Hamilton huddled at the edge of a small crowd with Gala and Eleanor Fawkes. Gala bounded to meet Christy, jerking Karen along behind her.

"Are they going to shoot the dog now?" Karen asked hoarsely.

"No, no," Christy said. "I'm just going to give him a tranquilizer injection and carry him back up here." He went to his Bronco to fetch the tranquilizer dose and Gala's blanket, mentally promising her another one. "Wait for me," he told Karen.

"That's what we've been doing," Karen said, but she found a smile to say it with.

Sam and the Navajo rancher, Ed Lee, were also waiting when Christy started back down the incline. Sam called to him, but Christy said, "Give me five minutes, Sam." He hurried to the dog. The acepromazine with which Christy injected the brindle dog began to take effect almost instantly. While Christy was at it, he cleaned up the dog's rear with the isopropyl alcohol he used to sterilize the injection site, not so that the musky odor of the anal-gland ejection would be less bothersome to the deputies, but so the dog, bound and unable to clean himself, wouldn't be as troubled by it. Then he slid the dog's limp body onto Gala's blanket. Sam stepped over immediately to take one end. The rancher took the other. Christy and Kee helped heave the dead weight of the dog out of the arroyo. Once on the top side, Christy said softly to Kee, "I want to keep the tranquilizer gun for one more day, okay?"

"Are you that convinced we've still got some hunting to do?" Kee asked.

"I think I am," Christy said.

Kee said soberly, "If you're right, we could have more killings."

"Yes. We'd better do the hunting fast."

"We might be wrong about the size and shape of the tracks," Kee said. "And we didn't pick up any tracks at all around Eli Tom's place."

"It isn't just the tracks," Christy said. "Ask Mrs. Lang if this dog growled and barked when he thought we were trying to hurt him. He did. He made plenty of noise before Brad Wilson shot at him. That doesn't fit our pattern, Tully."

Kee shook his head. "That isn't much to go on."

"Yes, but it's something. I've been so busy thinking about witch-wolves and feral dogs that I haven't given much thought to the domestic canines I've met that can't bark. Lots of city people have their dogs whisper-barked. Ever heard of it?"

Kee laughed abruptly. "How would I?" he said. "I've never known anyone who cared if a dog barks. Unless they yap too much at the moon and keep you awake."

"Whisper-barking is a fairly simple surgical procedure," Christy said. "I don't do that kind of surgery myself, but some people go that route if they have a barky dog in a close-packed residential development and have grumpy neighbors. If it's done right, you've got a dog that just whispers a woof at the mailman. The surgery can even tone down the growl, too. That could explain a lot. The point is, our hound dog in the blanket up ahead is a good, noisy barker. That, among other things, rules him out to me."

"What other things?"

The little crowd of hunters closed around, wanting to see the brindle dog, and that saved Christy from an answer. He saw that the dog was safely loaded into the back seat of the patrol car. Deputy Martin wouldn't hear of untying the dog. Christy checked the bonds and surreptitiously loosened the improvised muzzle while Martin was busy rolling down the car windows, then he peeled away, going to Karen and Eleanor. Gala sniffed him over with great thoroughness, finding out for herself what kind of animal he had been with and what he had been doing. She sniffed so hard that drops of moisture appeared at her nostrils, then applied the same treatment to Ann Lang when she joined them. Brad Wilson came over, and Gala did the same to him.

Brad looked apologetic. He reached to pet the Doberman's head. She jerked back, as dogs often did at the sight of a stranger's hand reaching over them. Brad said to Mrs. Lang, "Now don't you be mad at me for shooting at that dog, Ann. I wouldn't have done it if I hadn't thought you and Dr. Christy were in danger."

"Since you missed, I guess I'll forgive you," Mrs. Lang said.

"I'd better get back to the post," Brad said. "Bianca will be wondering what's happened. Stop with me, Ann. We'll have a cup of coffee."

"No, I'll just go back to the ruin," Mrs. Lang said. She looked unhappily at the deputy's car, which hadn't left yet, then drew Christy aside.

"I want to talk to you and Sam," Mrs. Lang said. "Alone. Can you come up to the ruin?"

"I've got some tall thinking to do, Ann," Christy said. "Can the conversation wait?"

"I . . . I don't know," she said. "It's what you said about finding the right dog. I don't know anything about that. But I know something that's been going on. I'm afraid it's confession time. Bring George with you, but not your girlfriends. All right?"

"If you think it's important," Christy said reluctantly.

"I'll be waiting."

Christy took Karen and the Doberman back to Karen's car. Karen looked at Christy searchingly. "I think it's time you told me everything that's going on here," she said. "I can help. I know I can."

"I'll take you up on that," he said. "But not just this minute. Do you mind just taking it easy at the ranch for another little while?"

"No," she said. "Not if that's where you want me. But I'm worried about you. No end of strange things have been happening, haven't they?"

Christy agreed. He agreed even more when, seeing Sam and the Navajo rancher waiting by his Bronco, he went to speak to them and the first thing Sam said was, "All clear? Ed Lee has something he wants to tell us."

"Oh? What's that?" Christy said to the friendly young rancher.

Lee glanced around. No one was close. "Sam told me the two of you might be interested in a story that was going around," he said. "I found out who started it. Maybe they can tell you more. You know the McCrea outfit, don't you, Sam? It turns out it was one of old Jake's wives who told a girl, and she told a girl who told my cousin."

Sam said eagerly, "The McCreas live next to the Fawkes ranch. Over on the east side."

Christy was having a hard time cataloguing his data. He prompted, "This is the story about . . . ?"

"The white wolf that floats across the sky," Sam said. "What if the McCrea outfit spotted it right on the Fawkes ranch? The thought's enough to make my heart pittypat a little faster."

The white wolf. Christy's heartbeat speeded up to match Sam's.

CHAPTER 15

Ann Lang was waiting for them in her living room. She had something concealed in her hand.

"Brace yourself, George," Mrs. Lang said abruptly. "You're not going to like being implicated in my confession."

The youngster stared at her glumly. "What are you talking about?" he said.

Mrs. Lang opened her hand. On her palm lay a tiny carving of a frog. She thrust it at Christy, and he took it wonderingly. It was light, apparently of bone, and the work was exquisite.

"I may not have mentioned it, but I occasionally dig a few artifacts," Mrs. Lang said. Her voice was gruff. "That's Hohokam, traded to the Anasazi."

Sam said, "You dug that up around here? Where?"

"No, I didn't find that," Mrs. Lang said. "Eli Tom brought it to me, along with some of the prettiest shell bracelets you could ever hope to see. They were special. Eli wanted me to sell them for him to some special collector. I told him it was out of my league and that it could take time to find the right buyer. He came back in three days, wanting the bracelets. I'm convinced somebody else had already found a buyer for him. Am I right, George?"

The youngster shrugged. "How would I know?"

Mrs. Lang faced Christy and Sam. "I guess you'll think I'm just jealous because other people started competing with me in pot-hunting. Well, pot-hunting is a growth industry, and I wasn't ashamed of it until recently. I said finders keepers on artifacts and to hell with all the archaeologists who screamed that only they should do the digging. I said they've already learned everything there is about the prehistoric cultures around here, so why should they keep grabbing all the best pieces for themselves?"

Christy said, "I guess that's one way of looking at things. But don't you think stealing panels of petrographs off somebody else's land is going too far?"

"How do you know about that?" Mrs. Lang demanded. "Eleanor Fawkes? Did she tell you?"

Christy said, "The source doesn't matter. But Sam and I already know about your pot-hunting, Ann. So there's really nothing you have to confess."

Mrs. Lang's cheekbones flamed. "Boy, that burns me," she said tightly. "Here I am saying *mea culpa,* and I choose you as priests, and you yawn in my face. Well, if Eleanor told you I was the responsible party on those petrographs, she was wrong. I've been quite content with pots and baskets. And I paid taxes on every cent I made from them. But what I'm trying to tell you nincompoops is that it was some of the kids who worked with Bianca and Brad Wilson who got too ambitious about the petrographs. And I'm thinking they got ambitious about other things. What about it, George?"

"Don't look at me," George said. "I never did anything."

"Didn't you?" Mrs. Lang said. "Didn't you and Eli steal the Hopi gods at Shungopavi?"

Sam slumped onto a sofa. "Oh, Lord," he said.

"Don't let her say things like that," George said. "Tell her she'd better not spread that kind of talk around."

Sam wouldn't look at his nephew. He looked at Mrs. Lang and asked, "Do you have any idea where the old kachinas could have ended up, Ann? Is there any chance of getting them back for the Hopis?"

"Not unless George knows," she said.

There was silence. The windows of the house were open, and the greater silence of the desert seemed to come in and settle in the room. Christy saw that bright patches of red had leaped to George's cheeks. He felt his way along the memory of George's edginess, his moodiness, and he said, "George, what are you so afraid of? Do you think it was because of the Hopi idols that someone killed Eli?"

George sighed. He glanced toward his uncle, but Sam still wouldn't look at him. George's shoulders slumped, and he said in a low voice, "I know that's why. And they're going to kill me next. Sam, won't you take me home? I've got to talk to that singer when he comes to get ready for tonight. I've got to get him to sing over me, too. Or maybe I'll go back to Denver with you. Maybe they won't look for me there. If they can't find me, they can't kill me." The youngster began to shudder.

"Whoa, wait," Sam said. He rose and put a comforting arm around his nephew's shoulders. "Nobody's going to hurt you," he said. "I wouldn't let them."

"How can you help it?" George said. "Those Hopis, they're the worst. They got more witches than anybody. You could feel it. That's why I wouldn't go down in the kiva with Eli. They said I was chicken, but, hell, the Hopi guys knew it would happen. They wouldn't go down, either. They said they couldn't get the kachinas because they were Hopi, but it wouldn't hurt Eli and me because we were Navajo. Damn liars. I told Eli not to go down there, but he wouldn't listen. They were all drinking. So I ran off, and I just sat in Eli's truck, but he came back to the truck with something all wrapped up, and just being near them is enough to kill you. That's why they're going to kill me, too."

Mrs. Lang said, "Take it easy, George. If you didn't help steal the idols, at least you're in the clear with the law. And the law will get you faster than any Hopi magic." She explained to Sam and Christy, "The Hopi elders tried to pray all their idols back at first, but they gave up and called in the police and the FBI."

Sam said, "George, you've got to tell us. What did Eli do with the idols?"

"I don't know," the youngster said. "He told me it wasn't any of my business since I wouldn't help him. But somebody sold them for him. I know they did, because he was sure unhappy about the price. He talked about that a lot. He needed money bad. He owed some guy a lot of money. I told him he shouldn't gamble. And he still owed on his truck."

"He had money," Sam said. "Tully Kee told Christy about it. Over fifteen hundred dollars."

George sighed again. "I guess that was for the kachinas," he said. "But Eli owed more than that." George looked at them with hopeless eyes much like the captive dog's. "It was after Eli and the Hopi guys got such a bad price on the kachinas that we took those cattle from Old Man Fawkes. I lied to you. I did sort of help Eli steal them. He shot them, but then he had to have somebody help him butcher them so he could load them in his truck. After he sold the meat, he gave me fifty dollars. Boy, did Brad Wilson ever get mad at Eli and me when he found out about those cattle. He said he didn't want anything to do with punk cattle thieves and we should just forget about trying to move those rock paintings. Eli said it wasn't stealing. It was his father's cattle and his father's rocks, and he had a right, but, damn, I got fired twice. Old Man Fawkes fired me over the cattle, and Brad fired me and gave up on the rocks. Now the damn witch-wolf is after me."

Christy said, "There is no witch-wolf, George. No white wolf, either. It's just a lot of talk. Rumors and fear."

George said nervously, "You don't understand. People have seen the white wolf. Everybody is talking about it. It lives out on the reservation."

Sam said, "Calm down. Maybe someone has seen it, and maybe not. We're going to find out right now. Out at the McCrea place. Ed Lee says they're the ones who started all the white-wolf talk."

"God, I can't go out there," George said. "I can't be around some white wolf. What if the Hopis made the wolf? It's got to be the Hopis."

Christy closed the gap and shook George's shoulder. "Listen to me, George," he said. "The animal we're looking for is real. It isn't a magic Hopi wolf out for revenge. It's not a magic anything. It's a plain old animal that somebody has been using. Abusing."

"You don't know that," George said.

"Yes, I do," Christy assured him. "The animal we're looking

for is just like my dog. It eats dog food, and it leaves tracks, and it answers to a special whistle."

Mrs. Lang said, "What whistle?"

Christy thought it over for the last time. "One of those high-frequency whistles, the kind that humans don't hear," he said. "It has to be that, or I would have heard it, too. Gala heard it twice last night. I think I knew it at the time, but I had spooks on my mind and I didn't stick to my guns."

Mrs. Lang said, "Last night? What happened last night?"

Christy said, "The white wolf paid a call at the Fawkes ranch. Miss Fawkes and I both figured we were out of our minds, but I'm betting everything it was a real animal. And it wasn't looking for you, George. Nothing's out to get you. It was looking for Eleanor Fawkes. Or me."

Thirty minutes later, Sam and Christy bucketed along a wagon track northeast of the Painted Cliffs toward the McCrea place, sending a trail of dust blowing in back of them. Over a red butte to the east, cottony white clouds sent a similar trail of streamers. Sam kept an eye on the clouds. Another rain today could fill the washes they crossed, leaving them stranded. The clouds remained white and puffy, but Sam's expression didn't lighten. Ann Lang had volunteered to run George to the one place he wanted to be, home. As Sam confided to Christy, the only reason he had let her do it was because he didn't want to talk to George until he'd had time to absorb and think about George's admissions of wrong-doing. Now he was sorry.

"I think you keep to the right here," he said. "Damn it, Christy, George is so scared that there's no telling what fool thing he might do. He might just cut out on his motorcycle and go to hell or Texas. I shouldn't have been so chicken about talking to him."

"Don't worry," Christy said. "George isn't going to go anywhere. He's a good Navajo at heart. He wants to be in on that Blessingway ceremony. Maybe in some way he needs to be, Sam. Maybe he needs the Blessingway to put him right with himself. Isn't that what it's supposed to do?"

"Sure," Sam said distractedly. "That's basically what all the ceremonials do—bring a person into harmony with the world." Thinking about it, he looked less tense himself. Sam began to drum his palm on the dashboard and chant, *"He-ye ne-ne ya-na.* That's how Blessingway starts. Kind of a signal, so the gods will listen."

"Does everybody sing at the ceremonials?" Christy asked.

"You chant along," Sam said. "It helps if you know the words, and I don't know too many. Some of the longer sings are as long as the *Iliad.* Longer. It's the same kind of oral tradition. But I've heard many a Blessingway." The worried look returned to his face. "But no ceremony is going to get back the Hopi idols. Hopis and Navajos are traditional enemies, but you've got to feel for them. They think their *talaotsumsime* were given to them by their gods. Their whole way of life revolves around them."

Christy had to agree it was big trouble. George would have to make a full disclosure to the law. With Eli Tom dead, things would go hardest on the two young Hopis—alcoholics, George had muttered—who set up the theft, but George wasn't totally in the clear. Finding out who fenced the idols was mandatory. So was finding the collector who presumably had bought them. But a bigger crime was on Christy's mind—the murder of two men and the possibility of more murders. How did the theft of sacred religious objects tie in to that?

Christy flirted for a moment with the thought that Mr. Fawkes, himself a pot-hunter and a renowned dabbler in odd money-making schemes, had masterminded the theft of the Hopi idols. Then were his death and Eli Tom's . . . ?

Christy shook off the idea. The jigsaw was puzzling enough without new pieces. "Sam," he said, "you've got a good mind. I need it."

"What for?"

"You've got a natural flair for investigation," Christy said. "You use it all the time to locate mineral deposits."

"We do it by computer nowadays," Sam said. "I just sit around and punch buttons."

"You still use scientific method. So consider: we have what you might call a mini-epidemic. It's killed two people. We can say at least tentatively that it attacked a third, Eleanor Fawkes. And the 'disease' is still not isolated. By projection, we anticipate that it will claim other victims."

"That's just anecdotal data," Sam said.

"Yes, so far," Christy said. "But the pattern they suggest is unmistakable. Our 'disease,' if you will, is distributed specifically, not randomly, in the available population."

"All Fawkes."

"Right. Now let's set up a fundamental assumption that our disease isn't occurring because of magic. That includes all the types of werewolves we can think up. It's occurring because there's a real vector—a carrier."

"Say 'murderer' and get it over with," Sam suggested.

"Okay, murderer," Christy said. "We can prove some things. We have the animal tracks. We know that a large canine was on the Fawkes ranch and had distinctly splayed toes, especially on the left rear foot, and we know the hound we caught this morning has smaller feet with no splaying."

"What else?"

"The whistle Gala heard. Attack dogs work selectively and usually on command. The whistle could be its signal for 'attack' or 'come back.' "

"Not proof," Sam said. "Guesswork. Scientific method leaves plenty of room for intuitive leaps, but sooner or later you're going to have to answer the question of why anybody would use a trained attack dog to kill off the Fawkes family when there are so many easier ways to kill people."

"I think I've got an answer for that," Christy said. "The Navajos were already talking about magic wolves before Mr. Fawkes was killed. Your brother-in-law said it was enough to get people excited. Then the killings started. More magic wolf. It obfuscates the real situation."

Sam's shoulders tensed. "It would take a damned cold-blooded murderer to risk getting innocent bystanders clubbed to death, just as a by-product. It seems that clubs and axes are the favored way to kill witches around here. Superstition. I hate it."

"We're going to get our disease carrier before anything else can happen," Christy said. "I promise, Sam."

"You can't promise. We don't have enough data about anything," Sam said. "So much for scientific method. Turn left. You'll see two hogans pretty soon. Let's see how fast we can attend to superstition and our floating white wolf."

As they neared the hogans, Christy heard a transistor radio blaring rock music. Sam grinned, and Christy grinned back at him. Progress had certain drawbacks.

A little boy popped out of one of the hogans, looked at the Bronco, then popped back in and turned off the radio. He scampered in back of the hogans to a shade house made of brush and came back with another little boy. In time, two women came out of the shade house. Both wore traditional velveteen tunics and long skirts, with tennis shoes. One carried a baby. A near twin to the Benally's black-and-white sheep dogs crept out from under an old wagon bed and stared silently at Sam as he got out of the car and went to speak to the women.

Christy waited, figuring it was better not to join them. In a few minutes Sam came back and said, "Drive on over to the summer hogan. McCrea's wives just slaughtered a mutton, and they want to finish dressing it out."

"Wives?" Christy said.

"You're deep in the reservation now, kid," Sam said.

An ancient woman, easily as old as Sam's grandmother, sat smoking in the shade house, a simple structure constructed of rough juniper poles as supports, with branches piled on top to give shade. The family needed it. Their place was treeless, and vegetation was almost nonexistent. Christy soon saw the reason. Goats, the common Spanish variety, wandered the banks of a freshly eroded gully. In their search for food, they had stripped the area bare.

Yet, it was a freshly slaughtered sheep, not a goat, that hung from an overhead support in the shade house. Hide and head were intact, and blood still dripped from the dead mouth, but the entrails had been removed and thrown outside. The little dog reappeared and rushed to the entrails as if to guard them from Christy. Christy went into the shade house and smiled at the aged Navajo woman.

"Hello," Christy said. "How are you?"

The old woman puffed out a small cloud of cigarette smoke. She smiled at Christy and replied in Navajo. She patted a cured sheepskin beside her, and Christy decided it was an invitation to sit. He settled himself on the ground next to the old woman.

Was she asking him a question? He couldn't tell, but he smiled and nodded. The grandmother smiled back. She had obviously helped in the slaughter of the sheep. Dried blood caked her fragile hands. She chattered something, pointing with her chin toward the hogans. Sam, the two younger women, and the children walked out. The woman with the baby in her arms seemed taken with Sam. For that matter, so did the other woman. They laughed and joked with him as they came to the shade house. Sam joked back, and Christy thought he was still joking when Sam spoke to him.

"None of them speaks English," Sam said. "I'll have to translate. They claim they haven't seen any wolves, white or otherwise, but the cute one didn't look like she was telling the truth. Now, here's the setup. You're still good old Dr. Christy, but you're not only a great animal doctor, you're a big wolf expert, and you're here on the reservation studying wolves. Every time I ask you something in English, just say whatever comes into your mind, and I'll translate it back as some question about wolves. Maybe I can edge them into talking about the white wolf."

The little boys each picked up a plastic bucket and trudged off over a rise. The baby was deposited in the grandmother's lap, and the two younger women began skinning the sheep while Sam talked amiably.

Strange, melodic language, full of explosive puffs and swallowed syllables. All the work seemed to be in the back of the throat, and the Navajo women's mouths had to move very little, except to smile at Sam as they replied to his questions. Eventually, Sam turned to Christy and said, "Now they claim the husband may see wolves, since he goes up in the Chuska Mountains a lot. That's north of here. But the cute one says thère haven't been any wolves around the outfit's place since the old woman was a girl."

"Which one's the cute one?" Christy asked. The plumper of the two young women flashed him a shy smile, then neatly ripped the sheepskin off the forelegs of the carcass.

"The one with the baby," Sam answered, then chatted on in Navajo, pretending to translate. When he next spoke to Christy, he said, "Their allotment backs up to Fawkes's ranch. I didn't know the old guy had so much acreage. He must have bought a few more sections. About six thousand acres, they say, most of it mesa land. The old lady used to graze sheep on his land, but Fawkes ran her off years ago. They say it's wild back in there."

"How come two girls both married the same man?" Christy asked.

"They're sisters," Sam said. "Nan and her own husband called it quits, and Betsy didn't mind, so after a while Nan married Betsy's husband, too. It used to happen all the time."

The two boys returned with the buckets, staggering slightly under their weight. They looked no older than six or seven. The women poured the water into a washtub, and the children pulled bits of cedar bark and sailed them in the tub. The family's dog finished off the sheep entrails and curled up in the shade for a nap. The baby fell asleep, too.

The grandmother began speaking with Sam. Christy waited. The clouds over the red butte to the east towered higher, a great white mountain of them. A light breeze came up. It blew away the smell of blood, fresh mutton, juniper, and the peculiarly sweet and pungent smell of human bodies that rarely encountered soap and water in a place where there was little water. Christy loved his Colorado mountains, and he had chosen them as the place he most wanted to live, but, looking over the limitless beauty of the empty land, Christy felt an inward stir. The Navajos had to endure poverty to live here, but there was grandeur all around them.

"So," Sam mused to Christy, "old Sadie says Hugh Fawkes was a flame of hers once. He wanted her to become the fourth or fifth Mrs. Fawkes, but she turned him down. That's when he made her stop grazing her sheep on his land."

Christy said, "Ask her if she knew the other Navajo women he married."

The younger women paused in the process of tearing the last of the sheepskin over the rear legs and peeped at Christy. Maybe they spoke more English than Sam thought they did. Sam chatted on a while. When he turned back to Christy, he spoke calmly, but his eyes were sparkling with excitement.

"She knew them both," Sam said. "Particularly the last Mrs. Fawkes. She was from over around Ramah way and Fawkes married her about twenty years ago. She gave birth to a baby girl about six months after she and Fawkes broke up, and get this: She named her Bianca."

Christy let his breath out through pursed lips. "Is it the same Bianca that's managing the trading post?" he asked.

"She doesn't know," Sam said. "She says she lost track of the woman years ago. Shall I pursue it? Or get on with the wolf? I figure we can push them up one avenue or the other, but not both."

Christy thought rapidly. Given the lead about Bianca Wilson's possible parentage, there should be ways of tracking down the name of her father. If not a hospital birth and a birth certificate, there should at least be people in the Ramah area who would know. Possibly even the mother was living. He said, "Let's go with the wolf. Tell them . . . tell them that animal doctors have to have special ways of doing things. Tell them that, like a stargazer, we have ways of seeing. Tell them I know there is a white wolf that can float above the ground, and tell them I have seen that *they* have seen it."

There were no more smiles from the two sisters. The conversation grew serious. The grandmother spoke shortly to the little boys, sending them away to play elsewhere. No voices were raised, but Christy didn't have to know the language to hear the intensity of their speech. Sam soon began to translate in staccato sentences.

"You scared them with that one," Sam said. "Yes, they've seen a wolf, and it's no ordinary animal." He listened, questioned. "True, the wolf doesn't walk on the ground. It floats a few inches above it. Don't pay any attention to that, Christy. It's a common superstition among the tribes. Blackfoot. Kiowa. They all tell about ghost horses or buffalo that don't leave tracks when they travel from place to place."

"This animal does," Christy said. "Ask about tracks specifically."

In a few seconds, Sam's eyes betrayed even more excitement, but he said quietly, "McCrea and the boys have seen its tracks, and they've seen tire tracks driving to the box canyon it lives in. The women have never been there, but they say McCrea keeps a weather eye on the wolf when it's in its pen."

"Its pen!" Christy said. "Where?"

"Quietly, quietly," Sam said. "We may have worked ourselves into a corner. They won't think you're much of a stargazer if you can't divine for yourself where the wolf lives." He spoke to the women again. Christy watched as the youngest woman's mouth set stubbornly. Sam gestured to Christy. They looked at him and quickly glanced away again.

Sam finally took a deep breath and turned a solemn face to Christy. But he winked as he said, "It's all ours. But you must promise to rid their grazing area of the wolf if they let the older McCrea kid show you the canyon. Sounds like they're still sneaking onto the Fawkes land to graze a herd. I have assured them that you have a special gun and special knowledge, and that you solemnly promise to rid them of the white wolf."

"I promise with all my heart," Christy said.

He meant it. Maybe the sincerity carried through his own alien speech. The clincher, though, was the dart gun that Tully Kee had borrowed. Sam brought it to the shade house to show them. While the gun itself didn't seem remarkable to the grandmother or the younger women, the dart that Sam produced made an impression. Feathered with a bright red plastic fringe at the end, tip a sharp needle, middle a clear syringe filled with tranquilizers, the dart resembled nothing they had ever seen before. Sam had Christy load the gun and point it at the little dog, declaiming that the dog would instantly go to sleep. Everybody seemed willing for a demonstration except the elder boy, but Christy wasn't about to dart an innocent little dog, and he put the gun away. The little boy looked relieved and not particularly uneasy when he climbed into the Bronco with them to guide them to the canyon.

The Navajo boy took them by the route his father traveled on horseback, not the route where tire tracks had been seen. They had to walk the last mile. It seemed a long way for a seven-year-old, but the child jumped from rock to rock, as agile as a chipmunk, and only Sam and Christy were breathing hard when the boy led them to the rim of a small box canyon. The rock here was all buff-colored sandstone. It radiated light back to the sun, together with so much heat that Christy cringed at the thought of an animal being kept in the airless canyon.

But where was the animal?

Christy whispered the question to Sam, and Sam whispered it to the boy. The boy backed away from the canyon rim, looking scared for the first time. Sam followed to question him. Christy scrutinized the canyon floor. By a jumble of rocks in one corner he saw a silvery metal post. Another. He realized he was staring at a small pen of conventional chainlink construction. Nothing was in it. Nothing. He called to Sam that he was going to check, and he worked his way over to the mouth of the canyon and clambered down the rocks.

It was even hotter than he had expected, although the walls of the canyon gave some shadow to the pen. The pen's sides were only four feet high, but more chainlink had been wired to create a top. Not much of a clue to the size of the animal for which it had been installed. The pen was God-awful small, though, for an animal the size of a wolf. Maybe eight feet by eight feet. A deep bare space had been worn in the sandy earth at the pen's front, as though the animal had paced, paced, paced away the hours of its imprisonment. A stainless steel bucket was half full of water. There was no evidence of a food bowl or food scraps. There were no individual tracks that Christy could make out in the scuffed dirt and rocks. But a type of evidence clung to the heavy cross-linked wire. Christy plucked off an airy ball of hair, as light as a cobweb, as purely white as new snow.

"Christy, get out of there," Sam called.

"But . . ."

"No buts. Get back up here."

"But we've got to look for the tire tracks."

"Not now," Sam said. "The kid says the wolf has disappeared three times this week."

Christy climbed out of the canyon. "So?"

"The first time was the day Hugh Fawkes was killed. The second time was the day Eli Tom was killed. The last time was yesterday, before that thing stalked you and Eleanor last night. But it's always back the next morning."

"Oh, Lord, and it's still gone," Christy said.

"That's right. Someone has some unfinished business with it, and it could be on the prowl tonight."

"After who? Eleanor?"

Sam was silent. "I'm not so sure about that," he said. He pointed at rust-red rocks on the horizon. "See that Supai limestone? That's the back of the Fawkes ranch. Pretty convenient, I'd say."

"You think Eleanor Fawkes is hiding the animal here? Good Lord, Sam, that's not possible. It was after her last night."

"But it didn't get her," Sam said. "That's pretty convenient, too."

"Where would she hide it?" Christy said. "She's got to put it somewhere when it's out of its pen. She couldn't just tie it to a clothesline out back of the house, not with Karen there."

"Who knows?" Sam said. "In her pool house maybe. Or the barn. All I know is that the animal is missing, and everyone knows you and Karen will be gone tonight, out at the Blessingway with me. That leaves the coast clear for the animal to operate."

Christy gazed at the cliffs and thought of Karen, chatting innocently with Eleanor Fawkes in the big, sprawling ranch house.

"We'd better go talk to Tully Kee," he said.

CHAPTER 16

The Blessingway singer was waiting for Christy and Sam when they came out of Tully Kee's office later that afternoon. Peter Madman waved, then spoke some last word to a Navajo man to whom he had been talking. The man walked on toward the chapter house, and Madman approached Christy and Sam.

"Got a message for you," the singer said to Christy. He looked measuringly at Sam, as if wondering whether to repeat it in front of anyone else, then said, "Well, okay. I've got to talk to Sam, too. Dr. Christy, I ran into John Klah this morning. He was out finding some lost horses for a man near Sanders, and he told me to watch for your car. He said tell you his dog was better, and tell you he saw something for you last night. He saw that what you're looking for is in a cave."

The old stargazer's message puzzled Christy. It must have puzzled Sam, too, because Sam asked Madman, "Did Mr. Klah say just exactly what he saw in a cave?"

Now it was Madman's turn to look puzzled. The singer was a robust man in his fifties, hair still raven-black behind the bandana headband he wore, but he apparently was not immune to the presbyopia that so often accompanied middle age. He wore horn-rimmed glasses that gave him an owlish look, and he blinked as he thought over Sam's question. He looked around at the tribal police substation, he looked at the road, he looked at some children playing in front of the chapter house, then he lowered his voice as he replied, "Klah didn't say, but they tell me you two have been looking for this human wolf, so it must be the human wolf."

Christy said, "I don't think it's a human wolf, Mr. Madman. I think it's a plain animal."

"Animals aren't so plain," the singer said. "Human wolves, neither. I could tell you a lot about human wolves. But you don't want to hear that. So I'll tell you this: Listen to old John Klah, and listen to yourself. Listen to what your blood and your muscles and the dark things in your brain are trying to tell you. Listen hard and don't just think with the front of your mind. Then you'll find this wolf."

"We're sure going to try," Sam said. "I haven't told my mother yet, but it looks like we're going to have to try tonight. I really wanted to be there for the Blessingway."

"That's all right," Madman said reassuringly. "The bathing and the second night are more important than the first night. You be there for that. But I got to tell you, I can't sing over George this time. Lois is the one with the bad dreams, and it was her that Klah saw the Blessingway for, so she'll be the one-sung-over. But Blessingway helps everybody. It'll be good for George, and I'll put in a shield prayer, and that's good, too. And then you get Klah or a hand trembler for George, and he'll tell you the chantway George needs. I was out at your place just now. That boy talked to me a little. He said he did something *báhádzid*. Well, so he said he thought he needed a big prayer, but that's not for me to say, that's for the diviner. So you do that, Sam. You going to be sponsor again for George?"

"If it'll make him feel better," Sam said.

"Sure it will," Madman said, "just like Blessingway is going to help Lois. Those bad dreams of hers, they're a warning. Now she'll avoid the misfortunes ahead that the dreams warned about, and there'll be happiness instead."

The singer looked so serene and confident that Christy envied him. Like a surgeon before an operation, Madman had apparently gone to the Benally place to see that everything was in readiness. He would sing and pray most of Saturday night and much of Sunday morning and all of Sunday night. It had to be very taxing physically, but at least he was faced with none of the uncertainty that Christy and Sam had for their own night's activities.

Their plan was laid. Sam hitched a ride with Tully Kee to the Benally place to break the news to his mother that he probably wouldn't be home for the start of the Blessingway, and Christy went to the Fawkes ranch to lie to Eleanor Fawkes.

The lie Christy chose was a simple one: He had to drive into Gallup to pick up vaccines for the Benallys' dogs before the Blessingway, and Karen would be going along with him so they could have an early dinner in Gallup.

Eleanor said tensely, "Oh, dear, I'll be all alone. I'll have to bolt all the doors. Be sure you knock up a storm when you come home, Karen, so I can hear you and let you in."

Feeling like a criminal, Christy asked, "How are you coming on your dad's paperwork? Got everything sorted yet?"

"No, there are simply bales of paper. But with nothing else to do, maybe I can finish them tonight. I wonder if I could get Bianca to come out and keep me company."

Christy took the plunge. "I wouldn't count on Bianca," he said. "Brad told us this morning he has to drive to Albuquerque, so it looks like Bianca will be manning the trading post tonight all by herself. And tomorrow—"

"What?" Eleanor said sharply. "Do you know something I don't know?"

"I might be talking out of school," Christy said. "It's something Ann Lang told me."

"That old busybody," Eleanor said. "She spies on everyone. Is it something about the Wilsons?"

"Mrs. Lang said they're planning to leave in the morning. Brad asked one of her helpers to feed and water the animals in the menagerie for a week or maybe two."

"And just what do they plan to do about the trading post?" Eleanor sputtered. "Close it down? If Brad wants to take his stupid bar exams, he might at least hire somebody reliable to look after the post."

"I believe that's why he's going to Albuquerque today," Christy said, spinning out his tale with all the credibility he could muster. "According to Mrs. Lang, Bianca knows a young couple in Albuquerque who are dying to come here. They ran a gift shop somewhere else, so Bianca figured they're experienced."

"It's not her decision," Eleanor snapped. "It's mine."

"Of course," Christy said. "She apparently just didn't want to bother you about it until she had a qualified person lined up."

"Damn that Bianca," Eleanor said. "I never did know why Father hired her in the first place."

"Didn't you?" Christy said.

"What do you mean by that?"

"Nothing. I just thought maybe you knew each other before she came to work for your dad."

"No, she's not from around here," Eleanor said.

"Maybe I shouldn't have said anything," Christy said.

Eleanor looked thoughtful. "No, you did right," she said. "I appreciate it."

Did Gala smell his treachery? When Christy and Karen took her out to the Bronco, she did her sniffing routine on Christy, ignoring Karen. He drove them directly to the Painted Cliffs Ruin. It was nearly five o'clock, and neither of Mrs. Lang's helpers was on duty. Mrs. Lang met them at the gate herself, locked it behind them, and took them into a small room in which Officer Kee and Sam were already waiting. The room was set up for television viewing. Rather a lot of it, since there were two TV sets and two VCRs. Mrs. Lang saw Karen's interested look and explained gruffly, "I tape a lot of old movies." But she was taping nothing now. She closed the door, glanced outside the one window, then plopped into a chair.

"Dr. Christy," Mrs. Lang said, "the floor is yours."

"No," Kee said. "I'll start." He looked about as pleased to see Karen as he had at the dog hunt. He asked, "Does Miss Hamilton know what she's getting into?"

"Christy has hardly told me anything," Karen said.

"I couldn't," Christy said. "Eleanor was always there. I couldn't tell you about tonight without ruining everything."

"What's so special about tonight?" Karen asked.

Kee said, "That's what I asked when Christy and Sam brought me a perfectly nice wad of white animal hair earlier today. We've got labs that cooperate with us, but they're closed for the weekend. That hair could be identified Monday morning without any difficulty. Then we'd at least know if it's a dog or a wolf. But Christy and Sam are convinced we don't have until Monday. They're convinced the animal is going to attack somebody tonight."

"Who?" Karen said.

Sam said, "That's the question. If someone is trying to get rid of all the Fawkes clan, the next victim has to be either Eleanor Fawkes or Bianca Wilson. Karen, we learned today that the last of Hugh Fawkes's Navajo wives had a daughter named Bianca. Tully has already been on the phone for us, trying to run it down, and every indication is that Bianca is just as much Fawkes's kid as Eli Tom was. That makes her every bit as much an heir to Old Man Fawkes's estate. And that's a pretty good motive."

Karen, who had remained standing, moved away from them slightly. "You think that animal Eleanor heard breathing last night was real? You think Bianca was trying to kill Eleanor with it?"

"Maybe," Sam said. "Or maybe it's the other way around. They both stand to inherit."

"I can't believe it of either of them," Karen said.

Christy said, "I know. But the animal is missing from its pen, and we're pretty sure it's going to make a try for someone. The one thing we know for certain is that it has to be either Bianca Wilson or Eleanor Fawkes who's running the animal and who sabotaged the generator at the ranch house last night. That's no maybe."

Mrs. Lang said, "So why does it have to be Bianca or Eleanor? Someone else could have messed up the generator."

Karen sat down, looking more certain of herself. "Oh, no," she said. "Christy is right. I like them both, but one of them had to do that. No one else was around. Christy's dog was with us. Gala. She would have told us instantly if any strange person was close enough to reach the generator."

"If that's good enough for you, it's good enough for me," Mrs. Lang said. "I've done my part. New batteries in the walkie-talkies. Nasty little lie dropped on the Wilsons about Eleanor being alone tonight for the last time. I told them she's going to Gallup tomorrow to see her fiancé and the lawyers, and she's not planning to come back until the estate is settled. If Bianca wants a shot at her, she'll think this will be the last chance. How did your lie to Eleanor go, Christy?"

"Okay, I hope," he said.

"You should have asked Karen to do it. Women are much better liars than men. We were enslaved for so many centuries that it's part of our genetic inheritance. Are you sure you don't want me to help you stake out the ranch and the trading post? I could take the trading post instead of Tully. That way he could stay loose. Float back and forth. Maybe even check in at the Benally place to keep an eye on George. I don't know where the stolen idols fit into all this, but that boy could be in danger, too."

"If he is, Harley will take care of him," Sam said grimly. "We'll leave Gala out there to help him keep an eye peeled. Harley will do anything that has to be done. He's a little bit of a warrior. Right now, I'm feeling like a warrior, too."

"What's your grand plan for me?" Karen asked. "Stay here with Mrs. Lang? Think again. If you're up to any highjinks, I'm going to be highjinking, too."

Christy said, "Are you sure? It's a big vicious animal that we'll be looking for."

With a smile that didn't seem to reach her eyes, Karen said, "If you're game, I am. Besides, I won't be all alone, will I?"

"No. We figured you'd want to help," Christy said. "Sam will be your partner. You'll park about a half-mile from the ranch and take up a position where you can watch the pool house and the barn. Tully and I will hide where we can watch the trading post. If Bianca makes a move, we'll stop her at the post. If Eleanor makes a move, you and Sam won't do anything but watch. You'll tell us on the walkie-talkie, and we'll intercept her before she can get to the trading post. Either way, the trading post is where we're going to settle this business once and for all. Tully will make the arrest, and I'll take care of the animal with one of the dart guns. There aren't going to be any white wolves floating over the reservation tonight. It's going to be sound asleep."

CHAPTER 17

The face of the moon, full now, lifted itself higher above the dark mesas to the southeast. Below, a train hooted past on the tracks bordering the remnants of the old Highway 66. Christy shifted, right knee twinging from long immobility. In twilight, they had climbed the rocks well west of the State Line Trading Post, near the cave where Simon & Avis had painted their names for short-term posterity. Christy had probed the back of the cave first. What he was seeking was in a cave. John Klah, the stargazer, had said so. But the back of the high cave held only a few Coors cans, unrusting scourge of the West, and Tully Kee had said there were no other caves from here up to the Painted Cliffs Ruin.

Sitting beside Christy on a narrow ledge of rock above the trading post, Kee fidgeted with Ann Lang's walkie-talkie. The reception hadn't been good in the rocky depression a half-mile away where they had left Kee's Suburban, but Mrs. Lang had assured them that the three-mile distance from here to the ranch house was well within the range of her favorite gadget. Christy fidgeted with his thoughts. If nothing happened tonight, Kee and Sam probably wouldn't say anything. A quiet laugh together. Navajos had a lively sense of humor. But Karen . . . if she hadn't already lost faith in him, how much longer would it take? How long before she started talking again about moving to Houston? Daddy Manybucks. Dermatology. How long before he lost her altogether?

The moon rose slowly, round and ripe, toward a heavy bank of clouds. A werewolf's moon. Scenes from his youth, Saturday afternoon matinees, stalked Christy's imagination. Lon Chaney, writhing in the darkness, suffering agonizingly as his cursed body metamorphosed, his face and hands grew shaggy, his teeth became fangs. The deadly man-wolf. Low fog rolling cold and damp across the moors. Distant howls. Shaggy feet padding through the darkness. Savage attacks without warning. Hot breath and rending jaws.

Christy listened attentively to sounds in the darkness behind him. That tiny stir. Just a rock cooling. Maybe an insect. He turned his thoughts to attack dogs. Had he read the data correctly? Followed them to the most logical hypothesis? Surely. Surely. But how could a potential murderer get hold of such an animal, Tully Kee had wondered aloud at the end of their planning session. All too easily, Christy had assured him. You could get an attack dog almost anywhere, as simply as buying a Saturday Night Special or a hunting rifle. More expensive, perhaps, but without the bother of a gun permit or signing some official register. Christy had seen posters himself in Denver. Mrs. Lang said she knew of several training centers in California. In the movie business, many of the trainers sold such dogs as a sideline and advertised attack training openly. "Let your dog make your life safer for you" . . . "Call now for free aggression analysis" . . . "A well-trained protection dog is not a vicious dog."

"Someone is moving," Kee whispered.

Christy stared toward the trading post. Soft lighting from its windows showed him Bianca Wilson's slender form as she moved from gas pump to gas pump, locking them for the night. The soft lights stayed on after Bianca went from the trading post to the house next to the animal compound. Night lights, Christy decided. A light came on in the front part of the house. It seemed to grow brighter as a cloud drifted across the moon, blotting out the natural light. Christy shifted, his knee complaining again, and looked down at the tumble of rocks that led from their high perch to the house. He and Kee had picked their hiding place carefully, looking for a quick way to get down to the trading post compound, but they had depended on the moon to help them find their footholds. If the clouds covered the moon at the wrong moment, they might. . . . Ah, there. The moon was emerging again. The rocks took shape in the darkness.

Floodlights came on in the animal compound. At the same moment, the walkie-talkie in Kee's hands squawked and sputtered. Kee hunched over it. "Shhhh," he said to the mouthpiece. "Wait a minute."

The wash of bright light in the animal compound didn't reach as high as their ledge, but Christy and Kee both crouched lower. Bianca came through a gate between the house and the compound, carrying two big buckets. Food? Water?

"What if it's Bianca, instead of Eleanor?" Kee whispered. "Where could she hide the animal? In one of the cages?"

"There's an empty cougar cage," Christy said, "but I can't think she'd use it. Any passing tourist could notice it."

Bianca went from cage to cage, but tonight she wasn't moving slowly and calmly, as she had before when Christy watched her with the animals. She was jerky and hurried. At the cage of Roberto the Coyote, she stopped and gazed up at the cliffs.

"Oh, hell," Kee said.

"Keep down," Christy whispered. "The coyote would know we're here. She's just looking to see what he's looking at."

"Shall I hoot like an owl?" Kee whispered.

If Kee knew how, he didn't demonstrate his talent. Christy stayed motionless and silent, hoping the walkie-talkie wouldn't squawk again.

Below, Bianca went back to her task of looking after the animals. She walked out of sight, apparently to the wolves' special compound. Christy couldn't see it from their ledge, but he had been aware of restless movement in the wolves' area, as if they, too, had nervously scented the strange humans on the rocks above them.

When Christy spotted Bianca again, she was already en route back through the gate to the house. The floodlights went out, leaving the animal compound in darkness. A door slammed. Kee grabbed the walkie-talkie and spoke into it softly but urgently.

"We're back on the air," he said. "Sam? Miss Hamilton? What's going on there?"

After a long silence, there was a spurt of static. Then Karen's voice said clearly, "Repeat, all is quiet here. What's going on there?"

"Nothing yet," Kee said. "Bianca's just been feeding the animals."

Another light came on in the back of the house. Christy could see part of a refrigerator. The kitchen. Bianca appeared at a window, and Christy ducked involuntarily before he saw she was reaching for a bottle of detergent on the sill. She seemed to look contemplatively out the window, then moved away from it and was lost to view.

Karen's voice said, "Repeat, all quiet here. Answer, please. What's the situation there?"

Kee said, "Can you hear me? Everything's okay here."

"What?" Karen's voice said. "Repeat, please."

"Oh-oh," Kee said. He switched off the walkie-talkie and nudged Christy. Below, just discernible in the moonlight, a form came through the gate to the animal compound. Heavy cloud drifted back over the moon, and the figure disappeared in the darkness. There was a metallic rattle and a clang, followed soon afterward by two more clangs. Christy felt his heartbeat accelerate with each second.

"Ohhhhhh, Lord," Kee said. For a moment, the shadowy form reappeared, going back to the house. It was not alone. Behind it, a white thing seemed to float along the ground. Then the moonlight failed. A gate latch clicked. In a moment, a door banged softly shut.

Kee leaped to his feet. "Damn it, don't lose her," he said. "Hurry. Down to the compound. The ground is dark, so be careful. Come on, Christy, move it."

In the fan of loose rock and boulders, they slid more than they climbed, tripping and stumbling in the darkness. Christy finished the last of the descent on his bottom, braking hard with his heels, tranquilizer gun clutched in his hand, while Kee, burdened with his handgun and the walkie-talkie, somehow managed to leap down as though he was descending a giant's staircase.

Christy heard scurrying feet and low growling to the left. He tensed, then realized it was the animals in the compound. They had come down in back of the Wilson house. The only light on now was in the kitchen. Bianca's head appeared again at the window, above the sink.

"She's back in the kitchen," Kee said. He ran for the house. Christy limped after him, but he was six feet behind when Kee slammed through the back door and leveled his handgun. Bianca Wilson whirled around from the kitchen sink. At the sight of Kee's pistol, she shrank back.

"Where's the dog?" Kee said.

She stared at him blankly.

"Damn it, where's the dog?"

She shook her head.

"The wolf, then," Kee said. "Where did you put him?" He nodded toward a closed door. "That room? Where?"

Christy edged in behind Kee, tranquilizer gun ready, eyes scanning the room. From the front of the house, outside, there was a solid thunking sound. A car door closing? A heavy motor throbbed into life. Kee rushed to a window in the next room as a vehicle pulled away.

"Oh, my God," Kee said, "it's someone else. Bianca, that's your van. It's turning . . . Oh, Christ. North. It's going toward the ranch." Kee clicked on the walkie-talkie. "Miss Hamilton!" he said urgently. "Miss Hamilton, can you hear me?"

Bianca held a soapy sponge. She squeezed it so hard that sudsy water began to drip on the floor. Christy heard two drops fall while he registered the fact that the left side of her face was bruised and swollen.

Then he said, "Who hit you? Brad?"

"No," Bianca said. She sounded weary. "Don't."

"I can't raise them," Kee said. "It must be the cliffs blocking us off." He glanced at Bianca. "What do we do with her? Lock her up?"

"No," Christy said. "We don't have time."

Kee's Suburban was parked well off the road, far enough away from the trading post that it wouldn't be spotted, and they wasted precious minutes scrambling across dark ragged ground to get to it. They hit the car at a dead run. Kee tossed the walkie-talkie to Christy, but Christy was panting so hard that he couldn't speak when he tried to get through to Karen and Sam. Kee gunned the Suburban toward the gravel road. Brush scraped under the frame. A spray of rocks spattered in back of them. Christy thumbed the walkie-talkie and tried again as they slewed onto the road that led to the ranch.

"I can't raise them," he yelled. "Hurry. Where's the damned van?"

"Way ahead of us by now," Kee said. He jammed the accelerator down, sending another spray of gravel flying behind them. They hit a bump hard and came down harder. Christy cursed, grabbing for the dashboard with both hands.

"Why Brad?" Kee said. "Why the hell Brad?"

"For the same reason we thought it might be Bianca or Eleanor," Christy said. "Money. He wants it all."

They rattled over another series of bumps.

"But you said only Bianca or Eleanor could have fixed the generator," Kee complained. "How the hell does Brad get into this?"

"It must have been Bianca who unscrewed the gas line," Christy said. "Maybe Brad made her do it to get Eleanor outside. Bianca looked awfully surprised when she found out Karen and I were there last night."

"You think she knows what he was doing?"

"I don't know," Christy said. "Maybe not. Or maybe she was afraid not to do as she was told."

Christy tried the walkie-talkie again as they neared the ranch, then sat up straighter. "I see the van. There, look. Parked off the road to the right. No, don't look. Watch the road."

It was only a gleam of moonlight on chrome, and it lasted only a moment. Now Christy could see nothing but the fan of headlights in front of them. Kee slowed, then braked. He flicked on his doorside spotlight and swung it to the right. The spotlight picked up a mass and turned it into a dark blue van parked beside a low ridge of rock. A second after Kee's spotlight hit the van,

Christy thought he saw a white form move on the rocky ridge toward the cliffs.

"Up there!" Christy cried. "Something moved!"

"Hang tight!" Kee said. He swerved off the road and headed cross-country, taking the most direct route to the van. Low-growing greasewood battered frantically at the underside of the car. Christy thumbed the walkie-talkie, shouting into it, "Danger, danger! Take shelter!"

Kee stopped ten feet from the van. Sam's voice blasted loudly over the walkie-talkie, saying, "Where is it? Where's the wolf?"

"We don't know," Christy said. "Take Karen and head for cover, fast!"

"Karen isn't with me," Sam said. His voice sounded steady but frightened. "She went up on the cliff to run away some sheep. They're straying around out here."

"Damn it, get her!" Christy squawked. "It might not be sheep."

"I'm on my way," Sam's voice said.

They leaped out of the car. Kee swung his spotlight up to the rocks, but moonlight picked up the first movement. It was on the rocky ridge. Something white. Something tall. Christy raised the tranquilizer gun. He was appalled to see that his hands were shaking. It was difficult to aim.

The spotlight caught a figure and held. "Hands up," Kee barked.

"What in hell for?" Brad Wilson's voice said. "What are you guys doing out here?"

Bianca Wilson's husband, wearing a white sweater, stepped cautiously down the rocks, pinned by the spotlight. He didn't put up his hands. He held them behind his body, like a child hiding cookies after raiding a cookie jar.

"Let's see your hands," Kee snapped.

"It's only a tire iron," Brad said, letting his hands swing in front of him. A heavy metal bar hung from one hand. The other seemed empty, though he kept his fingers closed in a fist.

"Drop it!" Kee said.

The tire iron clanged to the rocky ground. "Hey, come on,"

Brad said. "Point those guns somewhere else. Rattlesnake-hunting on private property might be illegal, but it couldn't be much more than a misdemeanor."

"What were you going to do, beat the snake to death?" Kee said. "Or was the tire iron for Eleanor Fawkes's window?"

"I don't know what you're talking about," Brad said.

"Where's the wolf?" Christy said. His eyes probed the darkness in back of Brad. Nothing. He swung his head to check the ridge. Kee was taking quick looks, too, then sighting again along his pistol barrel.

"What wolf?" Brad said. He moved closer to the van. "I haven't seen any wolf. For that matter, I haven't seen any rattlesnakes yet. I just got here. A guy said he saw a real biggie out this way before—"

"Cut the crap," Kee said. "Get over here in the light. Quick. Lean on the van. Legs outstretched. Christy, search him."

Christy switched the tranquilizer gun to his left hand and felt with his right hand around Brad's neck. A chain. Yes. He yanked.

"Christ!" Brad said.

"Shut up," Christy said. He yanked again. The chain broke, and he held it to the side to look at it, but on it dangled only a gold charm in the shape of a triangle. He dropped it on the ground and dug into Brad's right trouser pocket. Car keys. Plastic cigarette lighter. He saw Brad's left hand against the rear of the van, still closed in a fist. He reached up and pried the fingers open. There. Something slender. Something metal.

"Pay dirt," he breathed to Kee. He held up a long chrome dog whistle.

"I just found that," Brad said. "It was by Eleanor Fawkes's station wagon."

"Sure," Kee said. "And Eleanor's hiding a big white wolf somewhere on the ranch, right? How did you think you could make it work, Brad? Kill Eleanor and get people so worked up about Navajo wolves that they'd never look for the real killer? Or kill Eleanor and then shoot the animal, so it would look like her own attack dog turned on her?"

"You're crazy," Brad said.

Kee nodded. "And then here comes timid little Bianca out of the wings. How handy that you married the poor browbeaten girl when she didn't have a dime, and she just happens to be the only living heir to the Fawkes money."

"Where did you hear that?" Brad asked sharply. "I don't know a thing about that. If Bianca is related to Fawkes, she never told me. Maybe she's the one you ought to question."

"Oh, sure," Kee said. "Use the whistle, Christy. Call that thing and get it back here."

Christy raised the whistle to his lips, then hesitated. "I can't," he said. "I don't know what signals Brad uses."

"Make him do it, then," Kee said.

"He might not give it the right signal," Christy said.

"You damned fools," Brad said. "I don't need a whistle." His hand flicked to the back door of the van, and he jerked it open. "Snowball," he cried. *"Fass!"*

Mouth open in a silent snarl, tongue lolling, a huge white dog exploded out at them.

Christy was the nearest target. The dog flicked his eyes from Christy to Kee, scarcely pausing. In that second, Kee swung the pistol wildly at the animal and squeezed the trigger.

The sound of the shot was thunderous. Christy cringed. He saw Brad cringe. The white dog shifted his weight and charged for Kee.

Christy's stomach turned over. He tried to aim the tranquilizer gun before he realized that he had dropped it. The dog leaped, hitting Kee on the chest. Kee fell down hard, the pistol and dog both on top of him. The dog went for his throat, but Kee's arm got in the way. The dog shifted and went for the head as Kee rolled over, trying to protect himself. Just as rapidly, the dog snapped at Kee's wrist, then his shoulder.

The attack was so sudden that fear came late to Christy. Fear, trying to rush up from his cringing belly. Fear, trying to displace blood. He had time to hear an eerie sound, that of a dog growling viciously in a whisper, then Brad slammed his shoulder into

Christy's chest and knocked him to the side. They grappled by the open van door.

Kee cried out. Christy lashed out at Brad hard, then lashed again, driving him to his knees. Without thought, Christy darted toward the dog, yelling, and kicked the animal hard on the rump.

The heavy white animal twisted his whole body in one motion like a snake twisting to strike. The huge white head pulled back as he stared at Christy with set, eager eyes. Christy felt the fear surge through his body again. He cast an eye to the darkness. There. There was the tranquilizer gun. He started to move toward it, but the animal moved, too, balancing, poising himself.

Christy took a step to the right. The dog crouched. Kee rolled over, his arm hanging limply, and tried to get to his feet, but the dog ignored him. The huge animal had chosen a new target. He launched himself silently at Christy. The white head swung, teeth snapping audibly, but Christy had already jerked back, this time to the left. The dog sailed past Christy, displacing air like a gust of wind.

"Yaaa, you bastard!" Christy yelled. "Try again!"

The dog whirled and stared at Christy, poising himself for another leap. Christy spun around and ran. He dived for the only place he could think of, the open door of the big blue van. The dog bounded in right after him. Christy scrambled wildly over the front seat and tumbled out the front door. He slammed the door in the dog's face. Jaws snapped and heavy paws scrabbled at the window. Kee stumbled to the back of the van and shoved Brad out of the way. He slammed the back door.

"Got him!" Kee cried jubilantly.

The dog snarled soundlessly at the driver's window and tried to batter his way through the glass, but the door held. Christy stared back at the dog in awe, his heartbeat drumming violently in his ears, until another sound crowded in. Bodies thumping against the van, fists raining against flesh. Christy charged to the back of the van in time to see Kee struggling violently to keep Brad from reopening the door. Kee was weakening, and Brad's hand was getting closer to the handle. Christy moved in. Brad's eyes cut to him, and a look of despair crossed his face. Against the two of them, Brad must have seen the hopelessness of his attempt. He turned and fled toward the gravel road.

After all the fear, Christy felt a deep, sweeping rage. He scooped up the tranquilizer gun and used it. He sighted in on Brad's fleeing rump and fired. Brad jerked and kept on running. How black the red feathers of the dart looked in the moonlight. As black as the blood streaming down Kee's arm.

"Are you hurt bad?" Christy asked Kee.

"I've felt better," Kee said. "Did we get him?"

"We got him," Christy said.

Brad's pace faltered, slowed. They watched him stagger on until he fell. Silence rushed in. The moon passed behind a wisp of cloud and reemerged, stronger and brighter than before. Then rocks tumbled down the rocky ridge, and two figures appeared.

Karen called, "Christy? Christy, are you all right? We heard a shot."

"I'm fine," he called back. "But Tully got chewed a little."

Christy's gaze turned back to the van. The huge head of the white dog still jerked with the motions of whispered barking.

" 'Snowball,' " Kee said sadly. "Brad called him 'Snowball.' "

"The sonofabitch," Christy said.

"Which one?" Kee said.

Christy didn't answer. He started toward the ridge to meet Karen and Sam. Later he would check Kee's bitten arm, and he would go find Brad, and after that he would try to think of something to do for the dog.

But he knew there was nothing anybody could do.

"The sorry sonofabitch," he said again, this time to himself. Between man and dog, he knew which one he meant.

CHAPTER 18

All of the people who came the next night for the final phase of the Blessingway wouldn't fit into the Benally family's medicine hogan. Most of the Navajo men and women wandered about outside, but they moved back close to the hogan as midnight approached.

"I think the stew is nearly done," Mrs. Lang said. She pushed her black hair away from a sweaty forehead and leaned away from the heat of Christy's campfire. It had been a hectic several hours at the end of a hectic day. Sam's little grandmother had hoped against hope that at least ten or fifteen relatives and neighbors would come, but she had looked close to panic when she greeted the sixty or seventy who actually arrived for the start of the ceremony's big night. That the timing coincided with the evening meal may have filled the Benally women's hearts with joy, but it also meant they emptied all the pots of food cooked up in anticipation of supper, the midnight meal, and the several more times that food would be brought into the hogan before daybreak.

"Good old Ann Lang to the rescue," Mrs. Lang said now with her customary sourness.

"What about good old Dr. Christy and good old Karen Hamilton and good old us?" one of her young helpers said.

"You're pretty good at peeling potatoes and chopping onions," Mrs. Lang admitted, "but I never saw such a mess as Christy made chopping up the mutton. You'd think a veterinary surgeon could do better than that."

"It was awfully fresh mutton," Christy said defensively.

"It certainly was," Karen said. "Poor little sheep."

Theirs was not the only cooking project. Navajo women in and by the Benally house were making fry bread and what Mrs. Lang cryptically described as "Navajo tacos" to supplement the huge pots of mutton stew that Christy and the others had taken on.

"Need more firewood?" Christy asked Mrs. Lang.

"No, we'll just keep everything warm and start making coffee now," she said. "I think Madman is into the Songs by Which Pollen Is Applied. Pretty soon after that comes the deluge of hungry participants. Good time for a break, Christy. Where's that Scotch bottle? We'll take care of that, and you and Karen can take care of the dogs and give them a nice walk. Rufie is loose as all get-out from those hamburgers Karen gave him."

Karen looked contrite as she obediently went to Mrs. Lang's car for the big brindle hound dog. Her own first thought after the capture of the white attack dog had coincided with Mrs. Lang's —springing the brindle dog from his jail at the animal control center in Gallup. It had been late Sunday morning before Officer Kee could make the necessary phone calls, and Karen overrode Christy's objections and arrived at the center with a sack of six hamburgers. Emaciated dogs had to be fed carefully, and the hound's digestive system was predictably upset, but Karen was the dog's friend for life. So was Mrs. Lang, at whose house the dog had stayed until the Benally family's food emergency had called out Mrs. Lang and her helpers. She didn't trust the dog enough to leave him at home with her cat, so they brought him along and left him locked in her car.

Karen opened the car door. The hound was curled into a ridiculously small ball in the front seat. He looked at Karen with apprehensive brown eyes. The gaze he turned to Christy was even more uncertain. Hostile. He growled low in his throat. Karen looked anxiously at Christy.

Christy laughed. "Don't worry," he said. "My phobia has been pretty well 'flooded.' "

Karen snapped the hound's borrowed leash to his borrowed collar. He jumped quickly out of the car and came to her. Gala was watching from Christy's car. She barked once, imperiously.

Karen said, "Hurry up, Rufie. Do your business. Gala wants to walk, too."

As Christy had wondered and now finally thought to ask Karen, he said, "Why call this poor dog Rufie? He's so big. 'Rufie' sounds like a cute little dog. It doesn't fit."

"First Mrs. Lang thought 'Brutus' would suit him," Karen said. "Then she decided that was too stern-sounding, so she tried 'Rufus.' Within fifteen minutes he was 'Rufie.' I guess that's what he'll stay. There, that's a good boy. Now get back in the car."

Rufie turned his apprehensive eyes to Christy and bounded back into Ann Lang's front seat and curled up again in a ball. Karen closed the door and went to the Bronco for Gala. Gala lunged to the end of her lead, heading for the spring.

Karen said, "I have an idea that Mrs. Lang would like to keep Rufie. Would that be all right?"

"Sure, if she fences a yard and if he can get along with Margery Kempe," Christy said.

Ahead, tugging eagerly on her leash, Gala stiffened, staring toward the moonlit rocks near the spring. Her ears pricked forward, oscillating slightly.

"Is someone at the spring?" Karen said.

Christy could hear soft voices, then a clink of glass. "It's George and a couple of his buddies, I think," he said. "I saw George come out of the hogan awhile ago. He keeps a few bottles of beer in the spring. Let's walk back the other way. No sense in disturbing them."

Karen clucked to Gala and turned. "I thought George was all gung-ho about the Blessingway ceremony. Bringing himself back in harmony with the world. Long life and everlasting beauty. All the things Mrs. Lang's been telling us about."

"He was," Christy said. "I guess he still is. Maybe drinking a beer with a couple of buddies is part of being in harmony for George."

"Poor Sam," Karen said. "He's going to have his hands full trying to make something of that kid."

"George might be all right. He might be fine," Christy said. With some embarrassment, he added, "Sam and I have a plan. It was your dad and his, um, generous offer that gave me the idea. You know how Cletus is always after me to start investing my spare cash? Sam and I think we could both invest profitably in a little well-drilling operation. Sam's brother-in-law, Harley, could run it, and George could work for Harley. We don't know how much machinery we could afford at first, but they could dig all sorts of things. Irrigation ditches. Stock tanks. Can't you see George zooming around on a tractor, happily ripping up the world?"

Gala paused as they approached some parked pickups. Like Rufie the hound, she had business to attend to. Christy and Karen paused with her. Christy said, "Karen, about that offer of your dad's—I know you like Houston. I guess the idea of going back could be pretty appealing. It's home for you. But I just can't stand the idea of giving up Vail and setting up shop there. Can you forgive me?"

"Forgive you?" she said. "Don't be silly. It was just an idea. There's nothing to forgive."

"Then why have you been acting like you're mad at me?"

"It's because . . . you don't think much of me, do you, Christy?"

"Why, I think the whole world of you," Christy said. "I think you're wonderful, and I love you."

"No, I mean as a person. I'm like George to you. We don't *do* anything. We just hang around. And all any of you can think to do with us is buy us a tractor or a new car to play with. No, I'm not mad at you. I'm mad at me. I need to do something with my life, and I was so stupid. I thought up something for you to do instead. But it's my life, and it's up to me to do something with it, not you."

"We can do it together, can't we?" Christy said. "We could—"

"Shhh, there comes Officer Kee."

The Navajo police officer looked uneasily at Gala and touched the sling on his arm. "Does she know I'm a friend?" he asked.

"Of course she does," Karen said. "Don't tell me you've caught Christy's dog-aversion." In spite of her light tone, Kee turned his somber face to her and studied her before deciding to smile.

"I've got good news," Kee said.

"Brad confessed?" Karen asked. She passed Gala's leash to Christy.

"Nobody confesses these days," Kee said. "Much less Brad, with all his legal training. He demanded a court-appointed lawyer first thing. He's going to try to blame Bianca for everything, I think. But she's being pretty cooperative. I think he slugged her one time too many. Or maybe that attack-dog business was too much for her. Thanks to her, we know Brad really was the fence for the Hopi figures, and we've got a good line on the collector he peddled them to in Los Angeles. That's the good news. The Feds hope to seize the idols tonight or tomorrow."

"So the Hopis will be able to make rain," Karen said.

The hooded look came into Kee's eyes again. Beyond them, to the dull throb of a small drum, minor-keyed chanting rose and fell in the medicine hogan. Kee said, "Yeah, well, after the Hopis dance, the rain always falls. Call it coincidence if you want."

"How did the Hopi idols tie in with the killings?" Christy asked.

"Only periphcrally," Kee said. "Brad was apparently pretty disappointed at the price they got for the idols. Stealing artifacts wasn't making him the killing he figured on. I guess he got impatient. Here was this boozy, depressed little Indian girl he'd married. Her rich daddy wasn't coming across with much. Profits from the trading post were practically nil, and the old man pocketed most of them. So he went after Fawkes's money. All of it."

Christy shook his head. "Using a dog named Snowball," he said.

"What kind of dog was that, anyway?" Kee asked.

"A Kuvasz," Christy said. "They're Hungarian imports, like your Komondorok. The breeds are closely related. You might say a Kuvasz is a short-haired Komondor. Big, tough dogs with a pronounced guarding instinct. They're natural herd dogs, like Ed Lee's Ace and Queenie. In Hungarian, 'Kuvasz' means 'Protector.'"

Christy and Kee and Karen all exchanged an unhappy look. Kee sighed. "Our white wolf with the splayed toes," he said.

"What's going to happen to Snowball?" Karen asked.

Christy looked away, so Kee answered. "He'll stay at the animal control center in Gallup while they try to trace who sold him. More importantly, if it was really Brad who bought him. They'll start with the animal place where Brad bought the wolves. That was Christy's suggestion. Good one."

"And after that, they'll kill him," Karen said flatly.

"I don't think there's an option," Kee said. "The animal people in Gallup tell me you can't untrain an attack dog."

Christy's dog pushed against his knee, as if she had felt his distress traveling down her leash. His mental images of the big white dog so innocently named Snowball were images he hoped one day to forget. They had been forced to dart the big Kuvasz in the back of the van. There was no handling him otherwise. There was probably no handling him anyway. Fed and watered by Brad, but isolated, ignored, left alone in an eight-foot pen in a hot stone canyon day after day, the dog was demented. Even after the tranquilizer in the dart had taken effect and they were able to move the dog to the first secure place they could think of, the empty cougar cage at the Wilsons' menagerie, Snowball had tried, woozily and unsuccessfully, to bite everyone who came near him. Bianca Wilson had taken only one weary look at the tranquilized body of her husband, but she had stood for a long time looking at the caged dog, who, lying on his side, head wobbly, nevertheless had snapped, snapped, snapped at the chainlink of the cage. With a whispered growl.

Christy didn't know how deeply Bianca had been involved in her husband's schemes. She surely knew of the existence of the Kuvasz. When Brad took the animal out of the canyon, he couldn't have hidden it in the little cave hollowed out to serve as the wolves' sleeping quarters without her knowledge. What she knew wasn't Christy's business. It was the law's, and since she was still at liberty, even here at the Blessingway ceremony, perhaps she was in the clear. But Christy was privately convinced Bianca had had no role in guiding the dog's attacks, no role in keeping the Kuvasz at all. She liked animals too much to have stood aside and let a big furry dog suffer, as Snowball obviously had.

Gala pressed harder against Christy's knee. He leaned down and stroked her head. Black and sleek. Teeth as sharp as Snowball's, but a sound mind and a loving heart. He said to Karen, "It's midnight. I guess we'd better put Gala away and see if Mrs. Benally is about ready for the stew squad. Tell me something, Tully. How come Navajos don't put any salt in their mutton stews?"

Kee looked surprised. "I don't know," he said. "That's the way everybody cooks it. But you salt it. If you're a Navajo, you just put the salt in last instead of first." He stopped and half-turned to the medicine hogan, listening. "They'll be finished pretty soon now. That's the Twelve-Word Song."

"What does it say?" Karen asked.

Kee thought for a moment. "It says everything is blessed. When it's over, everyone in the hogan eats a pinch of corn pollen while they say a prayer in their own words. If you'll pardon me, I think I'll be on hand when the pollen's passed around. I'm like everybody else that lives around here. We all feel we could use some blessing after everything that's gone on."

Christy put Gala back in the Bronco just in time. The chanting stopped. Navajos began wandering out of the medicine hogan to join those outside. They chatted. A few lit cigarettes. A man called loudly to a friend who was sitting on the fender of a pickup. Sam and Harley Tsosie meandered out with the others and made for the campfire at which Mrs. Lang presided.

"Where are Eleanor and Bianca?" Sam asked Mrs. Lang. "Grandmother said they were here."

"They're somewhere around," Mrs. Lang said. "Bianca looks like she's scared somebody's going to knife her, and Eleanor is looking after her like a mother wolf determined to protect her young."

"Don't say 'wolf' around here," Sam begged. But he grinned and took a deep breath of the steam rising from the mutton stew.

"Ambrosial," he declared. He sniffed again. "Good grief, Ann, did you put lemon rind in it?"

Like a Navajo, Mrs. Lang pointed with her chin toward two big trays covered with dish towels. "Eleanor and Bianca have been at the Fawkes place baking for all they're worth. They brought about ten dozen blueberry muffins. That's where you smell the lemon rind. They're darned good. I stole one."

So did Sam and Harley. They looked happy and relaxed. Sam was his usual self, dressed in a sport shirt and slacks, but Christy thought he fitted easily into the crowd of dark-faced Navajos, some with long hair and some with short, some dressed much like Sam and others wearing a year's pay in silver and turquoise. *Dinéh,* Christy thought. The People.

Karen drew Christy into the shadowed edge of the campfire. Sounding wistful, she said, "I guess you and Sam will be all through here tomorrow. Are you still going fishing?"

"No," Christy said. "As George's uncle, Sam is going to be tied up with starting the arrangements for another ceremony. The family is planning to pull out the stops for a really big curing chant, probably in the first week of September. It seems that since a non-Navajo like Brad was the real human wolf, they think George should be the honoree in an Enemy Way ceremony. Four or five hundred guests. Dancing all night and horse races during the day. We're invited. Do you want to come down for it?"

"I don't know," Karen said. "September seems so far away."

"Well, I need to pick up some vaccine in Gallup tomorrow and give a few rabies shots, but after that I'll still have a few days free," Christy said. "Let's go to Texas and see your father."

"To hell with Daddy," Karen said. "Let's go home to Vail. I don't know what I want to do yet, but I'm going to look for a job."

"Want to open a detective agency?" Christy said.

Karen laughed. "Not on your life," she said.

They hugged each other happily. Karen drew away too quickly for Christy. "There's Eleanor and Bianca," Karen whispered.

Walking with the singer, Eleanor Fawkes and a timid, down-faced Bianca Wilson had approached the fire. Mr. Madman held something in his hand. He beckoned to Christy and Karen. His movements were solemn, but Christy saw that the singer's eyes were laughing behind his heavy horn-rims.

Madman said, "You made all the trouble go away, and you did a lot of other good things, and I brought something for you. Once we blessed a new school, and a lot of people came to see. People that didn't believe in Blessingway. So I sprinkled pollen on their heads. That's what I'm going to do for you. That'd be okay with you, wouldn't it?"

Christy said, "You bet it would. We need all the blessings we can get."

"Okay," the singer said. He nodded to Bianca. "But not you. You take a pinch of the pollen and you eat it. You're gonna learn to be a good Navajo."

Madman wasn't tall. Christy bent his sandy head and Karen bent her golden one so the Blessingway singer could have an easy reach as he went briskly from one to the next, starting with a pinch of pollen from his pouch for Bianca.

Sa-ah naaghei, Bik'eh hozhoo.

Long life and everlasting beauty in a world restored to harmony.